The Word of the Seer

GEORGE MURRAY WILSON

For Roy Pugh

"But Edinburgh is a mad god's dream
Fitful and dark,
Unseizable in Leith
And wildered by the Forth,
But irresistibly at last
Cleaving to sombre heights
Of passionate imagining
Till stonily,
From soaring battlements,
Earth eyes Eternity."

Hugh MacDiarmid

Contents

CHAPTER 1

The Last Fish Supper,
Monday 11th April 2022

Peter Marsh had endured yet another long and frustrating day at the administrative headquarters of the Kirk of Scotland in Queen Street, Edinburgh. He sometimes cursed the fact that he had taken on the role of 'General Secretary' two years previously, after leaving a relatively comfortable and similarly paid head of human resources role in a Scottish government agency.

It was essentially a managerial and organisational role rather than religious in nature - perhaps comparable to the chief executive officer of a large public limited company. But, of course, the Kirk was no company, it was far more complicated than that! As part of the 'reformed tradition', it recognised only Jesus Christ as, 'Head of the Church'. In terms of governance, it was via a convoluted, hierarchical system: Courts of Elders, including the Kirk Assembly, the Court of the Parish, representatives of Kirk Sessions from the Presbytery, along with area courts. At the top of this structure, on a national level, stood the 'General Congregation', with an appointed 'Moderator' as chairperson.

At the same time, the Kirk had a wide and complicated scope of operations, including councils, committees, parish churches, chaplaincies, overseas missions, retirement homes, retreats, youth and community projects, a huge property portfolio (including around, 4,000 ecclesiastical buildings, many of which were listed, 12,500 acres of glebe land, as well as valuable collection and heritage items), along with associated charities and groups (each with their own sets of trustees). Not to mention it had around 400,000 members, all with an interest and stake in its effective operation.

On the human resources front, there were around 800 ministers (who were essentially self-employed, rather than employees) and over 2,000 professional and administrative staff. There were all the usual 'corporate' functions of a large and multifaceted organisation, such as accounts, health and safety, communications, IT etc., within which the staff group sat.

Peter had to navigate this almost unfathomable matrix, dealing with a wide range of personalities, from pompous and narcissistic religious appointees (who typically viewed him as some sort of inferior lackey and gofer), and difficult trustees (often with competing interests and personal agendas), to the usual prima-donnas that are invariably found lodged within the cogs and wheels of a substantial and complex establishment. The phrase, 'herding cats' must have been invented with his job in mind, he considered.

And for all the long hours, hassle and stress, the pay was miserable. It was true that he could probably have earned more as branch manager of a local fast-food franchise or supermarket. But it was Peter's genuine commitment to the values and ideals of the church (membership and protestant religious observance being an essential job requirement) that kept him at it, slogging away every day, two steps forward and one back (at best).

It was also the case that he was a de-facto head of the Kirk in many respects - their most senior executive official. He was a little bit embarrassed to admit it, however, it gave him a sense of self-satisfaction when, at drinks parties with neighbours or his wife's work colleagues, such as at Christmas time, he was asked the inevitable question, "*What is it that you do for a living?*" Responding with, "*I am General Secretary of the Kirk of Scotland,*" would generally prompt a look of worthy respect as the person asking was thinking, 'wow, this guy has a cool and very important job'. Conceited of him, he knew, and of course, the reality of the day-to-day grind and shit-shoveling, was very different.

Despite the miserly salary, there was one undoubtedly valuable fringe benefit associated with his particular job with the hallowed institution. A historic grace-and-favour perquisite for the holder of the General Secretary position was the provision of a fine, family residence for habitation during the tenure of office. This was a four-bedroom, detached Victorian villa on one of Edinburgh's most prestigious streets, Dick Place. Peter would never have been able to afford such a place to live on an ordinary salary, and certainly not the Kirk's meagre remuneration. Such were the house prices in 'the Grange' locale these days, that most homeowners had either inherited the property, were endowed with considerable private wealth or had the benefit of lucrative share options, bonuses or such like in addition to their standard salaries. Even for a successful Edinburgh lawyer, accountant or doctor, such properties were out of reach of most, under the usual mortgage rules of up to 3.5 times the basic salary.

At the same time, however, the religious organisation's frugal estates budget meant that there was no proper heating or insulation within the large, high-ceilinged rooms, and the place was cold and drafty. This was not helped by the fact that all its substantial windows were single pane – not so much the Kirk's stinginess at play here, rather it was the city council's conservation area rules prohibiting the installation of double glazing. The property was not in the best state of repair either, with ancient electrics, plumbing and décor. Although Peter and his wife Gail, an accounts manager for the NHS at Little France, had made some progress with permitted modifications since moving there almost two years ago from their far more modest 3-bed semi in the Corstorphine area of the city.

The last weekend had been the start of the school's Easter weeks' holiday. Gail and the kids, Imogen aged 12 and Thomas, 10, both pupils at nearby George Watson's College, had travelled up to Beauly by train on the Saturday to visit her parents for the week. Peter had the coming Thursday and Friday off work, so would travel up by car on Wednesday night, straight after work, to join them for a long weekend and would drive them all back down to Edinburgh before school resumed the following week. But still only being Monday, this wee break seemed a long way off. At least it was 6.30 pm and he was heading home after the hard day's slog.

Another positive aspect of the Kirk provided residence was that it was not too far from the city centre, only really the other side of the Meadows. So, this allowed Peter to walk to and from work, the journey taking about 45 minutes and allowing him to clear his head before and after the days' onslaught, as well as get some much-needed exercise.

This evening, as he left the Meadows towards Argyle Place and the residential tenements of Marchmont, he decided to stop off at the Argyle Bar for a pint – his wee family was away after all. Following that, he thought he might pop into Salvatore's and pick up a fish supper to save the bother of cooking. With a presbyterian pang of guilt at mid-week drinking, Peter snuck in the side door of the pub hoping that none of the parishioners at St Mag's, his local church, had seen him enter. As he did so, he surreptitiously slipped off his Kirk of Scotland bronze lapel badge (displaying the Kirk's modern day 'logo' of a church building nestling within cupped hands, and underneath the motto, *pietate et humilitate*) to assist in remaining inconspicuous once inside the licensed premises and popped it into a small pocket on the inside of his plain, grey suit jacket.

He then realised that he need not have bothered as immediately spied one of St Mag's Elder's, James Murray, along with Session Clerk, Gary Rutherford, propping up the bar, no doubt putting the world to rights. This sight prompted him to smile. Greeting each other in a companionly manner, Peter then ordered a pint of Belhaven 80 Shilling ale. However, when the barman set it down in front of him, he made the excuse that he needed to ring Gail and went to take a bar stool up at a high table by the window. He did not want to come across as rude, but really just wanted some peace on his own after having Kirk folks yapping at him all day (due to his job, the local church officials were prone to start whinging and complaining about Kirk matters when he was in their company).

In any case, he genuinely was due to give her a buzz, as he did every day when they were apart. Perched on the bar stool he attempted to do so; however, she did not answer - this was often the case as Gail had never really got used to carrying a mobile phone around with her. He imagined that it had probably been lodged in the bottom of her handbag with all the other bits and bobs women seemed to keep in such places and that she had not heard it ringing. He resolved that he would try again later when back home.

Savoring the ruddy-coloured, hoppy but smooth ale, he gazed contemplatively out of the window at the passers-by coming and going along the pavements, most of whom were students with Marchmont being so close to the university. Looking at the youthful, energetic faces, full of eagerness and ambition, he found it hard to imagine that he, now a balding and middle-aged man, had once been like that. Almost to reassure himself, at the same time, he reflected that he was a fortunate guy and that life had worked out well for him since those student days - not least that he was blessed with having his lovely wife and two great kids.

Enjoying the mild buzz from the ale, along with a feeling of contentment and release from the stressful workday, when his pint was about one gulp from empty, he thought about ordering a second. However, that would probably lead to a third, he imagined, and then joining James and Gary propping up the bar for the rest of the evening. Definitely not a good idea as he had another full-on workday the following morning and needed to keep a clear head. In any case, his tummy was rumbling. So, draining the last of the pint pot, he said his goodbyes to the gents from St Mag's - who were now intently discussing the relative merits of different cask conditioned ales - and headed outside into the fresh, cool air. After repining his Kirk lapel badge, he stopped off at Salvatore's to collect a takeaway. Being originally a west-coaster, from Girvan, he had not cared much for the fish and chips when he moved to the capital first —

finding the peculiar chip sauce of these parts (a mixture of 'broon' sauce and vinegar), which was habitually and liberally dowsed upon a supper, rather unsavoury (or perhaps too savoury). Maybe it was a measure of how much he now felt at home in the east that he could no longer eat his chips without it.

After a short walk, he was soon back in Dick Place and eased open the large, wooden gate to 'Griffin House', the Kirk grace-and-favour abode. The garden was largely overgrown, with Gail and himself having had focused upon the interior of the villa since moving in. The verdant space offered lots of privacy though. Almost pitch black by this hour, he made his way up the garden path, fumbling around in his coat pocket for his keys. Fortunately, back in the previous August before the nights had started drawing in, he'd had the foresight to apply a small, stick-on solar powered light to the canopy of the outside porch which was automatically triggered by movement. As he got closer it engaged, casting a dim glow over the porch area, allowing him just enough visibility to find the right key from the bunch now in his hand and locate the keyhole. Once inside, he slammed the heavy, solid oak door shut, pleased that he would soon get to enjoy his fish supper - the enticing aroma of which had been teasing him on the last stretch of the way home.

On turning round and flicking on the vestibule light, all of a sudden, a metal-headed club hammer slammed into his mouth, instantly knocking out his entire front row of top teeth, along with some of the bottom ones. They splintered out and onto the tiled vestibule floor like beads falling from the snapped string of a necklace. Peter's mouth immediately welling up with blood alongside the broken tooth fragments. At the same time, there was splattering of fish, chips and watery-brown chippie sauce on the floor as the paper-wrapped takeaway package had dropped from his hand; the grip of which had been released by reflex under the shock.

A furious second blow then came at his kneecap from the same instrument, shattering the bones into pieces. Falling to the ground, Peter could make out two cloaked, hooded figures facing him, one with a meat cleaver raised, the other holding a weighty hammer in one hand, along with some long spikes or maybe fencing nails in the other, protruding through their fingers. The full force of one of the individual's boots was then applied to his jaw, immediately dislocating it to his agony. There was shortly after another blow to the side of his head and the General Secretary of the Kirk of Scotland passed out.

Sometime later, he was not exactly sure how long (it could have been just minutes or even hours), he regained consciousness. Lying on his back on the floor in the lounge, his arms and legs had been splayed out in a kind of starfish shape. The rug that Peter and Gail had bought on a Kirk youth mission visit to the Hindu Kush whilst courting in their twenties had been rolled away and he was direct upon the floorboards, whilst also stripped naked. There was some sort of muzzle or rag tied around his head - and what was left of his aching jaw and mouth - to gag him.

Peter's heart was palpitating in fear and dread. At the same time, he was having difficulty breathing through his bloodied and snottered nose.

The room light was off, but there was a flickering from candles. His blood ran cold when he realised that his captors had drawn in chalk around him a satanic five-pointed star symbol. It was then that he registered the excruciating pain focused upon his extremities. By moving his head gingerly to the sides and up and down as much as were possible, he could see that they had knocked the metal spikes he had seen earlier through his hands and feet, pinning them to the floorboards. He could not quite see, but from the fierce stinging sensation, he was sure that they had done the same to his scrotum.

A strange chanting was emanating from the hall and getting progressively louder. A moment later, he could see the two robed figures from before slowly entering the lounge and carrying ivory candles, like those commonly used by the Kirk itself. One of the individuals still had the hood of their cloak pulled up so that their face was obscured. The other, with a plumper and considerably shorter frame, had on some sort of ram's head mask with large, curling horns protruding out from either side at the top.

In the chilling reality of his situation, Peter sensed that he would never again see his beloved Gail, Imogen and Thomas.

He was correct. In an instant, the last words he would ever hear - uttered in a prim and proper Edinburgh male accent and laced with a cold and malevolent tone - were, "*Your Kirk owes John Kellie ... and you are going to pay on its behalf!*" The figures thereupon knelt down beside the church official.

Within a few minutes and before his fish and chips were even cold, Peter Marsh's heart had been cut and ripped out from his chest.

CHAPTER 2

The Habits

I loved Porty and was delighted to have my wee house there. It was a rather vintage bungalow dating from the early 1800's when Portobello (so named in honor of a 18th century British colonial purge upon Panama) had transitioned from being pasture lands of the monks at Holyrood Abbey, to a smuggler's haunt, and then a respectable seaside resort.

The hey days of the latter, however, had long since passed. Nevertheless, over the last ten years or so the area had undergone somewhat of a renaissance, with a renewed interest in activities on (and off) the fine sandy beach and the arrival of trendy cafés, bars and eateries along the pleasant promenade to Joppa. Property prices had soared, but I had been fortunate to buy my bungalow on Straiton Place at auction in the grey period between the amusement arcades closing down and the more urbane venues opening up. It had been a total wreck and you could see that most folks at the auction had thought that I was mad to bid on it with the work and money that would clearly be involved in getting it back to a habitable standard. There were only two other bidders who, thankfully, dropped out earlier than I had expected, allowing me to purchase the place at a very reasonable price. At the time, I was only 20 or so years of age. Sadly, both my parents had recently passed away as a result of a road accident and, as I was an only child, I'd inherited their two-bedroom property in the west of the city. After selling it, I had wanted to invest the proceeds wisely, rather than fritter it away on crap, hence, the purchase of the bungalow was ideal; the sum I'd inherited had been just enough to cover my winning auction bid, along with fees.

Being in no rush to do repairs, over the following decade I had, bit by bit, brought the property back from life support to become a comfortable and homely, if not a particularly fancy, abode. The various milestones of installing central heating and hot water, rewiring and putting in modern electrics, stripping the walls and papering, painting etc., were reached at different points whenever I had saved up enough cash for the work and materials. The first couple of years I had literally camped out there, with candles and a gas canister stove. One of the last jobs I completed was to scrape layers of sticky cigarette tar off the ceilings. This was particularly bad in the front room where there was a swirl of the cancerous residue above where an armchair must have been situated for many years. The spot had a fine view out of the rather splendid bay window to the wee park over the road, as well as further over to the promenade and beach. The old lady who had had the house before me, must have enjoyed sitting there, puffing on her fags, admiring the vista and observing the coming and going of the local residents and tourists alike. According to Joan, my neighbour, the poor old dear had been shuffled off into an old folks' home pretty much against her will. She had thought that the lady's 50-something year old kids had grown impatient with their mum's longevity and had been anxious to get their hands on their inheritance. Hence, the quick sale at auction. Joan was no spritely thing herself and one of the last remaining residents of her time who had moved to the locality in the 60s and 70s. The rest of my neighbours were of following generations and primarily younger couples with nursery and primary school aged kids, along with the obligatory docile family dog.

In fact, in the early days, I had been part of a couple too, however, my partner had flown off with a colleague from her work - about three years ago now - leaving me alone in the nest. Apart from the odd, transient girlfriend, that is how it had remained since. I still had custody of the family pet however, a black moggie named 'Déjà vu' (or, rather just Déjà), after the kitty in the movie, 'The Matrix' (a favorite flick of mine). A great wee - and undemanding - companion.

Although I loved Porty, I was totally scunnered with the parking situation. Not least that I had to pay for an expensive permit from the Council, then, at the same time, generally had to park a ten/fifteen-minute walk away from my front door. It was karma, I guessed, for driving a gas guzzling motor (a 2001 BMW F38, to be exact), which like my house, was of a bit of an antique - or as I preferred to describe it, a 'classic'. Despite its years, the car only had 14,000 miles on the clock when I had bought it off an elderly gent (in his mid-90s). It would seem that the car had been parked up in his garage for much of the previous decade and, even before that, had hardly been used since he had purchased it, split-new, years before that. It was like it had travelled from the past, a time machine, and was in mint condition. I liked the look and feel of the period, the silver body with a black leather interior, and a proper hand-brake - none of that electric nonsense that cars had these days. It gave a low gravely growl as I upped the gears and accelerated, but also in a kind of melodic way that modern cars seemed no longer capable of. It even had an analogue radio with a cassette tape deck. This was an item that never failed to cause bemusement to anyone under age 30 whom I gave a lift to. Not that I had any tapes, other than the few that I had discovered the old gent had left behind in the glove box, including Elvis Presley, and to my delight, Scottish country singer Sydney Devine. This was someone my granny had loved. I happily recalled her singing along whilst playing his latest discs on her old side-board style stereogram. On the discovery and playing of this particular tape, alongside the gritty melody of the car's engine, I had been prompted to name the big beast of a vehicle, 'Syd' - the car indeed was another vintage crooner! Mr Devine, of course, had sadly passed, but would live on to me each time I put my foot on the accelerator. My next car would be electric, I promised myself, so as to make up for Syd's certainly dreadful carbon footprint.

Up until February 2021, I had been working for a new town marketing agency, ClearSkye Communications. However, it had gone bust after losing its principal client. The firm had made the classic business mistake of having almost all of its eggs in the one basket with that main customer (a large private sector company), after previously ditching many of its cash-strapped, not-for-profit customers. When the client, without notice or concern, had upped sticks and took their custom else-where, ClearSkye had come down like a house of cards. More than thirty of us, both employees and contractors, had then found ourselves suddenly out of work.

Alongside looking for another job, to keep me occupied (and sane), I had spent the next few months researching and writing a book - something which had been an ambition of mine for some time. Previously, I had never had enough hours in the day to indulge myself in such manner. Hence, between filling in these frustrating online job application forms, I had undertaken work on it until completion. Some might have called my book 'fiction', others 'non-fiction', due to the disputable veracity of much of the subject matter, although the latter was the official designation. *Scotland - the Special-natural*, was essentially an examination of Scotland's links to the paranormal, the supernatural or as I liked to call it, the *special-natural*, something I had always had a keen interest in.

At night-time when I was a boy and prior to going to bed, I used to pester my dad to tell me stories. However, not the usual bed-time stories that parents would tell their children in order to lull them off to the land of nod and sweet dreams. Rather, I begged to be told ones that would scare me, and the more terrifying the better. Unlike most other kids, I had seemed to thrive upon the shivers that would traverse my spine prompted by the recounting of such tales, along with the chills that would cause my skin to flash with goosebumps.

On such occasions, my mother would invariably object and tell my father to ignore my pleas, "*Jim, dinnae go tellin' him these bloody daft yarns. He'll no sleep a wink ah night… and dinnae forget, he's got the school in the morning.*"

However, more often than not, once she had settled down to watch one of her favorite soaps on the telly, he would come along, perch on the end of my bed, and oblige. On reflection, I think that he had enjoyed telling the tales as much as I had done listening - and we became closer through the shared bond of storytelling.

He seemed to have an endless repertoire. Stories of peoples and events punctuating Scotland's history. Tales of myth and legend where the dividing line between truth and mere fable was unclear. For example: the Norseman, the Celts, the painted Pictish warriors (and their gods and demons); the standing stones and stone circles (what they were and why they were there); the Trows (the peerie, wee fairy folk of Shetland, who operated on a different time plane to the humans inhabitants - so that you could be captured by them for seemingly just one day, only to find out that you had been absent from friends and family for many months and even years); Thomas the Rymour and the Brahan Seer (foretellers and soothsayers - Scotland's Nostradamus'); the Banchee (the keening woman, whose wails and cries foretold of the death of a close one); the fisherfolk and their superstitions (such as the ill-fated call of the curlew), the Mermaids (with their mesmorising allure, leading to many a young, and not so young, fisherman's demise); the Loireag (a water and spinning fairy of the Hebrides); the Elm tree of the underworld; Goblin Ha' and Hugo de Giffard (the necromancer of Yester); the Winter Queen, *Cailleach*; the Baobhan Sith (vampiress of the Highlands); the Selkie seal-folk (beings capable of changing from seal to human form with the shedding of their skin); the Kelpies (the shapeshifting water horses of streams and rivers), along with the fearsome and similarly metamorphosizing Highland *Each-Uisge* (of the sea and lochs) and the - perhaps less terrifying, but mischievous - Shellycoats (of Leith and the Forth); the 'witches' of East Lothian and further afield; and, what had been a particular favorite of mine, Sawney Bean and his cannibal family of forty-plus souls (trapping unwary 16th century travellers for their cooking pot, with any leftovers pickled for future consumption).

It is a wonder I ever slept as a child!

It was perhaps due to my dad having hailed from fisherfolk that he had possessed such a stock of stories. His mother, my granny, had been from Findochty, a fishing village on the

Moray Coast. His father, my grandad, of course, had been one of a family of thirteen children, from the ancient fishing village of Newhaven, long since gobbled up by the city of Edinburgh in its urban expansion. Such families were steeped deep in superstition and tales passed word of mouth over the generations. Storytelling was generally done at the end of the working day and by the flickering light of the hearth or a fish oil lamp. These folks without exception had a harsh life. The men risking their lives upon the vagaries of the weather and the sea. On the return of the boats, the women - the fishwives - having huge creels of fish hauled (by two men!) upon their backs, to then make their way by foot to villages and towns, often many miles away, to sell the catch. The tales and superstitions, of course, had helped to provide these folks context and meaning to the often-delicate balance between life and death that they endured.

The aim had been for my book to be a compendium of such stories: the yarns, the myths, the legends. During that Spring, I had spent many, many hours, long days and weeks further researching the handed-down accounts, aiming to accurately record them in writing for posterity. At the same time, where texts and printed sources existed, to validate the stories as best I could, both in terms of their origin and the content. Further, attempting to do so with an academic rigor, the basic skills for which I had gained from a few years of PhD study (something I had undertaken prior to the university's research budget being canned, forcing me to make a career change and ending up in marketing).

I'd had another reason though for my interest in the 'special-natural' however, and my passion for the not inconsiderable task of researching and writing my book. The fact was that as long as I could remember I had been aware that I'd possessed certain psychic and related abilities. The extent of such aptitudes, I had been unsure of though. Initially, I'd guessed there had been only a modicum of latent aptitude. Nonetheless, I had known that the capabilities were indeed present.

The 'habits' as my mother disdainfully had referred to them, would inevitably surface from time to time. I could cite many and various examples of such occasions. However, there is one specific incident I recall in particular, perhaps more due to mother's reaction to it than the occurrence itself. At the time, I must have been perhaps five of six years old.

We'd had relatives visiting the house (an upper villa in Carrick Knowe) that afternoon and mum had the good crockery out on the living room table. There was my mum's cousin Jeenie, a rather peculiar elderly lady who was prone to quote from the bible at every given opportunity and whose tongue never halted, save as to even take a breath it seemed. Further, my older cousin Viv and her mother, my Auntie Catherine. Along with my mum, it made for a full room of yacking female relatives with stiff competition for airtime between them. Jeenie, who had sat adjacent to the door, looked a bit put out whenever one of the others managed to force a word in edgeways. I remember sitting, cross-legged on the frayed carpet just outside the room in our wee hall, with an odd, sickly feeling coming across me – a bit like the one you got just before the compulsion to vomit. My eyes then developed a kind of glow within them so that my vision blurred.

It was then, I recall, that a vivid daydream had come across me. It related to another of my aunties, Auntie Sheena. The elder sister of Auntie Catherine and my mum, and the wider family matriarch, she had not been able to visit and join the others that day on account of "*having to get her man's tea*" (as my mother had put it). Uncle Billy had been on early shift at Bilston Glen pit that day. In the daydream, I'd felt like I was up at the ceiling of their 4th floor tenement flat in Logie Green, hovering and looking down over Auntie Sheena whilst she was at her gas cooker in the kitchenette. This is something I later learnt was known as 'remote viewing'. She was stirring a large pan of mince, with a big, bubbling pot of tatties alongside. Presumably, fully cooked, I could then see her turn both burners off, drain the tatties and place lids over both pans, awaiting the imminent arrival home of hungry family members.

What she did not realise - but what I could sense - was that she had accidentally turned the gas oven on full; perhaps, inadvertently flicking the wrong dial round when turning off the burners on the hob. My sense of the situation included an awareness that unlit explosive gas was channeling into the oven apace and starting to escape, seeping out of its door. At this sight I remember experiencing an acute feeling of despair and hopelessness - that I could do nothing to alert her, rather that I was mute and inanimate, suspended in my aerial and ethereal vantage point.

Sheena had been a heavy smoker as many hard-working women of the day had been. A cig being a few moments of light relief in a day otherwise filled with an early rise, getting the kids up and - along with their man - fed and out the door for school or work, as well as making their lunch pieces in advance. That, together with going to their own job, doing food shopping, preparing dinner for them all, plus cleaning, laundry etc. Yes, a few drags on a fag were a bit of respite and release from the drudgery.

From my elevated position, I could see Auntie Sheena reaching for her pack of 20 Embassy Filter (the ones that had the red sash across the packet, contrary to their 'sister' brand, Regal, that had it in blue), taking one out and popping it in between her lipstick covered lips, then leaning over for the pink-coloured glass cube ornamental lighter at the side of the work top. This was used for the cooker, the gas fire (which had a troublesome ignition button that would often fail to engage), as well as for the purpose of regular ciggie lighting.

Standing over the cooker, one hand with a cloth wiping up some spills at the front of the hob, I could see her with the other, putting the pink cube to the end of the cig which protruded out from her lips and past the end of her nose. Sheena bore a look of concentration upon her face as she proceeded to depress the silver ignition button of the lighter with a "click." Her brow furrowed as no spark or flame came. A second attempt... and "click" - this time there were a few sparks as the barrel of the lighter agitated against the flint, but again no flame. Getting frustrated, she then gave it a third and more forceful depression... "click."

In an instant, a shock blue and purple flash burst out of the oven! The force blowing the door out and knocking poor Auntie Sheena backwards - clean off her feet and right out of the kitchenette through the mini-saloon style doors - as if she were a drunk being ejected from a bar in a scene from an old Western movie. I recall watching on helplessly as a shocked and bemused Sheena was carried by the blast's momentum to the other side of the hearth rug in the living room, cracking the side of her head on the solid wooden sideboard as she landed! A treasured picture of her and my Uncle Billy on their wedding day clattering off the top of it and setting down upon her, the glass now shattered within its frame.

It was then, I remember waking up from the daydream with a start, feeling sick and terrified. By reflex, as if fleeing from an attacker, I jumped to my feet and charged straight towards the living room and into the door itself, barging it with outstretched hands. It swung wide open on its old, rusty hinges, knocking cousin Jeenie's cup of tea clean out of her hands, so that its steaming contents spilt all over her tweed skirt. In the middle of the seated throng, I then bellowed, *"It's Auntie Sheena, she's been blown-up in her kitchenette!"*

As I urgently repeated this, the mouths of the assembled group hung wide open, aghast and speechless. In the moments that followed, I remember my mum, with some suspicion and reluctance picking up the receiver and dialing the numbers on our old rotary dial phone to make contact with Nessie, her bingo friend and Sheena's neighbour on the same landing. After a wee while, eventually getting through to find out that there had indeed been an explosion. By this time, Uncle Billy had arrived back from his work to witness the scene and a fire engine and ambulance had been called.

As I recall it, thankfully Sheena had escaped any major injury. After a night at the old Royal being observed for head injury as well as being treated for some burns, she had been sent back home to her Logie Green flat to recuperate.

Despite having sounded the alarm amongst the family, my mother had been none too happy with my intervention - I certainly remember that. To this day, I recall mum getting back from the hospital on the night of the blast after checking on

Auntie Sheena, and with a puffed, ruddy and irate face, giving me a rough clip round the ear, along with words to the effect:

"Cameron Guthrie, you MUST stop that NONESENSE – these HABITS. I mean it son. What will folks think ay us? I cannae understand how you knew about yer Auntie Sheena, but I raised ye tae be Kirk of Scotland and that funny, mumbo-jumbo stuff disnae hold wi' the Kirk. I dinnae want to hear or see any of that carry-on from you again, right… AH MEAN IT."

I had not really blamed her for that reaction, however. It was not considered a good thing to be different in those days, especially when it was something that would generally be regarded as crazy, weird, supernatural stuff… the embarrassment and shame of it! Scots of our station in society were taught not to stand-out or put our heads above the parapet. My mother had had that ingrained in her from an early age and had wanted to instill the same set of societal norms and rules within her child. And it was not her fault after all that I was, as my aunties and cousins came to describe me, an *"odd'en."* At the same time, even at that young age, I had felt the injustice in her treatment of me - chastising me for something that I really could not help.

It was experiences like that and many others, albeit generally less dramatic, that had led me to learn early on to keep the presence of my abilities to myself, at least as far as were possible.

Needless to say, despite this, I had continued to feel and see things including having premonitions and viewing future events that ultimately came to pass. Like that of my Uncle Bob having a heart attack and my dad losing his job in the 'Bru' office in Torphichen Street (albeit he had returned to the other side of the social security counter the following week). I would generally keep silent and feign surprise when I heard the news of such earlier foreseen events.

At the same time, over these childhood years and into adolescence I seemed to have developed an ear for those that had passed. Yes, the dead! Generally, this would be in my dreams at night, but also, occasionally, within daydreams. Commonly, the deceased individual would be asking me to pass a message on to a loved one, as if I were some sort of conduit from the place (or places) of the deceased, to that of the mortal world.

For example, this happened when I was around sixteen years of age and had my first proper girlfriend, Jill. I'd had a big teenage crush on her. We had perhaps been dating about three or four weeks when her grandfather, Donnie, died at the Royal Infirmary from cirrhosis of the liver. I had never even met him, however, a few days after his passing he called out to me in my dreams at night.

In a gruff voice that would have made Sydney Devine sound like a choirboy, Donnie had said, "*Son, I want yis to dae us a favor. Tell oor Jill to let her ma ken that I dinnae want my brother Kevin to get ma pewter tankard. It's a special tankard, belonged to my faither afore me. It served me well aw these years for ma beer - as ah nivir liked drinkin oot a can - and other drink. Rather, I want it tae go tae ma son Ally, Jill's uncle, as pairt ay his inheritance. Keeping it in oor ain faimly likes. And, as Ally loves a bevy, so ey does. Kevin wis niver much ay a brar tae me in any case. Ok? Thanks son.*"

This message was something that I had vividly recollected upon waking. It was as if he had written it on a bit of paper and put it in my pocket to read out as requested - that I was his psychic courier or telegram boy. On relaying this beyond the grave missive to Jill, she'd reacted badly, calling me a "*weirdo*" and a "*freak*" and I was promptly dumped. I never did get to find out who ended up with the tankard.

This experience of communication with the other side, along with others, had served to remind me that my special aptitudes - these unwelcome 'gifts' - could cause me far more trouble than they were worth.

Against this background, as I got older and into my later teens and early twenties, not only did I try to hide my abilities, but I would almost deny to myself that they ever existed in the first place. But, of course, that was not really possible - they would manifest themselves whether I liked it or not. Yet, I had actively try to suppress; this was the case, I guess, by force of ingrained routine and practice, even after my parents' passing. I had felt cursed with an infliction, a disease, a malign manifestation.

Perhaps writing the book had been a bit of an outlet for me, catharsis even - delving into the mysteries, myths and legends, including of the paranormal, as a third-party rather than taking part in directly myself. I contemplated that for me, working on the text had probably been a bit like that of a frustrated, out of work actor, jobbing as a poorly paid box office assistant at the Lyceum, 'to be close to the theatre'.

Well, it had been more than therapy. Due to my long hours of research and writing, by early July 2021, I had completed the book. Further, with help from an author friend, I had been introduced to a suitable agent who had been willing to represent me and assist in finding a publisher. After initial frustration and disappointment, to my surprise and delight, the work had been accepted for publication - and much sooner that I could have ever hoped for (I had heard so many tales of authors who had never managed to find a publisher after all their hard graft, something I had been prepared for). After requisite administrative hoops had been surmounted, an initial print run was undertaken allowing copies of *Scotland - the Special-natural* to be publicly available for the Christmas 2021 market. It had been with a curious sense of self-satisfaction that, in the week before festive season, I had walked into the 'Jeremy Thin' bookstore on the Bridges to see a pile of my hardbacks stacked up on one of the tables by the entrance.

To cut a long story short, following its release, the text had received a pretty good reception, even modest success. It had received coverage in Sunday paper book reviews, and I'd even had a short BBC Radio Scotia interview on their mid-afternoon weekday arts program, which was later replayed on Radio 4. At the same time, I had even earned a few quid out it - as had my agent, much to their delight (and possibly, surprise) - although, of course, that had never been a driver for my writing in the first place.

Perhaps, the most positive thing for me to have come out of this little bit of success was that it had prompted a number of invites to book-signing and reading events, such as at small book and community groups, festivals and the like. With a little embarrassment at my conceitedness, I'd had to admit that I liked the attention. Of course, I knew that I was hardly J.K Rowling, and my work was officially in the 'non-fiction' category, but I definitely got a wee thrill out of people coming up to me at such events, showing an interest, such as asking me a question related to its content or requesting that I sign a copy that they had purchased.

If writing the book had been an outlet for me in relation to my suppressed abilities, once written and published, it became a catalyst for me to 'out' such aptitudes. Yes, 'out' them was probably a good term for it. In similarity to a teenager, who with hesitation and no small amount of determination, had summoned the courage to tell their parents that they had the preference for the same, rather than the opposite sex, I had moved to be open - at long, long last - about my hidden self. Publication of the book had prompted me to tell the world (or at least those remotely interested) that I possessed psychic and related skills and capacities that most other people did not.

At the same time, it had seemed to generate within me the confidence and intent to harness and build upon my capabilities after all these years of seeking to suppress. Within just seven or so months from publication of the book, along with attending reading and signing type events, I had even started working with people on a one-to-one basis undertaking 'psychic medium readings'.

CHAPTER 3

Pilrig Community Festival

The Pilrig Community Festival, taking place in the June following the publication of my book, had kindly invited me to provide a reading. It was at this event that, for the first time, I had publicly announced in front of the small, gathered group in the main marquee tent what had driven me to write, *Scotland - the Special-natural*, including that it had been an outlet for my own, hither-to suppressed paranormal abilities. Further, that since its publication, I had decided to offer one-to-one 'psychic medium readings'. I had felt self-conscious at this announcement, a bit like I was engaging in some sort of self-aggrandizement and because, at that time, I had still to undertake any 'proper' psychic medium reading sessions. However, I made no big thing of it, rather slipped it into the biography I gave at the outset of the talk. In fact, nobody seemed to take much notice, other than a few polite smiles and nods, which really should have been no surprise to me. Yet, I felt a big sense of relief at making such statement in public, as this was all part of the new me – learning to be open and honest about my psychic and related skills. My public 'outing', complete.

To coincide with such an announcement, I had liaised with my agent and the publisher to update publicity and promotional materials relating to the hardback, including online presence, as well as good old fashioned business cards, to confirm that I was officially, 'Cameron Guthrie, Author & Psychic Medium Reader'. My ever-mercenary agent seemed to like this, saying that it would give, "*a new angle for sales.*" I had reflected at the time, that my poor mother would have been birling in her grave with the shame of my public descent into 'mumbo jumbo'!

After I had given my reading at the festival, there had been quite a few of questions from those gathered and I felt satisfied that I'd sparked interest and enthusiasm. After the Q&A came to a close, I sold and signed a few copies of my work and handed out some business cards to folks requesting them. As I was putting my notes and a couple of extra books into my backpack, preparing to leave, I noticed a middle-aged gent who had been at the session, milling around rather than exiting. He looked as if were about to come over and talk to me.

However, just then, one the festival organisers, Amelia, collared me to thank me for attending. She was a 30-something, earth-mother type, dressed in ethnic pantaloons and sporting a batic head scarf through which a greying, dreadlocked mane of hair sprouted. As Amelia and I chatted and made our way to the entrance to the tent, her semi-feral, five-year son, Shanti - who, also wore a shock of dreads, shoulder length and cherub light ginger in his case - was running around chasing another younger child. Whilst doing so, he ducked under a table at the 'Wholefoods Diner' stall opposite the opening of the marquee, bumping into it so that it rocked unsteadily upon its feet. The lady running the stall anxiously grasped the handle of a large cooking pot perched upon a camping stove on the now unstable table. The pot was bubbling with burning hot oil and browning falafels. Shouting and gesturing towards Amelia to grab the little Shanti, she shrugged in response and without great haste thanked me for coming along before making off to seek out her son who now appeared to be darting off with his wee pal to the park exit and busy road beyond.

Leaving the tent towards the wider festival grounds, I turned to see next to me the gent that had been hanging about. With a bit of a frown, he nodded in the direction of the disappearing Shanti and said with an unmistakable Edinburgh private school inflection, "*The youth of today, rapscallions the lot of them, eh! … Twas ever thus I guess.*" Then added, "*Mr Guthrie,*" as a statement rather than a question.

A tall, thin man with angular features, probably in his late 50s or early 60s, he was dressed in tweeds and wearing stout brogues, like a mannequin from the 'country living' department of the 'House of Bruar'. Hence, he stood out a little bit amongst the other festival goers who were mostly younger couples with their kids, with a smattering of more aged hip Leithers, as well as local teenagers of Asian descent who were there - in the most part it would seem - to see the 'bhangra' band that was shortly due to do a set on the makeshift stage. I imagined that perhaps he was a grandparent who had been dragged along for the afternoon to provide some childcare respite. If so, he was clearly failing in that task.

"*Yes, it certainly is,*" I replied with a smile, adding, "*… rather, it's Cameron.*"

"*I wanted to say that I really enjoyed your talk.*"

"*Thank you. Glad that you liked it and were able to come along. Great wee festival this, isn't it? It's been a privilege to be a small part of it.*"

The gent continued in his chiseled tones, *"Yes. I have enjoyed having a wander round and in fact, just by chance popped my head into the marquee as you were commencing your talk, Cameron. I must admit that I hadn't been aware that you were giving a presentation or, indeed, of your book. It got me thinking... I am a member of a gentlemen's club. ... Erm, well, sorry for the old-fashioned term, but really that is what it is. A talking shop for old buffers like me,"* adding with a chortle, *"Some younger buffers too, of course, ha ha."*

"A respite from wives, girlfriends and children generally," he continued, *"Somewhere where we might drop into after golf for a dram or two and a blether with like-minded company. Or just somewhere to escape to read a book or the newspaper in peace. We support a lot of charities and work for the community too, so not all hot-air, chit chat etc. We generally have a bi-annual meeting of members. It covers official secretarial and like matters in a private session, but then we move to an open session inviting guests, including wives, girlfriends and the like. For this we generally invite a speaker which would be of interest to the group. There is a buffet and drinks, along with plenty of good chat and cheer of course."*

"That sounds great. It certain seems a busy social group that you have," I responded politely, by that point guessing where the conversation was likely leading.

I was correct, as next he enquired, *"May I ask, if would you consider coming along to our October session as our guest speaker? I really think our members would be fascinated to hear of your book and the tales of Scotch myth and legend. We would, of course, pay a fee, plus your expenses. You could also bring copies of your text, which I am sure many of the members would be delighted to purchase, particularly if signed. I think it is on the third Monday in October but would need to confirm."*

"Oh ... my apologies ... I should have started by introducing myself. It's Farquhar... Farquhar Sutherland," he added.

As he said this, he extended a hand to me. Again, I could not help but be flattered by a further speaking invitation.

After Farquhar had outlined the venue location - near Gillane, a well-to-do wee community just outside of the city on the East Lothian coast, famous for its golf as well as the luxury villas of the retired 'great and good' of Edinburgh - I said that, subject to agreeing the exact date, I would be delighted to accept the invitation.

On this, he handed me a rigid business card with embossed lettering standing out as if in braille. This displayed his name, followed by various letters, most of which I did not recognise, indicating what I assumed were various academic attainments and professional accreditations. Underneath was written the designation of, 'Paterial Secretary to the Order', on the next line, 'The Noble Order of Eidyn' and, at the foot of the card, the address, 'The Manse, Gillane Bents, Gillane, East Lothian EH41 7FY'. I had some vague recollection from the media of the rather peculiarly named 'Noble Order of Eidyn' and it being linked to certain charity and public good ventures.

Before we had gone our separate ways, I'd handed him one my own cards with my contact details and updated professional designation. We had agreed to get in touch in due course to finalise arrangements, including the format of the talk in order to chime best with the members of his group.

CHAPTER 4

It's Doon at Tynecastle They Bide

In addition to the request to speak at the Gillane gentlemen's 'Order', similar invitations from community-type groups had been arriving, to the point that, by mid-August 2022, my diary for the next few months was pretty full and I'd had to start turning folks down. In any case, I had wanted to leave time to focus more upon providing one-to-one psychic medium readings and developing my skills there, rather than just giving talks related to my book. The fact was that many such personal commissions were also being put my way. The change in publicity and promotions relating to the book, including that I was a 'psychic medium reader' as well as author, were clearly paying off.

As I was a relative novice (at least in terms of doing formal one-to-one sessions), I made it patently clear to potential clients that I was not yet experienced at undertaking readings - rather, that I was officially starting out and honing my skills 'on the job', so to speak. Nevertheless, that I would do my best to relay with honestly and clarity, any feelings or insights which I gained from such sessions.

Clients were typically individuals who, for their own personal and legitimate reasons, wanted to communicate with the deceased; invariably persons they had been close to who had passed. In such sessions, I sought to use my psychic capabilities to act as a channel for communication with the departed. Although, more generally, the basic aim of my readings was to see if I picked up on anything regarding the client's past or potentially their future; as part, were there any events or issues that should be relayed to them, along with positive guidance (even words of caution or warnings)? It really depended upon what the client sought and contact with the deceased was not always a feature. In any case, I informed (or perhaps more aptly, cautioned) clients at the outset that any input or feedback that came from 'the other side' may not always be welcome and could perhaps reveal things that they would have preferred not to have been aware of. I was particularly wary and careful in relation to this latter point.

On such basis and subject to suitable caveats, I agreed with a number of individuals to proceed with private consultations. At least initially, I did not charge for the sessions as I felt it would be wrong whilst developing my skills.

By trial and error, as well as via research of works written by psychics and mediums within the profession, I learnt a method which seemed to gain some modestly successful results.

Assuming the client was comfortable, I would generally meet with them at their home and take a walk around the premises to get a feel for the place and what it revealed about the person themselves. At an appropriate point, I would talk at some length about the process and endeavour to find out what exactly the individual wanted from it, deal with any unrealistic expectations and answer any questions that they may have. It was then that we jointly decided whether or not to proceed further.

If we chose to do so, we would then sit down, typically facing one another and I would ask to hold their hands or to place mine lightly upon their shoulders. On doing this, I would seek to meditate for a period - typically, ten or so minutes. As part of the process, I would endeavour to empty my mind of the cluttered thoughts of the day; then concentrate on my breathing... inhaling in, slowly... and, exhaling out slowly..., ... in, slowly... and out slowly..., and so on - feeling my chest, gently rise and fall.

In most cases, slowly, bit by bit, I would begin to have thoughts, pictures and scenes enter my mind - what might be described as visions related to the person. For example, I might see an image of a name, an object, a location, a date or such like; or view the individual in the company of family members or friends. I would often hear or see a presence from the other side saying something that they wanted passed on to the client. It was important for me then to be a filter and articulate what I thought was positive information and feedback to be relayed. Sometimes, the images appeared much more quickly with little or no meditation required, and at other times, not at all.

That was generally the extent of it. My feelings were that this method allowed me to form an elemental psychic bond with the client. Future meetings would typically permit me to build upon such foundation and engage with the individual further, such as to address particular questions that they had. In certain cases, however, just one meeting was all that seemed to be required in order to meet the client's purpose and expectations. Subject to my aforementioned 'filtering' so as not to cause any unnecessarily alarm or hurt, I would share, as candidly as possible, what I saw, heard, felt or witnessed.

Following such a basic method a typical example of a one-to-one psychic medium reading session I had undertaken during this early period was that for Marion McKie - a kindly lady in her early 80s, residing in a lower villa in the Magdalene area of the city - a sprawling post-war, council-built housing scheme.

With a patchwork of furrow lines upon her face, she was clearly someone who had worked hard for a living all her days. During our initial chat, she had specifically asked me to try and contact her late husband, Alec, who had passed away about ten weeks previously of lung cancer - *"I just want to ken ays alright on the ither side, that's ah. If yeh dae that, I'll be at peace and no bother trying to contact him again. I'll wait until ah meet him in that world."*

After having a wander around her immaculate home, of which she was clearly proud to display, we sat in the kitchen, and I asked to hold a personal item of Alec's which I felt would assist with her request; further to see a photograph of him. In response, she disappeared off to the living room and I heard a drawer opening and her rummaging around. Moments later she returned and handed me a beautiful brass box, a little dull, but not tarnished.

"His baccy box… belonged tae his faither afore him, although the faimily got given it efter Alec's grandfaither had been bayoneted tae death in Battle ay the Marne… just a laddie, aged 19, but married aw the same… his wife wis left with two wee yins to bring up on her ain efter that. All the sojiers or thir grieving families got yin whether they liked it or not."

Examining the box in my hands, I could see that it was stamped with the text, *'Christmas 1914'*, *'Imperium Britannicum'* and had the cameo of young, regal looking female standing out, with the letter '*M*' aside, along with other markings. I guessed that the 'M' was Princess Mary, although my knowledge of the British monarchs and aristocracy was poor, due to lack of interest, despite my historical bent.

Marion went on, "*Alec, awis said that it wis ah 'fuckin' disgrace' that the lads - oan both sides, mind - wir sent to their deaths for the pleasure of cowardly toffs squabbling ower land an' territory. … An' that pampered royals geeing a fucking brass box wi cigs or chocs in it didnae make up fir thir slaughter!*"

Excusing her swearing, she continued, "*But he also said, it wis a fine baccy box aw the same, an' reminded him of his faither and the grand-faither that he niver got tae meet. So, he made guid use ay it. Aye… he used it fir his baccy an' papers for as long ah kent him, and wid started courting in wir teens. Even when he wis sitting propped up in eys death bed at St Columba's Hospice in Granton, he used tae have it on eys lap, making up eys rollies.*"

"*It's perfect Marion, just perfect,*" I responded.

At the same time, she had brought another item through from the living room. Passing a framed photograph to me, she explained, "*This wis us on oor diamond wedding anniversary a couple ay years ago. Just afore we headed to a do the faimly had organised fir ayhs at the Ken Buchanan Hotel oan Ferry Road. The Evening Herald hid sent someone roond tae the hoose tae take it - it wis printed in the next day's edition as pairt ay a feature-thing oan the city's 'elderly citizens', the war generation, ken. I wis real proud and it's a lovely photae ay the baith ay us, don't yeh think? This is the original colour version they sent ayhs.*"

"*It certainly is Mrs McKie … you look fabulous, the both of you! … And it is another perfect item for this session,*" I replied smiling. Indeed,

Marion looked resplendent, all done up for the occasion. Alec looked like he had been a little bit uncomfortable getting his photo taken for the paper, but nonetheless wore a cheek-to-cheek grin - no doubt under Marion's strict orders - his pleasant, but ruddy and bloated face betraying a lifestyle common to men of his vintage in central Scotland.

At the kitchen table, placing the baccy box and the framed photo in between us, I gently cupped each of her palms in mine. I then took a deep breath and lightly closed my eyes. As per the aforementioned method, I focused upon my breathing and cleared my mind of the days buzz and thoughts. Next, I let the image of the photo diffuse into the empty space created. Gradually, in my mind's eye, I could see the outline and then its more exact form. This became clearer still, thereupon the image morphed into something more than what was portrayed in the photograph. It was two of them, Marion and Alec, getting ready for the photographer's arrival. At this, the scene became animated. It was a bit like I was watching a film clip, although more akin to me actually being present as a witness.

Marion was straightening Alec's tie, evidently something he wore a little reluctantly - he circled the tight collar with his index finger, clearly not used to such awkward restriction. She then patted down his jacket and picked a couple of seemingly non-existent specs from the lapel. I could then hear the sound of the doorbell and witnessed the lady of the house adjusting her skirt and looking into the 1930s fan mirror over the sideboard in order to - once again - check her hair and make-up, before going to the front door.

Moving my focus from this vision, I released my left hand from Marion's, and proceeded to place it, fingers spread, over the top of the brass baccy box. Almost immediately I felt a tingling sensation. It travelled from the tips of my fingers to the back of my hand. I could feel my veins as if they were lightly vibrating, almost tickling the skin on top. A clear, sharp visualisation suddenly arrived in my mind's eye. It was Alec, as if he were standing right next to of me, with the red cheeks and worn face of the photograph. Like we were two mates standing at the bar of a pub enjoying a pint and some banter together. He looked round at me and said,

"Tell my Marion that ahm fine … that she's no tae worry and I've nae pain anymair. That it's no sae bad here, ken."

It was as if he had been listening to my initial discussion with his wife.

"An' tell her that I'll be here waiting fir her when her time comes. But, ken, there's nae need to rush on ma account."

I took my hand off the baccy box and reached for her free hand, so as to hold, once again, both. Speaking out loud, I replied,

"I'll tell her Alec, I'll tell her… thank you."

On hearing me say this, Marion gripped my hands tightly, and with a surprising degree of power for an elderly lady. Leaning close towards me and with a trembling voice she asked,

"Tell ahys what Cameron? Is that Alec speaking tae yeh?"

"It is Mrs McKie. And I can tell you that he is looking well." I then relayed Alec's message verbatim.

"*Oh, my … that is amazing,*" Marion managed to choke out as she began to sob. "*Tell him thit ah love him. That I'll see um when god decides it's ma turn.*"

Alec looked towards his dear lady, then back to me, his eyes focused directly upon mine. Smiling serenely, he said, softly, "*She's a good un, a'wis wiz. Ma mither said that way back when we wir courting, and she wisnae wrong. Son, yeh can tell her thit ah miss her too. But, as ah says, I'll be here fir her, waiting.*"

I passed on the message to Marion who was now fully greeting.

I then felt a tap on my shoulder - it was Alec, "*Can I ask one mair question son?*"

"*Yes, of course,*" I replied.

"*It's fir you though, rather than the missus - she disnae like fitba. I want tae ken if the Herts won the cup? Ah had tickets fir Hampden to go with ma mates, Tam an' Ally fae the bowls at Brunstane. But fuckin well had tae pop ma clogs the week afore! Nivir got tae ken the score.*"

Smiling, I replied, "*Hearts won 2-1 Alec, after extra-time*" - the Scottish Cup final having been played between Heart of Midlothian F.C. (Hearts aka 'the Jambos') and Rangers in mid-May. I could sense Alec's relief and joy as he started to sing a song with some gusto, a song that always took me back years to when, as a wee boy, my grandad used to take me to Tynecastle Park, the Edinburgh home-ground of Hearts.

"*Herts, Herts, Glorious Herts,*
It's doon at Tynecastle they bide,
The talk of the toun are the boys in maroon,
An' Auld Reekie supports them wi' pride…"

Alec bellowed this out. The volume of his singing, however, gradually reducing, as he started to melt away into the distance and from the imagery of my mind,

"This is ma story, this is ma song,
Follow the Herts and yeh cannae go wrong,
Fir some say thit Celtic and Rangers are grand,
but the boys in maroon are the best in the land..."

Opening my eyes, I was met with a beaming smile from Marion, whilst tears of joy were rolling down her cheeks. *"Thank yeh son, thank yeh so much! Yeh dinnae ken how much this means tae me. I'll rest easy now until my ain time comes,"* she said, taking a paper hankie from inside the cuff of her cardigan and dabbing at her eyes.

No follow-up session was required – my client had received the confirmation and reassurance that she'd sought from our psychic medium reading session.

CHAPTER 5

Golden Girl, Sunday
16th October 2022

I t was the evening before Chloe Rennie was to take part in the heats for the World Highland Dancing Championships.

The next day, the event was to take place at the Emirates Arena in Glasgow from 9.30 am. A minibus had been scheduled to collect her and fellow local competitors at 7.45 am from the door of the Norwegian Seaman's Church on North Junction Street, Leith, the erstwhile home of the Vivienne Leitch School of Traditional Dance. Being invited to attend the heats was on the back of Chloe's success earlier in the year, winning a silver medal in the South of Scotland Championships for her age category (11-13 years), along with the progress that she had made at training since then. If successful, she would be competing in the World Championships event itself in August of the following year, taking place at the Cowal Highland Gathering. To compete at that renowned fixture had been an abiding ambition of Chloe's since her mum and dad had started taking her to highland dancing lessons at the Vivienne Leitch School as a 7-year-old child. Hence, to say that she was excited that evening to be attending the heats the following day would be a big understatement.

The anticipation was equally shared by her mum, Helen, who knew that she would find it difficult to concentrate through her 11 am to 7 pm shift at Asda at the Jewel the next day. Dad, Jim, would be exactly the same - he was down for the Monday back shift at Turnball's, the grain processing plant on Leith docks. Over the years, Chloe's parents had taken her all over Scotland to compete at dance competitions, including in the Western Isles, as well as twice over to Ireland. They would have dearly loved to have been able to attend the Emirates in the morning, the pinnacle of their cherished daughter's dancing career to-date, but neither were able to get out of working.

The foreman had simply laughed at Jim when he had asked for the shift off, before adding bluntly, *"Nae chance, wiv a big order tae process. If yeh dinnae like ma answer, yeh can take yer jaiket wi' yeh… fir good!"* And Helen knew better than to ask her supervisor for the time off as she'd had a long battle to get put on a standard day shift pattern and proper contract in the first place. Any perceived ducking out of work might have led to her being put back on weekend working and an unpredictable 'zero hours' regime. The family needed the guarantee of regular work and wages, not least to be able to afford to pay for Chloe's class and competition fees, along with the shoes and various outfits for the Highland dancing - outlays, of course, that they never begrudged shelling out for. In any case, her parents knew that their daughter would text with the results of the heats as soon as they were announced.

Chloe's wee brother Jamie, 10, was not quite so excited as the rest of his family were about the competition. He fully expected his sister would be arriving back the following evening telling them all how she would be competing on the big stage at the next World Champs. The fuss they would all make of the golden girl after that would be a pain in the arse to put up with, he had no doubt. That said, Jamie was secretly quite proud of his big sis; he had always looked up to her, despite the usual sibling rivalries and fallouts they had from time to time.

Before bedtime, Chloe packed her kit bag with her doting mum's help and laid out clothes for the bus rather than leave it until the morning, partly due to the excitement and part, just to be super-organised. Comfy trackies were placed on the wee dresser next to her bed and would be worn for the journey and arrival at the Emirates - Jim, through the week, had nipped into Ocean Terminal at his dinner break to buy her the Nike pair that she had been after for the special event. In order to afford them, he had carefully managed to put aside money from his wages over the previous few weeks.

All prepared, the household had an early night. That was all except for Jamie who, unbeknown to his parents, was at his computer games terminal with headphones on until the early hours.

CHAPTER 6

Grand Patter, Monday
17th October 2022

October had always been one of my favorite months in Scotland. There was a feel of winding down. The days were shorter and with a chill in the air, but there was a special quality of light different from the rest of the year. The sun tended to linger low in the sky at early morning and late afternoon, casting a golden glow in the sky and enunciating the fine yellow, orange and red autumn colors of the leaves as they fell. Such beautiful crisp, sunny days served as a hiatus before the pall of winter drew up from the horizon. Most recently, however, the weather had seemed unseasonably mild.

It was the morning of the day of my talk at the Gillane gentlemen's club. Settling down with a freshly made coffee from my wee machine, I opened up my laptop to check on the arrangements. My diary confirmed that 12.30 pm was the agreed time for my arrival. The presentation I would give was pretty much pre-prepared as it followed a now familiar formula. This was something like the fifteenth that I had given, and I had learnt to pitch at just about the right length for most speaking events - not too short to infer that I did not have enough to say for myself, but not too long so as to bore the pants off the audience.

Off course, there were tweaks according to the nature of the particular group or gathering. For example, the East Linton & District History Society the previous week had wanted more detail on the research I had undertaken to validate the topics in my book, whereas the Kirkcudbright Book Festival in August, had preferred to hear my reading of passages from the text, along with my feelings and emotions with regard to the content. In relation to the day's event, when we recently discussed over the phone, Farquhar Sutherland had requested a particular focus upon the 'Fiosaichean' (a topic which I had included outline reference to in my Pilrig Community Festival talk which, of course, he had attended); needless to say, I was prepared to oblige.

Over the weekend, I had also undertaken some background study on the client, the 'Noble Order of Eidyn'. This was something I always endeavored to do before such speaking occasion, although usually at the last minute. Hence, on this occasion I was better prepared than usual. Upon various sources on the internet, in line with what Farquhar had said, it was a described as a 'gentlemen's club' - although I was not exactly sure if, strictly speaking, such groupings were still permitted in these days of LGBTIQA+ rights, equality and discrimination laws, etc. Of course, the gent's group also had a rather pretentious title, redolent perhaps of the masons. At the same time, it appeared to be a registered charity. That chimed with my earlier recollection on hearing the name of the Order and that it was known for doing good works for the community. According to one local, Edinburgh news website, it had, "... *over many years, provided valuable support and funding to all sorts of worthy causes and community ventures in and around the city."* Indeed, there was gushing praise from different quarters for these 'good samaritans'. On reading this, I pondered whether I should perhaps be reducing my - already modest – attendance fee in view of the obvious magnanimity of this client?

So, feeling well prepped, prior to heading over to Gillane, I had the time to indulge in another of my passions. As perhaps indicated by my encounter with Alec McKie - deceased of Magdalene – I to, had certain 'Jambo' loyalties, although had not been to a game in years. I did, however, have a hobby of collecting originals of old match-day programs of the club. Those of special games and victories, such as the 2012, 5-1 Scottish Cup victory against city rivals, Hibernian F.C (Hibs aka *'the wee team fae Leith'*… although, to be honest, that was a rather unfair moniker), or the Scottish League Cup, 1-0 win over Kilmarnock in 1962. In fact, earlier in the week, I had put in a bid on e-Bay for a much-coveted program from the 1-0 victory against Bayern Munich in the 1988-89 UEFA Cup quarter finals - this first leg match having been played at Tynecastle Park on a February evening in 1989. I was keeping a close eye on the bid, although there was nearly another week to go until the close of the auction. Hence, with time to spare, I spent the greater part of the morning perusing various auction sites for other interesting match programs, comparing 'bid' and 'buy now' prices, as applicable.

Late in the morning I got properly dressed in smart, khaki chinos, white shirt and blue blazer and packed my leather case with what was required. Once ready, I then started on my way up to Gillane. Whist guiding Syd towards the A1, en-route with one hand on the steering wheel I rummaged around with the other in glove compartment, pulling out one of the cassette tapes left by the auld fella who had sold me the car. Glancing down, I could see it was the album, 'Independence', by Scottish pop-stress of yester year, Lulu. Feeding into the retro dashboard tape deck, the title track began to play.

Along to a high tempo pop beat, our wee diva gied it laldy! I could not help but join in, singing the catchy chorus in unison with her. Other drivers must have seen my profile at the driving wheel swaying from side to side, with my head bobbing away merrily as I did. But what the hell did I care, I thought smiling. As the other tracks continued to play on, I reflected on the fact that Lulu definitely had 'it', both then and now. A class act - rivaling even the esteemed Mr Devine.

Before I knew it, I was attempting to ease my lump of a car out of the sharp, left angle turn at the High Street in Aberlady, having left the A1 at Gladsmuir. I then headed onwards upon the North Berwick Road to Gillane. We were now firmly in premium east coast golfing territory. On this stretch of the road, with fairways either side, well-manicured greens punctuated the scenery at various intervals. Retired Edinburgh professionals, clad in Lyle and Scott and pastel-colored breeks, were busy whiling away their time as the hourglass sands of retirement ran on. I imagined that the members of Farquhar's Order would themselves have been peppering the links today had it not been for their function.

Gillane itself was a pretty wee place, with a quaint village centre that would not have looked out of place in the English home counties. However, this particular area was hidden from view as I drove up the main road and out of the other side of the wee town. Farquhar had given me meticulous directions from hereon and it was not long before I had to swing Syd into an anonymous side-road that he had assured me led to 'Gillane Bents'. Although I did wonder if I had taken a wrong turn as it looked as if it just led just to farmers' fields, rather than anywhere in particular.

The road passed through a clearing in some trees, turned a tight corner and then ascended a small hill. Before reaching the top, I was met by elaborately black-smithed metal gates fixed in between two, large stone pillars - which must have been at least twelve foot in height - and high fencing. The gates bore the lettering, 'The Manse'. Closed shut, I was thinking that I would have to get out of the car and look for some sort of entry phone system. However, as if by magic, the gates opened automatically and inwardly, like two great mechanical arms outstretching in the direction of the top of the hill. Passing through, I noticed a large sign saying, 'Private property, trespassers will be prosecuted'. I could also see security cameras attached to the stone pillars which swiveled round, following the slow progression of my vehicle.

As I reached the crest of the hill, a large mansion house was visible down in the distance. It appeared to be of the Edwardian period, in traditional sandstone, and was surrounded by park land and well-maintained gardens, with what seemed to be further fencing encircling the more immediate perimeter of the property and its grounds. From my elevated position, a pristine lawn was in view rolling out like a fine carpet from the back of the house and graduating down to the shore of the Forth. There stood a long and substantial jetty protruding into the waters and mooring a number of fancy boats - or rather, yachts - along each of its sides, some of which were truly enormous.

Slipping Syd into third gear and leaving the top of the hill, an extended and impressive driveway then led down towards a full-frontal view of 'The Manse' of Gillane Bents. This was no Kirk 'Manse' as the name might have suggested, however. Its ostentatiousness far removed from the typical practical and austere clergyman's residence. Presumably, at one time, it had been the church house for the minister of the nearby Gillane village Kirk, however, under its current ownership, had been added to and transformed into the rather brash and grandiose mansion house of the present. The driveway then led to another gate, this time already open and allowing access to a wide circular area in front of the building. This curled around a large, shiny gold statue: a life-sized figure, representing some sort of preacher man, clutching a large book - presumably a bible, albeit looking more of a manuscript of some sort - in one hand and raising the other in a kind gesture to the heavens, although rather oddly, it came across as more of a salute. I thought it looked a bit like a John Knox in polished gilt and then chuckled to myself thinking that if it were, the legendary Calvinist would most certainly not have approved! Coming off the driveway and on to the circular area, Syd crunched upon white chucky stones which glistened in the sunlight. Probably crushed Italian marble I thought, half-joking ... not your average B&Q gravel, that was for sure. Parked side by side along the edge of this circle, were perhaps thirty to forty cars, expensive looking ones, gleaming like gems on a necklace.

Now, I am not the sort of guy with a geeky knowledge of modern, fancy motors (ok... yes, I do like my more vintage ones), so a fair number of the makes and models of the vehicles I did not recognize at all. But perhaps that was because they were so exclusive, I considered. From what was parked outside the Manse, it was patently clear that there was some serious wealth inside. In fact, I had never seen so many luxury cars in one place, not even behind the glass at the Aston Martin showroom at Sighthill. No parking spaces left, I could see a small exit from the circle which led to an overflow car park in between the house and its pristine lawns. I eased Syd through to find a space there. As I did so, I noticed that behind some grand, old oak trees, towards the parkland, were three different helicopters parked up on the lawn... yes, bloody helicopters!

Billionaire-type pad, yachts, super-extravagant cars and now helicopters ... who the hell were the members of the 'Noble Order of Eidyn', I wondered? Some secret club for the uber-wealthy, tucked away in deepest, darkest East Lothian, but masquerading as a charity? Definitely not the sort of not-for-profit entity I had been used to working with during my earlier days at ClearSkye Communications.

After finding a parking space, I grabbed my leather case which I had packed with some copies of *Scotland - the Special-natural*, along with the paper with my talk, business cards, and a banana (which I had taken in case the buffet turned out a dud - although, after seeing the Manse and its surroundings, I was now anticipating fare prepared by a Michelin-starred celebrity chef!).

Heading back along to the circle in front of the house with the fancy motors, I then made my way upon the opulent, sparking gravel towards the entrance of the building. As I did so, it made a crackly, squeaking noise, a bit like I was walking on fresh snow. The Manse had a magnificent, antique wooden door, situated under an equally grand entrance portico. The door must have been ten feet high and almost the same in width. Just below half-way up, at chest height, there was an ornate, brass knocker of unusual design, fashioned like an antique quill pen;

upon use it had been crafted to meet an equally decorative but curious looking book or manuscript reminiscent of that that held by the statue figure I had just encountered, again created in brass and embedded in the wood. As I was just about to use this fine fixture to alert of my arrival, the bulky door suddenly swung open. Thereupon, I was greeted by the sight of a rather stunning young lady, probably in her early-20s, definitely not more than that. Dressed in a kind-of maid's uniform, she smiled and beckoned me inside saying, with a hint of an accent from somewhere in eastern Europe, "*Welcome to the Manse, Sir.*" The uniform was a rather old-fashioned 'Victorian tea-room' style, black and white, with frilly lace, however, rather incongruously accompanied by a bum hugging, short black skirt - all together, the outfit was reminiscent of a 1970's Benny Hill sketch. I had little doubt that the poor lassie must have felt rather humiliated having to wear such daft work garb.

Once inside, she led me up some steps and into a rather magnificent hallway with a decorative tile flooring and wood paneling half-way up the walls. Above the panelling, an eclectic mix of curiosities were festooned. These included a taxidermied ram's head (with great, circular twisting horns as part), various rather gruesome and medieval looking items of weaponry, along with what appeared to be a WWII German soldier or officer's uniform jacket. Upon the latter, I recognised embroidered on collar the *Schutzstaffel* 'SS' insignia in lightening strip, logo fashion - I knew from my wider book research that these symbols were actually those of the 'Armanen Runes' and claimed by the Nazis to be symbols of Aryan priest-kings. The sleeve of the jacket bore a spread-winged eagle resting upon a circle with a swastika in the center. By way of reflex, a shudder ran through me, and I promptly averted my gaze.

In fact, separate from the uncomfortable feeling prompted by these rather strange 'curiosities', I got a general sense of foreboding from within the Manse, detecting a rather sinister 'atmosphere' and a feeling that bad things were present and afoot on the premises. I tried to dismiss such reaction, rather to focus upon the talk that I was shortly to give (and which, of course, I was being paid as a professional to deliver).

The young maid had disappeared off into a side room and a minute or two later a short, stout middle-aged gent appeared, dressed in tweeds. He had a bloated, ruddy face and rubbery lips, accompanied by a small triangular beard and neat moustache. The sort of beard and tache combo that men on the continent, particularly in Germany and Austria, appeared to be rather fond of. Grinning at me, he extended his hand and with an anglified and genteel Edinburgh lilt, welcomed me:

"*Greetings dear boy, you must be the eminent Mr Guthrie?*" A resident of the Grange, rather than Gorgie, more Barnton than Bingham, I thought - no surprise there.

He continued, "*We are most pleased to have you join to our little event. I've heard a lot about you and your book from Farquhar whom I understand engaged you for this afternoon's proceedings. We are very much looking forward to your talk and I wanted to welcome you personally. I'm Alister Forbes-Fleming, Grand Pater of our Order.*"

Beckoning me down the hallway, we engaged in some small talk as we meandered along. As he spoke, I caught a whiff of whisky emanating off his rather rank breath. Politely (but not entirely truthfully), I complimented him on the surroundings of the Manse, saying how wonderful I thought the building and grounds were. As part, I mentioned the golden preacher man statue at the entrance, enquiring as to whether, perhaps, it was fashioned upon an original minister of the Manse? At this, the portly gent looked quizzically at me and replied -

"Well, it is representative of a minister, but not of Gillane parish. He is, or should I say was, a fellow by the name of the reverend John Kellie who passed many, many years ago. A renowned thinker and skilled philologist - that is in addition to his undoubted ecumenical skills. Somewhat of an inspiration to the foundation of this Order, if I may say. Poor chap was an innocent victim of a most terrible miscarriage of justice by the Kirk of Scotland - a long time ago now, but certainly not forgotten!"

Just as I was explaining my surprise that, with my keen interest in Scottish history, I had never heard of this celebrated individual, Forbes-Fleming mumbled something like, *"He wouldn't appear in your history books,"* and promptly changed the subject. I found that rather strange.

Bidding me to follow him, he guided me through the doorway of a large galleried hall and onto an elevated entrance area. Here, I was greeted by the sight of a sea of mostly grey and balding mens' heads, indicating perhaps sixty to seventy Order members in attendance. Interspersed amongst them were a number of young ladies, similarly attractive and kitted out as the eastern European lassie I had encountered upon my arrival. They were circulating and serving champagne flutes from little silver trays. You could see the hungry eyes of a number of gents in attendance darting eagerly in the direction of rear ends and frilly cleavages as the waitresses busied themselves dishing out the champers.

Dotted around the hall were large circular tables and chairs, with ample room between for the current chatting and mingling of those in attendance. As we descended three steps to join the throng, I noticed that crockery and glasses for a buffet were being set up at the far away side of the room. Just then, came a loud knocking from behind me. I turned to see a chap in full penguin-type tails, rapping the silver covered top of a dark, wooden cane upon the substantial door to the hall; the latter stood open and at a right-angle to the expanse of the room. It was as if he were the pantomime 'Black Rod' at the London Westminster parliament. This prompted a hush and after a moment the fellow announced, in clipped and nasal tones, "*Let the open session commence.*"

As he did so, he signaled to two of the waitresses at the back of the hall, upon which they proceeded to open up a set of concertina doors set within the wall revealing a further fairly substantial room. This contained a large group of finely dressed ladies - clearly, these were the wives and girlfriends of the gentlemen members present, the 'WAGs' if you like. The women started to make their way through the open partition and into the main hall, accompanied by lots of high-pitched chatter and giggling. As they paired up with their respective men folk, I could see that they were generally of a much younger age demographic to their partners. It did not surprise me, of course, that there appeared to be no same sex couples at the event - it was obvious that the rams and ewes had distinct roles in this rather stuffy and old-fashioned set-up.

Forbes-Fleming thereupon ushered me over to a couple of 60-something gents before promptly flitting off, clearly an accomplished social butterfly. The two looked like what I imagined the typical denizen of an exclusive Scottish golf club would resemble. They seemed pleasant enough, all the same. One of the impossibly attractive waitresses, who was effortlessly weaving in and out of the gaggles of members and their partners with her wee silver tray, handed me a glass of champers. This was well-received.

I could not help but notice the jewelry that adorned the necks, ears and wrists of the wives and girlfriends, it was something else! Invariably showy, with lots of shiny gold and sparkly stones, but clearly exclusive and expensive rather than of the costume variety. At one point, a noticeably well-oiled Farquhar Sutherland bounded up to me with his tall lanky frame, effusively thanking me for coming along and apologising for not saying hello earlier as he had been busy organising the day's event.

Before long there was a tap of a spoon on a glass. Thereupon, the chatter quietened and the folks started to move to take up seats at the various tables within the hall. Forbes-Fleming then lumbered with his ample frame up the steps to the raised entrance area and to behind a microphone stand which had been set up. He was not helped by the rather ridiculous 'Knights Templar' style, purple velvet robe, which was now adorning him, complete with swinging, golden tassels. After a moment to catch his breath he spoke, "*Welcome, welcome … a guid afternoon to yin an' aw!*"

This was done with a mock timbre as if he were trying to recite Rabbie Burns and much to the obvious amusement of the audience. After some minutes outlining the fine charitable work of the Order over the previous six months, he moved on to introduce me in his booming baritone:

"*As Grand Pater of our Order I have the pleasure and privilege to welcome local author and historical sleuth, Cameron Guthrie, to our little gathering - our bi-annual meeting - to deliver the talk. I am delighted to inform you that he will tell us about his simply wonderful book, 'The Scotch and the*

Supernatural'. This work, as you may be aware, has prompted much interest since its release."

At this, I gulped down the last of the champers from a second glass I had managed to purloin off one of the waitresses' silver trays as she had breezed past me a few minutes earlier. I really did not like public speaking and found it sought to steady the nerves. Suitably fueled, I made my way up to the raised area next to Forbes-Fleming. He made room for me behind the stand, and in a friendly gesture patted me on the back before moving down to take a seat amongst the throng. Smiling to the audience, I made polite little head nods to the left and right and then - after elevating the microphone some inches - began.

As per the now standard format for my talk, I commenced with the usual *"thanks for inviting me along"* and gave a wee personal bio, explaining what had led me to write the book (the correct title of which I recited). Of course, this now included the fact that I was a 'psychic medium reader' (... and, since the summer, even a moderately experienced one). I then moved on to provide a very broad summary of the content of my book - the tales, the various myths and legends. In addition, I gave a brief outline of the research I had conducted to validate the stories (in terms of both origin and content) as best I could. At this point, I progressed to the area that Farquhar Sutherland had asked me to provide a particular focus upon.

"Ladies and gentlemen. May I ask which of you are familiar with Michel de Nostredame, known as 'Nostradamus', the 16th century French astrologer, physician and reputed seer?"

Almost all heads nodded in recognition.

"Thank you… Okay, how many of you have heard of Merlin – he of the sword and the stone and the legend of King Arthur?"

Again, heads were universally nodding. *"Thank you once again,"* I said in recognition, before asking,

"Now… how many of you are familiar with Scotland's own reputed prophets, Thomas the Rymour and the Brahan Seer, who were supposed to have been able to foretell the future, amongst possessing other special abilities?"

In response to this, virtually no-one indicated recognition, both Alister Forbes-Fleming and Farquhar Sutherland being notable exceptions. Of course, this in no way surprised me - the question had essentially been rhetorical and I'd fully expected a such response. Likewise, I had not anticipated that many of those in attendance would have actually read my hardback in advance of the day's talk - although it had received a good reception, such as from book critics and media, it was of niche interest and certainly no bestseller. More particularly, I was familiar with the fact that Scotland's own history and cultural figures had long been overlooked in the school curriculum, at least within the generations of most of the gents in the hall, along with many of their female companions. This was generally in favor of history and figures of another country - typically, England - so that the Scottish schools' syllabus focused on the Norman conquest, the Magna Carta, Henry VIII and Shakespeare (… and all that), to the detriment of our own nation's history and cultural figures. This proved true for both state and private sector schooling. The latter, no doubt, being where most of the gents (and ladies) present would have been dispatched and processed through in their formative years, I was sure - they were the Fettesians, Herioters, Lorettorians, Watsonians, etc. Indeed, the history of wider European nations and even that of America was frequently afforded superior status and importance. The result of such sidelining, needless to say, was a general ignorance of our own, indigenous Scottish history and persons of note within.

I went on to outline that the Brahan Seer of the 17th century, and Thomas the Rymour of the 13th century, were Scotland's own Nostradamuses.

"The Brahan Seer, Coinneach Odhar, was originally from the Isle of Lewis. He had been a farm worker on the Brahan estates in Strathpeffer and gained notoriety for having the gift of prophecy - then referred to as, 'the sight'. Making many forecasts and predictions which came to pass, including those related to the Battle of Culloden, the Highland Clearances, construction of the Caledonian canal and more recently, the discovery of North Sea oil, as well as the re-establishment of the Scottish parliament in 1999."

Moving on to Thomas the Rymour, I explained,

"He was a gentleman by the name of Thomas Learmont, a Laird from the village of Ercildoune in the Scottish Borders, now known as Earlston. Thomas was reputed to have had 'special-natural' powers, including those of prophesy which he often relayed via his poetry. As part, it is claimed that he accurately foretold of events including the manner of the death of Alexander III, the Battle of Bannockburn, Mary Queen of Scot's defeat at the Battle of Carberry Hill, along with the union of the crowns (with the rule of James VI and I)."

My provision of details and elucidation of these home-grown historical figures clearly sparked some interest from those assembled judging by the number of heads nodding, along with vocal and facial affirmations apparent.

At this point, I briefly went over a summary of the research I had undertaken confirming the existence of these individuals from our country's past, along with available evidence which I had interrogated concerning the veracity of their predictions. Further, indicating that such research had confirmed in my mind that the 'special-natural' powers that both appeared to have possessed had been considerably broader than mere soothsaying and not always used for positive purposes. Thereupon, I gave a number of examples. This included Thomas the Rymour's fabled curse of the 'weeping stones' - that Fyvie castle in Aberdeenshire would never pass in direct line between more than two generations and, as part, that no eldest son would live to succeed their father.

"This did indeed this came to pass, with a series of tragedies befalling such male heirs," I confirmed, before adding, *"Another thing I can say for certain is that the scope and extent of these individuals' powers and abilities - and more broadly that of the 'Fiosaichean' - are largely unknown."*

At this, I received a few curious looks from those assembled. I continued,

"Both the Brahan Seer and Thomas the Rymour were what was described going back to the ancient times as of the Fiosaichean - the 'Seers'. Individually, each Fiosaiche was thought to have been blessed (or cursed, dependent upon the viewpoint) with considerable special-natural power.

Around 3,000 years ago, the Celtic tribe, known as the Votadini, who ruled what is now southern Scotland and northern England - from hill forts at Dunpender (Traprain) Law in East Lothian and later to Suidhe Artair at Din Eidyn (Arthur's Seat, Edinburgh) - relied upon the Fiosaichean to assist them in retaining their power and wealth.

Indeed, Scottish history, has other examples of the Fiosaichean throughout its eras. Illustrations may include, Hugo de Giffard, the warlock and necromancer of Yester of the 13th century; further, the Winter Queen of legend, Cailleach, who is referenced to in literature from at least of the 8th century. Sadly, time constraints today, do not permit me to elaborate further upon these particular individuals."

I then added, with a wry smile and a wee chuckle, *"However, if you wish to find out more, copies of my book are available for sale at the end of this talk."*

"As is indicated by the presence of Nostradamus - almost certainly one of such gifted individuals - the Fiosaichean have been present not just in Scotland, but in other countries and cultures all over the world and again, throughout history. By different names, of course, for example, the 'witch doctors' of many indigenous and tribal societies - the Shamen, the Shamankathe, the Śramana of Southeast Asia, the aboriginal Kurdaitcha etc. Not all of such individuals through the ages were of the Fiosaichean, however, a few - the very special ones, the most gifted - may well have been. Specific examples might include, the ancient Greek priestess, the Pythia, and possibly even Merlin himself… although, not as he is portrayed in the Arthurian legend, rather the bard, mystic and prophet, Myrddin Wyllt, of the 6th century. A reputed example from the 20th century is Maria Orsitsch, the Croatian psychic, whom Adolf Hitler and the Nazis engaged, along with her long-haired 'Vril Gesellschaft' followers, to assist in developing weapon's technology from the future."

Curiously, there were quite a few nods from those in attendance at the mention of this Nazi occult, lady-legend. Generally, to most audiences, she was unheard of.

I went on, *"There are possibly even Fiosaichean living amongst us today, however, I must stress again that they are an extremely rare breed and phenomenon. Hence, not every individual with special-natural or psychic abilities are of their number - far from it."*

I smiled before adding with an exaggerated tone, *"If that were the case, then even I might be a Fiosaiche!"* This drew some laughs from the audience.

"Rather, those of the Fiosaichean are exceptional individuals indeed, with extraordinary powers and skills. As rare a phenomenon as perhaps a Pablo Picasso or an Albert Einstein… perhaps even more so. Further to research, reliable examples throughout world history and the ages are scarce indeed."

After around an hour of speaking, despite continued keen interest from those assembled, in line with my initial instructions from Farquhar, I decided that it was time to wrap up my talk. As I drew it to a close, the gathered Order members and their partners gave what appeared to be genuine and energetic applause which, of course, I was delighted to receive.

As the clapping died down, a shiny-faced Farquhar Sutherland, now also wearing a heavy velvet robe (albeit with fewer golden tassels than that of his fellow Noble Order high-heid yin, Forbes-Fleming), made his way, rather unsteadily, up to join me at the elevated entrance area from which I had delivered my talk, nearly tripping with his foot on the lengthy garment in the process. Clapping and smiling effusively, saying, *"Bravo, Bravo Mr Guthrie!"* He then invited questions from the audience.

Of course, I was happy to deal with any, although was mindful that I must not elongate my time slot too much further. After taking what I thought was an appropriate number, I thanked the audience again and, to further applause, made my way down from the podium to a vacant chair adjacent to my leather case which contained a few signed copies of *Scotland - the Special-nat-ural* which I would shortly offer for sale.

As I sat down, with a little relief I reflected that this was another gig effectively done and dusted. There would be the oppor-tunity shortly to enjoy the (likely gourmet) buffet - without more wine, unfortunately, as I was driving - before the event came to a close, according to Farquhar Sutherland, at no later than 4 pm.

CHAPTER 7

The Heats, Monday
17th October 2022

First thing on Monday morning Helen prepared a breakfast of porridge and fruit juice to set Chloe up for the big day ahead. She also packed cheese and ham pieces wrapped in tin foil, some fruit, along with an energy drink into her kit bag. Money too, in case that were needed at the venue.

At about 7.20 am there was a rap at the front door. Abbey, Chloe's classmate from Leith Academy and the dance school and who was also taking part in the heats, had arrived to chum her up the road. They lived just a few doors apart in the same street. The two girls were hyper, laughing and joking as they departed towards the turn-off to Bangour Road and onwards to the bus collection point. Both Helen and Jim had, of course, given their talented daughter a big hug and kiss before she could get out the door. Even Jamie, a little reluctantly had wished her good luck, not managing very well to hide the smile of admiration upon his face for his big sis.

After the day's event at the Emirates Arena was complete, the minibus was to drop the girls, along with the rest of the kids, back in Leith by 7 pm, latest, having made its return journey east down the M8.

As it turned out, the minibus arrived back at the Norwegian Seaman's church a bit earlier than expected, at around 6 pm. Despite nervous exhaustion and, inevitably, some of the kids having won and others losing in the heats, there had been a lot of fun and high jinks in the bus as it travelled to Edinburgh along the motorway. In a kind of battle of the bands, songs were sung along to from two separate smart phones, with the minibus roughly divided into a pair of competing singing groups. Sat up front was Vivienne Leitch, along with her husband Rupert who was driving - they could not have been prouder of the girls and boys. En-route they had stopped at the McDonald's at Showcase Leisure Park, just off the M8 not far out of Glasgow, and treated everyone as a wee thank you for their efforts and commitment on the day.

Abbey had missed out on the takeaway, however. She'd informed Chloe earlier in the day that her mum, at the last minute, had arranged for her to stay with her Auntie in Partick that night, meaning that she would no longer be able to join her friend on the return bus journey or the short walk back home from the North Junction Street drop-off as had originally been the plan. Chloe had not really minded at all though - she had plenty of other pals in the group being a popular and chatty girl. In any case, she was on cloud nine, so much so that when the bus arrived back at the church, she thought that she would probably float home on the air of exhilaration that she felt having come through the heats and booking her place in the World Championships the following August!

Earlier in the afternoon when the results had been pinned up on the noticeboards in the stadium, she'd gathered with the huddled group of girls in her age group peering anxiously up at the list of names: those who had made the cut and those who had not. This was always a nervous moment at any event, however, at this one, of course, it had been super-duper anxious.

Chloe's heart had leaped nearly out of her chest at seeing her name on a far shorter list - the favored list, the winners list! Immediately, she texted both her mum and dad, simply saying, *"good news got n2 champs... will tell u all bout it wen I get home,"* followed by two emojis (a smiley face and a gold medal) and three kisses.

Helen had been on the tills at Asda when she felt her phone buzz in the lap pocket of her green and white pinnie. Having to wait until she finished serving a customer before opening it had felt like an eternity. Shrieking with joy when she eventually got the opportunity to do so. Tears of joy ran down her face as she excitedly explained to those in the queue, *"My wee lassie, Chloe, just gone and won hersel' a place at the World Highland Dancin' Championships!"*

Cheers and claps came from shoppers and Helen's colleagues on the other tills. Leith was the sort of place and community where folks were always happy to celebrate one of their own doing good.

Jim had needed to wait until his tea break before he got the news - phones being strictly forbidden in the grain hulling area of the works. He choked up a little on reading his daughter's message, however, he had just about managed to conceal the tears in his eyes from his workmates. Before putting the mobile back in his coat pocket within his locker, he tapped out a short return text with his calloused digits, weathered from the years of hard graft at the processing plant earning a living for his family, *"you are my wee champ! well done + c u soon love dad x."* Jim could not wait to see her beaming face when they were all back home, with her beautiful, sparkly blue eyes, so full of life and ambitions for the future.

Chloe knew that her folks would be rightly delighted for her, not least due to the years of ferrying her back and forward to classes and competitions all over the place, along with the associated cost. Now that she was going to the World Champs, it was a way of demonstrating to them exactly how much she appreciated their sacrifice.

On getting off the minibus back at the church Chloe thanked Mrs and Mr Leitch, the well-mannered and brought up girl that she was, and waved goodnight to the other kids, some of whom were already getting collected having messaged their parents to alert of the earlier than expected arrival back, whilst others were heading towards the Commercial Road junction. Unfortunately, no one was going in Chloe's direction to chum her along and, hence, with the absence of Abbey, she had to make her way home alone.

As she crossed over the bridge at the Water of Leith, there was a biting wind coming across from the east. However, lost in her thoughts, she hardly noticed. Chloe was picturing in her mind's eye the ecstatic reaction of her parents as she arrived back home in what would be less than ten minutes time - it was not a long walk at all. Her annoying wee bro would surely be jealous at the attention she would receive, she reflected with a smile. He would ignore her most likely, focusing instead on his Xbox. Chloe loved him to bits really but would never let him see that. She was also looking forward to the certain enthusiastic welcome she would receive when coming in the front door from wee Dougall, the family's miniature, wirehaired dachshund.

Turning into Bangour Road, it was only a short distance to Barlington Wynd where Chloe and her hard-working, but happy wee family lived in their three-bed 1970s concrete-built, terraced council house. On her left, she passed the Saly Army Building, then the Ebenezer Church. Only half an hour before it would have been busy with folks leaving the early evening service, but it was all shut up and quiet now.

Passing the entrance to the small industrial estate on her left, she suddenly became aware of footsteps behind her. Glancing back over her shoulder, she could see a dark figure emerging from the estate and towards her. Chloe's happy and jovial mood instantly evaporated as, at the same time, a ripple of primeval fear ran through her - intuition telling her in an instant that she was in danger. Whoever it was seemed to be wearing some sort of long cloak and promptly started to quicken their pace in her direction. She tried to run, to scream out - she was nearly home after all and people, the neighbours, would likely hear her - but she simply could not. A leaden inertia of terror gripped her, and she was paralysed like a rabbit caught in the headlights. Suddenly, a gloved hand came from behind her and forcefully clasped itself upon and over her mouth. Chloe fainted.

The next thing she knew was that she was in some sort of industrial premises. Her mouth, she could feel, had tape over it. There were two men there (at least she thought they were men), both wearing dark cloaks like she had seen upon the figure emerging from the shadows earlier, with hoods obscuring their faces. One of them, tall with a lanky frame evident despite the robe, started to drag her across the floor by her feet towards a large machine which she could see bore a big stainless-steel funnel at the top of its frame. The other, not so tall, plump judging by the girth of the cloak, was pressing a button which appeared to be closing a roller-shutter door. The first man deposited her up at the base of the machine. She could smell alcohol off his rank breath as he huffed and puffed from his exertions. His accomplice who was now making his way from the shutter door towards Chloe, gripped a hammer menacingly in his right hand.

The taller man, in a posh Edinburgh accent - like she had heard from some of the fathers of the highland dancers from private schools - said to the other, "*Best check she really IS a virgin.*" The hammer man responded brashly in similar a tone, "*Not many of them in Leith, that's for sure, even at this chavvy wee tart's age.*" Both sniggered at this. Thereupon, Chloe felt her new trackies that her dad had got her for the special day, together with her underwear, being tugged down. She continued to be speechless and motionless, in abject terror, thinking of when it might end, as there was a hard crack of metal upon skull bone.

Chloe had no more mortal thoughts - they were gone forever.

CHAPTER 8

Essential Oil, Tuesday 18th October 2022

The morning after the Noble Order of Eidyn gig I had a lie in and then a leisurely breakfast before tackling some work on the laptop. After a few hours, needing a second caffeine buzz of the day, I took a break from my desk and put a pot of coffee on. As I did so, I flicked on the kitchen radio to catch the lunchtime news bulletin on Radio Scotia. Why I bothered, I really did not know - force of habit I guess - it was always the same format: a murder, a dour story related to Scotland or the Scots, a disproportionately long sport's slot (generally, almost in its entirety, filled with football punditry to the exclusion of all other sports), and then a cute-kitten-stuck-up-a-tree type feature.

Sure enough, that day the headline was that a body - or at least, some remains - had been found in Leith in rather gruesome circumstances. The account was rather graphic for the early afternoon news, I felt. The anchor, Lesley Brunton (a typical, Bearsden-accented, Radio Scotia show host and some-time journalist) passed to a reporter at the scene, an excitable and over-zealous (at least for the grim circumstances) Tom Miller.

"Thank you, Lesley. Yes, I am at the scene. A grisly discovery has been made in a small warehouse off Bangour Road, Leith - the business premises

of 'LeithLife Juices & Oils Ltd', an organic fruit juice and essential oils producer. I am led to understand that this was further to a local resident, Karen Nicol, alerting the Polis... erm... Police, this morning, to the presence of human remains in the vicinity.

Further to investigations, the constabulary found that the premises had been broken into. It has now been confirmed that, upon entry, they discovered an industrial, cold-press machine into which human remains had been fed. From detritus evidence at the scene, it would appear that a thick ruddy black 'juice' had been extracted from the body parts by such cold-press process which, thereupon, had been further treated to a steam distillation procedure via the firm's large copper purification vats and equipment.

The presumed final output - a small amount of refined excreta oil made from the pressed and distilled human matter - is thought to have been collected in one of the firm's glass essential oil vials. This is thought to be no longer present at the site.

The crushed organic remnants of the cold press and distillation activity appeared to have been hastily scooped up by the culprits and put into plastic refuse sacks which they had then slung on to the top of the business estate's communal bins. However, this was only for urban foxes through the night to climb up and rip the sacks open, exposing the contents and allowing them to scatter down Bangour Road in the wind.

I am led to understand that Mrs Nicol had been in the kitchen of her premises in Barlington Wynd cleaning up after the family's breakfast when their cat, Timmie, arrived through the cat flap. She said that the animal had been chewing upon something that looked rather odd, which it then proceeded to proudly drop at her feet. Curious, Mrs Nicol had then moved to pick it up with a piece of kitchen paper and, on closer inspection, was horrified to discover that it resembled that of a human finger, albeit in completely flattened form.

I have spoken to a number of nearby residents who say that they were alerted to the strange and gruesome course of events by the shrieks coming from Mrs Nicol's flat upon this shocking discovery. In the words of one, '...they were so loud that they could have been heard all the way up to the top of the Walk'.

Police Scotland are continuing with their enquiries, including liaising with forensic and pathology services to identify the human remains."

The broadcast then reverted to Lesley in the studio, clearly rather flustered with the macabre content of her colleague's report on daytime radio news. I could not help chuckling a little at this, but then felt a sense of guilt due to the horrific nature of the incident. What was the city coming to? Who the hell, would want to murder someone and then make a vial of essential oil from their corpse?

Jezzus, clearly some twisted shit going down in the old Port! I considered. Probably linked to a dispute within the city's drug and crime underworld I imagined - something that reared its ugly head from time to time. In fact, the news report prompted me to recall of a likewise weird discovery and grisly murder earlier in the year. It was that of a church guy and happened in his house in the affluent Grange area on the southside. Poor fucker had been found by his wife and kids stark bollock naked and nailed to the sitting room floor - baw sack and all - with a satanic cross scribbled around him and his heart gouged out!

Just as I was pouring the fresh, steaming coffee into my mug and reaching to turn the radio off so as to return to my desk in the front room, Lesley Brunton piped up again just after the Radio Scotia sports reporter had given a long-winded low down on the signing of yet another new goalie at Hibs. She had an update on the Bangour Road murder:

"Police Scotland have just released a statement confirming the victim to be 12 year, Chloe Rennie, a student at nearby Leith Academy and accomplished junior highland dancer with the Vivienne Leitch School of Dance. The family have been informed and the police continue with their enquiries."

CHAPTER 9

A Familiar Voice

The rest of the week, I pretty much kept my head down and did quite a bit of research on 'extrasensory perception' techniques (apparently of the mystics of Ancient Egypt). These were methods that I was considering incorporating into future psychic medium readings, where appropriate. I also did some work improving my website, along with a little marketing.

It was uneventful, apart from an odd thing that happened on the Thursday. I'd popped out in the afternoon to stretch my legs and when I got back, there was an alert flashing on the landline indicating that I had a missed call and a that a voicemail had been left. On playing the message, it was short and a little garbled, but went something like this,

"Son, listen tae the lady, you MUST burn it."

A strange message that made no sense to me whatever. After I had played it over a number of times, however, I realised that there was something familiar in the voice. I did not get it initially, but by the Friday morning, something clicked - the message sounded as if it had been left by my mother... it was her voice, it genuinely seemed. The only thing was that my mother had been dead coming up for thirteen years!

It was true that with my psychic medium abilities I could commune with those who had passed during reading sessions (and sometimes in my dreams) - albeit, never with one of my parents - but I certainly did not have the deceased ringing me up and leaving voicemail.

So later in the day on Friday, tutting to myself for flights of fancy, I tried to convince myself that it must have simply been a wrong number from someone with a similar tone of voice to that of my mother - that I must have misheard the message in any case. Nevertheless, still curious, on the Saturday I'd tried the caller enquiry '1471' service to see if I could determine the phone number of who had rung me. However, it said that this was 'unknown'. I then resolved that it was better for me to forget about the incident, and promptly deleted the peculiar message from my landline voicemail.

Thereupon, I successfully managed to put it out of my mind... at least until the even more strange events of early the following week.

CHAPTER 10

The Comasach

On the Monday morning, exactly a week after the Noble Order of Eidyn talk, a generous cheque arrived in the post from Farquhar Sutherland containing almost double the fee that I had quoted him for the event. He said in an accompanying note that the additional sum was to cover any 'incidental expenses'. It was decent of him, I thought, and in any case these gents could certainly afford it from what I had seen on my visit to Gillane Manse.

That cheque, plus the numerous books sales and orders that I'd made at the end of the gig, had certainly made it quite a profitable booking.

It was a good morning indeed, as I also received a message from e-Bay informing that I had been successful in my bid for the Hearts v Bayern Munich UEFA Cup match program. On hearing this news, I punched the air, exclaiming in broad Edimburgo, "YA' BEAUTY."

The icing on the cake was that my winning bid had not been so high for such a prize piece of 'Jambo' memorabilia. As I was in the process of arranging payment and express delivery, I noticed that the seller was based in the capital itself and had flagged an option allowing for collection of the item from them directly. Being impatient to get my hands on it, I promptly made contact and arranged to go round to the seller's flat that evening in order to collect - around 9 pm after he got back home from a late shift at his work.

Before that, earlier in the evening, I put together a light dinner. Just a bowl of lentil soup and some toast (I really did need to do a food shop and get some more substantial mealtime items, I reflected).

After dinner, I decided to get out of the house and headed to the gym for a wee sesh - something I had been neglecting of late. I always felt better, both in mind and body, after a work-out. Thereafter, at about 8.45 pm, I made my way to collect the football program.

For a collector of Heart's memorabilia, perhaps surprisingly, the gent (in his late-30s/early-40s and a rather unkempt and peculiar looking character) lived in Edina Place, just off Easter Road and up the road from the Hibs stadium. Mind you Porty, was not exactly a hotbed of Heart's support. As he opened the door to hand me the prized item, a waft of stale chip fat channeled towards me from the dour hallway. In any case, on close inspection I was pleased to ascertain that it was indeed the genuine article.

Back at Syd, I tucked it safely and deeply within the inside pocket of my leather case which had been in the boot since the talk at gentlemen's group. I then made my way back to Porty. Once there, I drove past my wee house in the forlorn hope of finding a nearby parking space. And it appeared to be my lucky day - almost unbelievably, the space right outside was free. This must have been the first time in a year, I thought. But just as I was preparing to reverse into the vacant space, this gaudy colored, spoiler-plated wee Fiat zoomed straight into it from the other side of the road - head-first and nearly causing a collision.

Instantly, I felt my blood pressure rising but resisted the temptation to yell out the window at the scrawny looking teenager who was grinning behind the wheel. Mind you, I did momentarily wave a fist towards him through the glass demonstrating my displeasure, before thinking how daft I was being. The wee shite just smirked back.

Thereafter, I drove around the local roads until I eventually (after about 15 minutes) found a parking spot at the top of Bellfield Street. After easing my beast of a car into the vacant space, I grabbed my leather case out of the boot and started to make my way down the pavement in the direction of Porty Baths.

Not far before the turn-off to Straiton Place, I clocked a woman standing on the opposite side of the road, down at the corner where the Victorian swimming pool building stood. She appeared to be watching me, keenly observing me even. I just ignored her as if I had not noticed and continued to make my way towards the left turn into my street. As I got nearer, I glanced nonchalantly in her direction. Under the hazy glow of a streetlamp, I could see that she was perhaps in her 50s, plainly dressed, frizzy grey hair and with a rather wild look in her eyes. And yes, she was definitely watching me and not clandestinely at all - clearly unconcerned that I might notice. Rather, she made herself obvious and stared right at me!

This struck me as rather strange, although Portobello did have its fair share of oddballs and jakies hinging about, especially later in the evenings. Just as I was turning into my street, I took another quick keek and was prompted to halt for a second in surprise.

The lady was now raising her arm, straight and pointing at me, as if in an accusatory manner … like a judge gesturing to the accused in the dock. At the same time, in a sort of slow motion, she opened her mouth and gradually started to say something to me. As I was still a good 20 metres away from her, I could not quite hear what she was saying - it was a bit like a question or request of me perhaps?

But all of a sudden, she got very animated, into a kind of frenzy, and started screeching and shouting along with jabbing her finger at me in a hostile manner.

"*BURN THE BOOK, BURN THE BOOK, BURN THE BOOK,*" she yelled repeatedly, her face contorted as she did.

Jesus, a shudder went through me, and I could feel my hair stand on end. Without any further dalliance I took to my heels, putting my head down and striding at pace down the pavement towards my bungalow. As I did so I took a couple of glances back over my shoulder to check in case she was following me. Thankfully, she was nowhere to be seen. I could still hear the shrieks though albeit they were waning as I put more distance between myself and where presumably she still stood.

As I neared my house a recollection of the strange voicemail that I'd received on my house phone the previous week flitted into my mind. I reflected upon the odd congruence of that weird message with what I had just heard from this crazy woman. The voicemail, albeit a bit hard to make out, had also given an instruction for me to 'burn' something; furthermore, it had said that I should listen to 'the lady'?

Relieved to reach my gate, I bounded up the wee path to my door and unlocked it quickly, slamming it shut once inside the vestibule. Flicking the light on I went straight into the front room in order to pull the curtains shut around the bay window in the front room.

Just as I was tugging the heavy cloth over the rusty old curtain rails, I noticed a figure standing in Straiton Park over the road. It was perhaps forty meters away. Once again, the gentle light from a streetlamp allowed an outline view. The figure, positioned just the other side of a small privet hedge marking the boundary to the park, was clearly looking towards my house. This was not, however, the figure of a woman, rather more likely a male from the stature, I concluded.

I wondered for a moment, was it the Fiat driver that I had almost certainly antagonised earlier by raising a fist to after he had nicked my parking space? Perhaps he had been waiting for my return home to give me a fright by filling my windows in? However, as I continued to observe it was evident even in the dim light that the guy had a far heavier build than that of the boy racer and was older. A feeling of anxiety once again came over me.

Shaking my head as if waking myself from a tiny moment of slumber, I sought to regain my composure concluding that I must be weary from the day and getting paranoid. Without further ado I jerked the ends of both curtains the final inch to block out any view from the outside - and from the inside out - and headed to the kitchen to open up a nice Portuguese Douro valley red that, along with a bottle of oak-aged Rioja Gran Reserva and a special Chianti Classico, I had stored in the press. That would sort my sensitive nerves and overly fertile imagination out, I felt sure.

This Douro valley red was a bottle that I had resisted the temptation of opening the previous night, being conscious that I had been drinking too much of late. I was trying to have the odd night without a glass, but to be honest was finding it a little bit of a struggle. Indeed, such nights were few and far between, but I had managed it on occasion. Tonight, was different, I reflected, as I really did need - or at least deserved - a drink after my encounter with the strange, shouty women, never mind the creepy guy in the park.

Carefully, from my vinyl collection, I placed Led Zeppelin's 'Houses of the Holy' on the turntable of my reclaimed record player (circa early-80's) at a low volume. Listening to and collecting vinyl was a recent and emerging passion of mine. The metal door of my wee woodburning stove then creaked open as I put some kindling in over a firelighter and carefully arranged a couple of logs on top before sparking it into life with a pencil-like lighter. I then melted into my old, worn leather armchair, sipping at the sumptuous red. Déjà jumped up on my knee looking for a wee clap - she was not the most overtly affectionate cat so I liked when she did that. In the mesmorising and flickering flames, along with comforting warmth emanating from the stove, by the second glass all thoughts of crazy ladies and possible stalkers in the park were forgotten.

At something like 3am I awoke in the armchair with a start. It was now cold in the room and I badly needed a piss. Arising, I stumbled half-conscious to the bathroom, my foot knocking over an empty wine bottle as I did so. When I eventually reached the comfort of my bed I must have been back sleeping as soon as my head hit the pillow. I dozed on until around 7 am the next day when I was awoken by Déjà. She was trampling upon me over the duvet, purring loudly and evidently trying to arouse me in order to get her breakfast. The wee blighter was always wanting fed.

Not having had a proper dinner the previous evening I was also feeling pretty hungry myself. I had a fancy for French toast - a few glasses of wine the night before often prompted a desire for such fried breakfast. However, after getting up and inspecting the fridge I found that I had no eggs left. Further, the few remaining slices of bread in the bread bin were stale - one with signs of greeny blue mould growing on it, the sight of which made my stomach churn. Hence, I decided that I must head to the shop.

Thankfully for Déjà, there was still some cat food left. As I squeezed out a sachet of cubed, jellied mystery meat into her dish I caught a whiff which set my tummy off again and I was near boaking. Pulling on my jeans, a previous day's t-shirt and hoodie which were lying in a pile on the bedroom floor, I shoved on my trainers without bothering with socks - I was on an urgent mission for the ingredients of French toast after all!

Leaving the house, I headed towards the Coop at the top of Bath Street. Again, it was a strangely close day for the month of October. As I marched past the tenement doorways en-route, with a pang of hunger, I was thinking of how best to make my chosen breakfast. As per usual, I decided, with a little cheese grated over the top so that it went properly crispy in the pan, then plated up with broon sauce and plenty of salt and pepper... yum.

My thoughts of food, however, were interrupted as I spied an elderly lady standing on the pavement up ahead. Sporting an old-fashioned head scarf and raincoat, she appeared to be watching me. Instantly, I recalled the previous nights' strange incidents and feared that I might be about to experience something similar, before promptly dismissing such a notion - considering that I must be getting paranoid once again and needed to get my shit together.

However, as I got closer to her, I could not help but notice a suspicious look upon her face; her brow was puckered and her eyes locked onto mine. Steeling myself, I simply smiled as I walked past, cheerfully greeting her with, "*Morning, it's a warm day out today, eh.*" Without slowing down at all I just continued up the street. Yet, as I did so, I could feel her eyes following and penetrating me; then she said something directed at me. She wasn't shouting, but the tone was forceful enough. However, as I was travelling at a fair pace and already moving away from her, I could not entirely make out what it was, but it sounded a bit like, "*Burn it, burn it… listen tae us laddie, will yeh?*"

Trying hard to convince myself this was not really what she was saying and that it was probably just, "*… aye, the weathers awfy mild fir the time ay year son*" or such like in response to my greeting, I continued up the road shaking my head and exhorting myself to keep calm. I was relieved upon reaching the doors of the Coopy.

It was the familiar comings and goings of a busy morning with the good folks of Porty getting their messages. Grabbing a basket, I made my way up the fruit and veg aisle thinking that some of these wee, piccolo cherry tomatoes would go nicely with my French toast, perhaps grilled or softened in the pan.

But just as I was mentally preparing my breakfast, for fuck's sake, a boy, perhaps eight or nine years old, standing alongside his mum (who was picking items from the organic produce section) was gawping at me intently. In fact, he was even screwing up his eyes as if trying to gain maximum focus upon me. Jeez, not again, I was thinking.

With a wary and troubled expression upon his coupon, he proceeded to raise a finger and point at me; then, utter in a whiny, high-pitched tone, "*Burn the book... You MUST destroy it, Cameron, PLEEEASSE.*"

This time I had no trouble in making out the words and it stopped in my tracks by reflex. Responding limply, I simply said, "*Pardon?*" Thoughts were swirling around my head at yet another weird encounter – and this time, my name had even been used!

By now the mother had noticed something was going on and proceeded to shield her son from me with her arm as if he needed protection and was eyeballing me with clear suspicion. The laddie then spoke again, this time louder and even more shrilly, "*BURN THE BOOK... BURN THE BOOK... BURN THE BOOK,*" jabbing a wee finger at me accusingly as he did.

The mum, a stern looking thirty something - with ponytail, in gym gear and whose hubby was probably already at his well-paid office job in the city despite the early hour - looked at me with unveiled disgust, like I had been trying to touch the lad up for fuck's sake! ... and that that had prompted the wee raj's haverings.

She now tugged the boy right behind her, then leaned towards me, directly shouting in my face like she was deranged, *"LEAVE MY SON ALONE YOU VILE PAEDO FREAK."*

Taken aback in horror at the accusation and literally speechless, I instinctively backed away up the aisle. As I did so, I noticed other shoppers looking on wondering what the commotion was. They were eyeing me with suspicion as if they had already passed judgement.

At the top of the aisle, I glanced back to see the mum approaching a security guard and saying something, gesturing to her son (which she had one arm tightly around), then pointing in my direction. The boy was now sobbing and the guard moved to kneel down as if to ask him a question. My heart was now racing.

Shit, I must get the fuck out of here and *fast*, I could not help but conclude.

Dropping the wire shopping basket on the floor I promptly made my way down the adjacent aisle towards the tills and exit. I sensed the presence of the security guard not far behind me so quickened my pace, squeezing past a group of folks queuing at the till. Numerous eyes were upon me. As I reached the exit door and stepped outside, the voice of an older male, with an air of desperation, followed me saying, *"Listen tae her… Destroy it, get rid ay it!"*

Outside the shop, in somewhat of a panic at the probable pursuit of me, I darted off up towards the High Street. Then quickly and deliberately lost myself amongst a throng of morning commuters who were heading to the bus stops to be transported for yet another day of drudgery in the offices, shops and other workplaces of the city. Not that I had done anything wrong, of course, but if the police were called, they would almost certainly take the gym-clad, stay-at-home mum's word over mine - an unwashed, hungover 30-something guy, wearing days' old clothes and no socks. That bolshy, overprotective mother and her strange son would be saying god knows what shite and I could do without such grief, that was for sure.

Once I felt I was a relatively safe distance away, I peeked back down towards the shop entrance and could see the security bloke out on the pavement, scanning up and down the street. I considered that I would need to find a new local shop.

Doubling back down Regent Street, I headed home at what I hoped was a non-suspicious jogging pace. Nothing particularly odd looking about that, I reflected, as Porty had lots of morning joggers - although I was probably the only one wearing jeans. En-route a dog barked angrily at me from behind a garden gate as I approached. However, the beast took a few steps backwards and turned to whimpering as I trotted past its wee front yard, displaying rather fearful eyes and demeanor.

Back home, I closed and bolted the door with some relief. It would just have to be granola and UHT milk today I grumbled to myself.

After this perfunctory breakfast, I took a strong coffee over to my desk which faced the bay window. Deciding not to bother opening the curtains, rather I pulled the chain switch on my brass advocate's lamp; this emitted sufficient light for working especially when directing the green glass swivel shade as required. After the recent spate of strange events, focusing on work would help get my head straight, I concluded. I was beginning to think that all this deliberate and proactive dabbling with the paranormal - the psychic medium readings that I was now regularly doing - had perhaps unleased something unpleasant, maybe even evil? It was one thing me having latent abilities, but I was now engaged in developing them, perhaps even exploiting them - had this been a mistake, I contemplated?

Were these people staring at me and saying strange things to me, perhaps ghosts? Or the 'undead' walking around the streets of Porty? Surely the fuck not? For me, communication with spirits and those that had passed had hitherto been limited to visions in my mind's eye, such as at the reading sessions or in dreams, not as physical entities out and about on the city's pavements and in the local shops!

I wondered, was it only me that had been able to see and hear the 'starers'? Of course, the Coop guard had been speaking with kid and his angry mum, so I surmised not. Another question, of course, was whether all the recent, weird events were linked?

I really did not know what to think, but my gut told me something uncanny and otherworldly was definitely afoot. Although, I thought - or perhaps, hoped - that I was over exaggerating it all in my mind. Maybe there was a simple and rational explanation for what had been going on? *Work... focus upon work Cameron*, I told myself, at least as a distraction. Taking a slurp of the bitter-sweet, dark brew in my mug, I opened up my laptop to do just that.

It was difficult to focus on work however, as my mind kept wandering back to the recent, strange events. Around noon, I was then disturbed by a knocking at my door. I resolved to ignore it as I still had the jitters from the Coop experience.

Curious, nevertheless, I went to peak out of the heavy curtains at the side of the bay window to see who it was. For a moment, I felt a twinge of panic that the security guard had called the police and that they had somehow got my address - maybe from a local shopper who had recognised me and knew where I lived. It was certainly a bit late for the postie and no one I knew would generally be knocking at my door at noon on a weekday, I pondered with a sickening feeling.

On pushing the substantial and rather dusty curtain fabric back - just enough to get a wee keek, but not enough to be noticed - I observed a young lady, maybe in her early to mid-twenties, standing and waiting at the door. She was petite in stature, wrapped in a long, black raincoat and with a black leather satchel bag on a strap over her shoulder. I could not fully see her face as she was side-on to me and with the curl of dark brown hair from her bob hairstyle partially obscuring it. She was clearly attractive though. From the base of her raincoat, I glimpsed black tights and sober, dark brogue style shoes. I assessed that she must either be a funeral director, an Edinburgh lawyer or the police. Of course, the polis generally went in twos, so I sighed in relief observing that she appeared to be on her own.

Quite insistent, after a few moments she reached out a second time to knock. In normal circumstances, I would have been most happy to open my door to a pleasant-looking, young lady such as this. However, on this occasion, I still had the heebie-jeebies, so I simply took my hand away from the curtain, letting it gently swing back into place, and quietly resumed working at my desk, grateful for the return of peace and quiet.

But for fuck's sake, barely an hour and a half later, she was back again chapping at my door - as confirmed by another covert look out of the curtains. There was no way I was going to open it though, I decided - I was not being disturbed further. This time, directly after her knocking had ceased, I heard the brass letter box's familiar clatter and knew that she must have posted something through it. After a few moments to allow her to leave my wee front garden and return to the street, I skulked to the vestibule to see what had been left.

Sitting alongside a free newspaper that appeared to have been delivered that morning (and would shortly go straight to the recycling bin), was a small, rectangular business card. On picking it up and taking a look, it read,

> **Aoife Gilfeather**
> **Solicitor**
> **Gilfeather & McLean LLP**

This was along with an address in the new town and contact details. Upon turning it over, I could see that there was also a hand-scribbled note, just squeezed onto the limited space of the small white rectangle of the back of the card -

> *Please ring me Mr Guthrie asap.*
> *We really need to speak — I have something*
> *for you.*
> *Ms Gilfeather*

A lawyer … I was right, I reflected. Why was it that Edinburgh lawyers were always so predictable and staid in their attire? Those in Spain that I had had dealings with in the past due to work had been far more colorful and relaxed in their dress and, of course, the legal eagles down the other end of the M8 had a certain and customary gallusness about them which generally extended to their business wear. All the same, even in her sedate outfit she was definitely fine looking, … or perhaps even more, I thought - in a Miss Jean Brodie type of way.

I wondered whether the fact that she was trying to make contact with me was in some way linked to the strange recent events? Further, what was the 'something' that she had for me?

It was then that I recalled that I had an unpaid parking fine in relation to which an aggressive private firm had been writing me copious letters for going on nine months now (all of which I had ignored). Perhaps she was trying to serve me with some sort of legal writ in connection with that? Yes, that was probably the 'something' she wanted to deliver to me.

Deciding not to dwell on it, however, I put her wee business card in my pocket for the time being and resolved to make a brew and get back to work.

In fact, I worked pretty non-stop the rest of the day, doing more research on 'extrasensory perception' techniques, as well as some prep for a talk I was to give in a few weeks' time at the Stockbridge Writers' Guild. Still not having been for a food shop thanks to the Coop debacle there was little in the house, so that evening it was another basic dinner - this time a couple of the stale slices of bread (with mouldy looking bits cut off) toasted, along with baked beans and with a little bit of over-mature cheddar - which I found lurking at the back of the fridge - grated on top. All accompanied by a liberal grinding of black pepper, of course. As I prepared this, Déjà hovered around my ankles leaving me in no doubt that she was also wanting feeding. So, before I sat down to eat, I squeezed the one remaining cat food sachet into a paper bowl whilst she purred in anticipation. As I put it down for her, she was straight in there, her wee head bobbing away as she gobbled it up.

After doing this, I took my not-so-grand meal on a tray to the front room to have it on my knee sat on the armchair. I was just about to turn the telly on to watch the 6 pm news as I ate, when there was yet another bloody rapping at my door! Déjà, replete having wolfed her dinner down, had only just settled on the sill of the bay window for the evening having snuck under the curtains to jump up there. This was a spot she favored greatly due to the location of the radiator underneath, as well as the vantage point to the outdoors. Well, she clearly got one a hell of a fright at the knocking ... in an instant projecting upwards like a furry missile and out between the curtains ... then, scrambling upon landing and into a dash to the kitchen as if her life depended on it - like a scene from a Tom & Jerry cartoon.

Surely it cannot be that bloody nuisance lawyer again? I was thinking apprehensively. Reluctantly leaving my dinner for a moment to check, I once again peaked out the side of the curtains and saw that, indeed, it was her. Jeez, what was up with this dogged women? It was after office hours as well - did she not have a home to go to? Sighing in frustration, for a moment I contemplated opening the door to ask her what the hell she was playing at, however, resolved to ignore a further time - perhaps more out of spite than anything else.

During the evening, I set out to finish the last few chapters of an old Scot's classic which I had been reading, 'The Private Memoirs and Confessions of a Justified Sinner', by the late 18th century writer and poet, James Hogg. At the same time, in the background, I had the original of Black Sabbath Vol 4 on vinyl playing at a low volume on the record player. The book had been a little hard going at times, with the multiple narratives and archaic vernacular. But at the same time, I'd found it a compelling and rather masterful tale of Calvinistic religious fanaticism, murder, folklore and the supernatural - a menu that I certainly enjoyed (… and let's face it, one that was a damn sight more appetising than that of my stale toast, beans and musty cheddar). This served to pass the time and keep my thoughts from wandering too much. At the same time, I accompanied the reading with some rather fine Rioja Gran Reserva. As per the rather flowery description on the back of the bottle, it did indeed appear to have 'luscious velvety, vanilla and woody tones upon the palate'. On finishing both the book and the bottle of wine - clearly, my resolve at drinking less was failing somewhat… mind you, at least I had resisted the temptation to crack open the Chianti Classico and it remained sat in the press - I headed for an early night, resolving that first thing in the morning, after (hopefully) a good night's sleep, I would head to the large Asda up at the Jewel and do a big shop.

CHAPTER 11

Leith Waterworld

W hether it was the wine - drink heavy with sulphites often gave me a headache and upset my stomach (although, that never seemed to put me off consuming!) - or the odd events of the last day or so, I did not know exactly, however, that night's sleep proved to be fitful and restless. As part, I experienced strange dreams, wild dreams, awaking at numerous intervals through the night with the shivers and sweats. Stirring at around 5am, my pillow felt uncomfortably damp, so I turned it over - the cool, dry side feeling good against my head. That was me awake though.

Laying there, I reflected upon what I could remember of the dreams within my spells of sporadic sleep. I could only recall certain snapshots and they were already fading. These glimpses nevertheless indicated that I had been in Edinburgh in my unconscious mind. Yet, it had not been the place I really knew, rather that of a different time period. Not the city from the past, which I would have recognised from history, rather, one from the future - and a deeply unpleasant and disturbing version of what was perhaps to come.

This Auld Reekie of my dreams had large portions of it underwater. My broken recollections included an image of myself and the attractive door-knocking solicitor, Ms Gilfeather, travelling in some sort of amphibious craft. It was fiercely hot - quite uncomfortable - with hazy sunshine burning down through a noxious looking, yellowy smog. We were travelling down Leith Walk and at one point seemed to traverse from solid ground and onto water, our transport wobbling slightly in transition.

This occurred around the site of what I knew as the 'Spey Rest' a rather dingy bar of the current waking day, not too far from the foot of the Walk. In my dream, however, it had been renamed the 'Spa Rest', presumably in honor of its now waterfront location. Through the enclosed windows of the craft, I could see some auld Leith worthies sat around a small, circular table outside the bar and under a large canopy. They were on some sort of wooden dock, with small waves of murky coloured water (complete with floating fag-ends, an empty 'Tennents Supra' lager can and discarded takeaway food wrappings) lapping up near their feet. Playing dominoes, each had half-pint and nip glasses in front of them. Bedecked in shorts and t-shirts, they bore the ruddy faces which were just visible through plastic-like bubbles - about the size of large watermelons - which encased each of their heads, zipped at the neck. Hands, arms and legs visible upon each of the gents looked uniformly blistered and red-raw with sunburn. They appeared to be consuming their drinks via straws protruding from the head-cover globes. However, one of the gents, a shilpit craitur with badly blistered lips, appeared to be consuming his beverages intravenously via a syringe - dipping it into each glass, pulling the plunger to sook the drink up, then fixing the top of it to a plastic tube sticking out of the side of his stomach - thereupon depressing the plunger and, little by little, pumping the alcohol into his system. Other than these devil-may-care Leithers, I could see no one else outdoors - presumably as they were shielding from the sun, heat and harmful pollution. The only other souls visible seemed to be cowering behind tenement windows or passing in similar window encased vessels to which we travelled.

Continuing to lay upon my bed and seeking to further remember my dreams, my recollection moved on as if I had pressed a fast forward button whilst watching a movie. The two of us were now going along a waterway in the craft, but with half-submerged tenements at either side. Appended to the top corner of one of the buildings was a sign jutting out over the water; it read, 'Great Junction Canal' and underneath, 'Strictly No Unauthorised Vessels by Order of the Governor, North Britain Archipelago Sector, Her Majesty's UK Government'. Alongside it was some sort of surveillance camera, swiveling to scan the scene. Our amphibious carriage progressed and took a right turn onto another, but narrower, canal. I was guessing that this was a semi-submerged Henderson Street as I recognised the building - or at least the upper floors of it above the waterline - which had long ago housed Lanny's Ice Cream Saloon, where my Uncle Billie had used to take me as a boy. Another sign then came into view giving directions to 'Portobello Keys' and 'Joppa Island'!

From what I could recall from these snapshots, the lower half of Leith and surrounds had become a Venice of sorts, but definitely not a very appealing one (and, using another famous city comparison, the 'Athens of the North' moniker was clearly no longer appropriate, other than perhaps in relation to the insufferable heat). Small vessels, many with tinted windows, were going to and fro on either side of ours. The driver/skipper of our craft, from what I could see sat behind him, was a burly, middle-aged man. He was wearing a baseball cap which sported the logo-styled text of 'Central Waxis' curling over the back. His chunky forearm clutching the steering sported a tattoo of a cup - a football trophy - with 'HIBS' in green lettering arched over the top, then at the base, 'Scottish Cup 2081'.

The craft progressed down some smaller side streets - now waterways - along to what I seemed to instinctively recognise as the Shore of my waking daytime, albeit looking very different. Only the upper sections of tenements and buildings were visible, with many seemingly, fully under the water. Perched on the ridge of a pitched roof of one, were two monkeys - yes, monkeys! Baboons to be specific (or at least I thought so from years of watching David Attenborough wildlife documentaries). One sat with its back to the other as it had its fur groomed by the nimble fingers of its partner, which at the same time eagerly nibbled up bits of - presumably - lice and fleas with its dexterous tongue and lips. They had perhaps escaped long ago from an abandoned Edinburgh Zoo, I guessed; part of their own wee colony - and were probably the only current inhabitants of the city enjoying the baking temperatures.

At the same time, various run-down dwellings, shops and cafes, were present on stilts, tethered to or embedded upon the high floors, attics and roofs of the part-sunken buildings. The few customers that were visible were huddled inside, generally behind plastic canopies and drapes (a bit like those you get at the entrance to a butcher's shop chiller-room). One such premises had an illuminated digital display panel hanging from above its jetty, bearing first the temperature ('44°C'), then flashing to the time ('3.10 pm') and lastly, the date – '1st November 2082'. A putrid stench from the water, of sewerage, human waste and god knows what, was uncomfortably discernable despite the closed windows of the vessel. Upon one of the stilted structures, the festering carcass of a dog was being feasted upon by a huddle of large, black sewer rats. I winced particularly at that mercifully fleeting but unwelcome recollection - no wonder, it had been a troubled sleep.

At this point, I contemplated getting up from bed, however, decided it was better to continue to seek to recall glimpses of my strange dreams before the memory of them completely evaporated; I had a queer sense that they had - or at least would have - significance in some way. Focusing once again on the snapshots remaining from my slumber, I recollected a different dream scene, even more vivid to the previous. I was not sure whether it was from a future Edinburgh, an earlier version or, indeed of the present?

This time I was lying on my back in bed. Not just lying, but in fact I was being pummeled hard by a woman on top of me! Facing towards me, she had both her hands on my shoulders, pushing herself upright as she leathered into me, gasping and groaning. Each time she was thrusting her crotch as far as it could possibly go towards mine… and then some - her wild, dark brown hair hanging at either side of an athletic frame. As she heaved and pushed, bits of spit splattered and dropped from her mouth with the heavy breathing and exertion. I felt them land on my chest, face and into my open mouth, tasting a saltiness. At the same time, I breathed in a sensual odour of pheromones emanating from her pores and a waft, not unpleasant, of what was surely her vaginal secretions.

Almost like an object, unable to move in paralysis, I was being used to satiate this creature's carnal desires and was not sure whether, in the dream, I had been enjoying or hating the experience or even if she had forced herself upon me? She had a primal look upon her face, a beautiful and mysterious visage, with eyes almost like that of an animal, a tigress, drilling into mine. Reaching a crescendo, she bucked furiously, screaming and wailing, rivulets of sweat running down her arms and heaving breasts, her face contorting with intermittent moans and gasps. This seemed to go on and on and on … until, finally, I heard relieved panting emanating from the fecund beast, as if she had finally satiated a great thirst and need… a need for my seed.

Thereupon, she abruptly dismounted me, with some drips of sperm and discharge falling from her swollen vagina onto me as she did, then disappeared out of the room to the bathroom - presumably, I had served my purpose. As she did so, she displayed further her exquisite, powerful, yet womanly physique. My spent penis - the erection rapidly dissipating - was raw and sore; indeed, my whole abdomen was aching after the pounding it had been subject to.

My recollection of this dream painted it so vivid and real, such that I wondered for a moment, had it actually happened, before dismissing such ridiculous notion.

Suddenly, I was jolted from these recollections by the sound of a persistent tapping at my bedroom window. Christ, it must be that bloody pest of a solicitor again, I immediately thought… wondering how the hell would she have been able get to the rear of the house? (which was not accessible from the street). With some irritation and annoyance rising within me, I promptly jumped up and yanked the curtain back. But there was no human form at the window responsible for the disturbance. Rather, there was a big, black crow perched on the outside window ledge upon its scaly, hook-clawed feet. Tap, tap, tapping its stout pick of a beak upon the glass and with a small bristly patch of feathers covering its nostrils. The creature's dark, beady eyes were fixed up at me as if it were trying to communicate, to alert me to something.

Suddenly, Déjà jumped up from the bedroom floor to the windowsill, no doubt wondering what the commotion was, as well as wanting her breakfast. This prompted the bird to squawk loudly and fly off.

Feeling the strong urge to take a morning piss, I made my way to the bathroom. As I pulled my boxers down, I realised there was a sticky mess upon me - my pubic hairs were matted and glued together. A whiff also fanned upward that did not seem entirely of my sperm. As I made to relieve myself, my foreskin suddenly ballooned with urine due to it being bonded all round to the head of my penis by dried-out sperm. In panic and by reflex, I hastily pulled the skin back, mercifully breaking the seal and allowing the pent-up piss to cascade down to the lavatory pan, along with the continuing flow.

Jeez, I reflected that I had not had a wet dream since I was a teenager (surely, that is what had occurred?). And even in those days, it had only taken place once or twice (not least due to the incessant masturbation of a kid that age). But, to have one at 33 years of age? - for fuck's sake, how embarrassing. What is more, my penis and abdomen were tender and hurting, just as they had felt under the recollection of my dream. It was like I really had experienced that rough fucking from the wild, mysterious *dama de la noche*. Perhaps what had happened, I mused, was that I'd had a fairly vigorous nocturnal wank in semi-consciousness - the erotic dream prompting the urge to do so - and I had simply forgotten about it? All a bit odd, that was for sure.

After taking a shower and cleaning up, I decided that I would go straight to Asda to get my food shop as it opened at 6am. I was thinking that at such early hour it would be quiet and that I could hopefully get my provisions without any similar dramas to the Coop venture of the previous morning. Getting quicky dressed, I then jogged up to Bellfield Street where trusty Syd was waiting and, thereupon, headed up to the Jewel.

The supermarket was indeed near empty and thankfully, the trip was uneventful. No 'starers' or folks saying weird things to me were present, at least not any that I had noticed (and I had been keeping an eye out). Perhaps I had been imagining or, at least, misinterpreting the recent odd events, I tried once again to re-assure myself. Stocking up with plenty of grocery items to keep me properly fed for the next wee while, I also wanted to make sure that I avoided any need to venture back to the local Coop. Of course, I also got plenty of pet food sachets for Déjà (along with some tins of tuna in spring water and a packet of cooked chicken). Needless to say, in addition I bought a few bottles of some half-decent red wine to keep me company me in the evenings, along with the cat, whilst relaxing in my old leather armchair by the wood-burner.

One thing that did unsettle me, however, was the fact the Asda workers were all wearing these wee tartan ribbons pinned to their lapels. Not really the fact that they were wearing such items, but rather the reason behind it. I found out that it was in respect for a fellow worker's daughter who had been brutally murdered recently. The lady on the till told me that the poor girl, just 12 years old, had been a star highland dancer, the apple of her mum and dad's eye. That she had been abducted off the street in Leith just over a week previously. With a tear in her eye, she told me,

"Yeh dinnae really want tae ken what they did tae the puir wee soul. Her ma, Helen, has no been able to make it back tae work since, she's in such an awfy state. Her and her man only had a flattened and chewed up finger ay the lassie to bury, along wi' some ground up remains that had been strewn doon Bangour Road. Sick, bloody sick!"

This prompted a lump in my throat to develop, whilst at the same time I recalled the report of the atrocity on the Radio Scotia lunchtime news bulletin recently. Before I departed, the till lady also told me how the supermarket was now looking to dock the mum's wages if she didn't get back to work, stating that her miserly entitlement to paid 'compassionate leave' had been exhausted - that's 'caring' big business employers and how they treat the 'family' of employees for you, I pondered ruefully.

On returning to Porty, I was fortunate to find a vacant parking space at the end of Straiton Place just as one of the neighbours pulled out, presumably on their way to work. Grabbing my shopping bags, I headed along the pavement towards my gaff. As I got closer my heart sunk to spot ahead the solicitor lassie standing at my gate. Jeez, it was not even 8am and she was already back on my case! I reflected, shaking my head in annoyance.

Approaching the gate, she clocked me and uttered in a rather fretful tone, *"Mr Guthrie, we really need to speak… I called for you yesterday. Did you get my business card and message?"*

Thinking that I was about to get served with some sort of writ or summons related to the unpaid private parking firm fine, with a rather stern look, I replied brusquely,

"I am busy I am afraid and need to work. Email me if you need to get in touch - I have no doubt that you will have the email address seeing as you

clearly know my home address. It's just not right turning up at folks' door-steps like this all the time - it's an invasion of privacy and not welcome. If you are really a solicitor, then you should know that. So, move on please, and gie us peace!'

Evidently undeterred, she implored, *"Please, please listen to me. I simply MUST speak with you. I have a document for you, one that you must take from me."*

At this, Ms Gilfeather started to shuffle her hand around inside her leather shoulder bag looking for something.

'Aye, aye', I thought … she did indeed want to serve me with some sort of legal document related to that bloody parking charge. I resolved not to take any bit of paper from her, re-calling that I had seen something on social media indicating that until you voluntarily took a writ or summons in your hand, it was not valid and had not actually been served.

"Don't come any closer, otherwise I'll call the police," I said bluffing. *"You really shouldn't be harassing people where they live, it's not at all funny. May I ask you again please to MOVE ON AND AWAY from my property and home."*

Proceeding to brush past her - and moving the supermarket bags out of her reach whilst I did (just in case she tried to issue the writ/summons by dropping it into one of them) - I hastily proceeded up my wee path and steps to the front door. All 'fingers and thumbs' and juggling the various bags, I unlocked it as quickly as I could and snuck inside; thereupon slamming it shut with some force and turning the key to employ the Chubb dead lock, alongside the Yale latch which had automatically engaged.

For the second day running, I decided not to open the heavy curtains veiling the front bay window which looked onto Straiton Place and the wee park beyond. Although I did wonder why I should let this stranger upset my routine? I pondered also if perhaps I really should ring the police? Good sense, however, soon prevailed - I had learnt over the years it was best to keep the constabulary out of things unless there was no realistic option other than to involve them. Taking some deep breaths, I decided to put a pot of coffee on and make some scrambled eggs on toast with the fresh shopping supplies. I would then, I thought, check the solicitor and her firm out on the internet.

Back at my desk with a steaming mug and breakfast, I lifted my tablet, which immediately sprang into life. An email notification pinged in from one, Ms Aoife Gilfeather of Glifeather and McLean LLP. The email was marked with a red exclamation mark as of "High Importance"; on opening, it read, as follows:

"Mr Guthrie, I truly apologise for coming to your house yesterday, as well as this morning once again. I appreciate now that it was unwelcome and perhaps has been unsettling for you. But we simply must speak and do it without further delay.

I have a document - a special and unusual one - addressed to you personally at your house on Straiton Place. My solicitor's firm have been holding it within its safe for you, by name, for over 130 years. I know that this sounds far-fetched, but please trust me that it is true.

Please note that in order to comply with your wishes, I have currently moved away from your residential premises, and I promise not to trouble you there again. However, may I ask a further time please that we speak - as the assigned representative of my firm, I am duty bound to provide you the document, by hand and sit with you whilst you read it - all according to our late client's wishes.

May I suggest meeting later this morning? Perhaps at the 'Espy' pub, on a corner of Bath Street and the Promenade? The sign on the door says it opens at 11am. I'll wait at the Bath Street entrance for you at that time.

I hope very much to see you.

Yours,
Aoife Gilfeather"

Reflecting upon the rather bizarre contents of this email, I wondered whether it was some sort of practical joke? Well, at least it did not seem to have anything to do with the parking firm extortionists, I thought with some relief.

Albeit a little freaked out by what lady lawyer was saying, on top of the recent strange events with the 'starers' and folks saying weird things to me, I had to admit that I was more than a little intrigued. Did she seriously have a letter addressed to me 'personally', 'by name', that had been written nearly 100 years before I had been born? I contemplated that maybe she meant me as in a distant relative or descendant of the author, as a great, great nephew or something? That maybe I was due some sort of long, lost inheritance? But how could it be addressed to me at my 'house on Straiton Place'? How could someone all these years ago know the address of where their descendant would be living well over a century into the future?

None of it made sense and, in any case, I was perhaps reading too much into her presumably hastily written communication. I wanted to know more though, that was for sure. Admittedly,

I was also a little taken with the demure Ms Gilfeather (despite the hostile reception I had hitherto given her), especially now that I'd had the chance to properly see her face for the first time when she was at my gate – she was certainly attractive, with a kind and warm visage of natural beauty and the most striking of eyes, almost amber in colour.

I decided that there was no harm in meeting with her at the Espy to get to the bottom of the mystery. In fact, I thought, roll-on 11am!

CHAPTER 12

Aoife at the Espy, Wednesday 26th October 2022

T o get a bit of fresh air and clear my head, I decided to walk through Straiton Park and along the promenade towards the Espy, rather than to take the shorter, direct route along Straiton Place. As if in disguise, I put on a baseball cap, the brim of which was pulled down my forehead to just above my eyes, along with a black and white patterned, Palestinian-style keffiyeh scarf, partially obscuring the lower half of my face. Paranoid maybe, but I thought that this might put any potential 'starers' off the scent - if indeed such individuals truly existed outside of my imagination. Best that I could meet Ms Gilfeather in peace, I considered.

It was an overcast day, with moody and ominous dark clouds hanging over the Forth towards Fife. At the same time, even though it was towards the end of October, there was an unpleasant mugginess hanging in the air. Something odd was definitely happening to weather and climate, I reflected - an observation I had been increasingly prone to make as the seasons changed and the years went by.

As I turned into Bath Street from the Promenade, the attractive young attorney, sure enough, was standing, waiting at the entrance to the pub, and looking as prim and proper as ever in her staid, lawyerly attire. A little petulantly, I had deliberately kept her waiting a short while and she was eyeing her watch (it now being near 11.20am) presumably wondering whether I was actually going to show up. On seeing her, I took off my cap and, with some relief, loosened my scarf. On looking up and seeing me approaching, she could not help but break into a wee smile - no doubt with relief that I had decided to come and that she would be able to discharge her legal duties. I imagined for a moment how nice it would be to be greeted by such a smile if we were meeting for a date, rather than for dealing with matters of the law.

I nodded to her nonchalantly and went straight into the bar through the side door. Dutifully she followed and we took up seats on a polished maroon leather circular bench in a quiet and private snug area to the left of the door. Ms Gilfeather kept what she must have thought was a comfortable and appropriate distance from me on the seating. Within a moment an artsy-type waitress, sporting two metal studs in one eyebrow, approached with a menu and asked a little disinterestedly, *"Morning. Is it breakfast or just drinks yous' after?"*

"Well, I have eaten, but I could certainly use a drink. A pint of Tennents, please," I replied and then, looking towards my companion, prompted, *"... How about you Ms Gilfeather?"* She smiled and ordered a sparkling mineral water.

The door then creaked open and a couple of auld-fella barflies sloped in for their liquid breakfast, taking up their - no-doubt all-day – perches on stools at the front of the bar. To my relief, still a little anxious about 'starers', neither of them took any interest in myself and Ms Gilfeather, other than perfunctory, as they began to scan the racing pages of the paper and discuss bets for the 2.30 pm at Musselburgh.

"Thank you for agreeing to meet me Mr Guthrie," the lady lawyer opened with an air of sincerity.

"Well, it certainly looked like I was not going to be able to shake you off without agreeing to meet, so here I am," I responded a little glibly, before adding, *"After reading your email, I have to say that I am a little curious as to what this is all about?"*

"Well, it is good to properly meet you Mr Guthrie and that I shall have the opportunity to explain," she replied.

"It's Cameron, please… you solicitors are always so formal."

"Yes, of course. And, likewise, it's Aoife." She pronounced, *Eee-Fa* in an unusual accent that I could not quite place - it was Edinburgh, and then again it was subtly different. A crisp and clear tone, but pleasantly hushed to the ears. The sort of voice, I reflected, that I might enjoy listening to for listening's sake.

Without further ado, she proceeded to hand me a document. Rather, an antique looking circular scroll. It was on stiff parchment type paper, weathered and with brown stains blotched upon it. Tied with a red ribbon and embossed with wax seal, it felt weighty and of significance in my hands, and not just in terms of grams and ounces.

"This is for you Cameron.

As indicated in my email, this document has been in my legal firm's safe for some 130 years, addressed to you personally, by name - Mr Cameron Guthrie - and at your home address at 40 Straiton Place, Portobello.

My firm was founded by my great, great grandfather, Tavish Gilfeather. The document had an accompanying instruction letter from a Miss Sgàthach (I am not sure whether this is her first name or surname), originally addressed to him - and opened read and by him - but which has since been passed to me all these years later.

As part of this original instruction, at noon on Tuesday, 25th October 2022, the document was to be passed to you by hand. That was, of course, yesterday and, clearly and regrettably I failed in that task. I can only hope that the one-day delay will not be material. Perhaps this might explain my persistence at knocking at your door yesterday and, again, appearing at your house this morning Mr Guth ... erm, Cameron. May I apologise once more for such intrusion. It's just that myself and my firm take our client instructions very seriously and this being so unusual and a very long-standing commitment, all the more so. So, I hope that you are able to forgive me. I am so glad that you kindly agreed to meet me here as, otherwise, I would have been at a loss as what to do.

Before you read the document, please be aware that I do not know the exact content, although a rather curious summary was provided in the aforementioned instruction letter. After reading and re-sealing the client instruction letter, my great, great, grandfather had left implicit orders that it must not be re-opened by a firm's representative (or indeed any party) until the Friday in advance of the scheduled delivery of the substantive missive to yourself. This directive had since been passed down through the years by the various partners in the lineage of our firm. Hence, it was only last Friday, that I was provided the opportunity to read the instruction letter for the first time. As the only solicitor in our firm to be a direct descendent of Tavish Gilfeather, it was felt, that despite my relatively junior standing, it was most appropriate for me, rather than another representative, to personally follow through with our client's stipulations and wishes provided some 130 years in the past."

Taken aback, I looked at the curious article in my hand. Shaking my head in disbelief, I responded, *"Aoife, it simply cannot be. My bungalow on Straiton Place was never in my family and I have only been living there for around 12 years, after buying at an auction. I can't even say if it had been built 130 years ago! And I'm just 33 years of age, so how on earth would your client know of me - to personally address a letter with my name all that time ago? There has got be some other explanation or that this is an elaborate hoax of some sort, on you or me ... or both of us perhaps?"*

"Please bear with me Cameron," Aoife replied in an effort to provide some calm reassurance, then continued, *"May I suggest that you open the document and read it in full before we speak further."* As she went on to beckon me to do so, she added, *"Lastly, I would ask you please to do your best to keep an open mind and to try to suspend disbelief."*

With a gulp of anticipation, I proceeded to tug at both ends of the ribbon around the document, the action of doing so clearly designed to break the aged wax seal upon the center of the rolled-up scroll and allow access. It needed quite bit of force to do so, whereupon the parchment paper sprung open revealing not one, but a number of such leaves, each bearing distinctive, quill-style writing in black ink.

Carefully, I flattened the pages down. The inner ones, all numbered, appeared to be in better condition and less stained than the outer leaf, which seemed to have served primarily as a protective layer. The document or scroll was in fact a rather lengthy letter. Looking a little hesitantly at the text on the first page, I could not help but gasp upon seeing my name and address. But I experienced perhaps an even greater intake of breath when I registered that above this, not only was the letter dated 130 years in the past - I had been prepared for that from what Aoife had said - but it was simultaneously dated sixty-odd years in the future!

I looked towards the assigned representative of Gilfeather and McLean LLP with wide, questioning eyes - clearly, I was finding keeping an open mind and suspending disbelief a little hard. She gave me an understanding smile and nodded in recognition - I guessed that she had been expecting such a reaction. How could the letter be dated both in the past and the future? A letter from the past locked in her firm's safe to-date was perhaps plausible to a certain extent, but a letter from the future was clearly an impossibility. Was this something Aoife had been aware of and had decided to keep from me (maybe the client instruction letter had been similarly dated)? If so, presumably she had not wished to add a further layer of incredulity upon matters before convincing me to meet with her - this was quite literally a 'riddle, wrapped in a mystery, inside an enigma'. Shaking my head, again I was questioning whether all this was just some crazy wind-up?

In a supportive and welcome gesture, Aoife then lightly placed her hand upon my shoulder and smiled at me warmly. And with equally impeccable timing, the waitress arrived back with our drinks, plonking them unceremoniously in front of us. My hand shaking, I promptly tanned about two-thirds of my pint and then ordered a large whisky before the waitress had had the chance to depart back to the bar.

Casting my eyes back down to the mysterious artefact whilst remembering Aoife's final comment, I began to read in full …

15th March 1892 (and 18th September 2082)

Mr Cameron Guthrie,
40 Straiton Place,
Portobello EH15 5BQ

Dear Cameron,

You will surely be most confused at receiving my letter and will rightly have many questions that you wish answered. Although I will certainly address some of these here, I am afraid that many more will remain, and new ones shall surely arise further to your reading of the content.

Where to start? Well, let's commence with 'time'. It can be said that I am both writing this letter many years prior to your birth, but also many decades after you are to first read it.

Confused? I have no doubt that that you are, however, this missive shall seek to explain how this is possible.

To unravel the complexity and understand you firstly need to appreciate that 'time' is not what it seems, or at least how it has hitherto appeared to you.

Reflect upon that notion if you will. As you do so, perhaps let me try to focus upon why I am writing to you. To be blunt, I must explain that you have a task that you need to carry out Cameron. Rather, a job that you MUST undertake, one that you have been 'chosen' to do, in fact. 'Fate' itself, has selected you! As such, it is your duty of to undertake, or at least make every possible effort to successfully perform.

I shall no doubt sound dramatic in saying this - but the truth is dramatic - the fate of the world rests upon your successful completion of this assignment. I do not say this lightly, but that is the reality of the situation.

You will surely be surprised to hear that I know a lot of things about you - I shall explain shortly how this is so. As part, I am aware that you are well versed in Scottish history. Most particularly of myth, legend and the paranormal, or the 'special-natural' as you like to call it. I understand also that you are cognizant of your own psychic and wider abilities and have begun to explore, develop and expand upon them more recently, including undertaking 'psychic medium readings'. At the same time, you have, I believe, written a book linked to your interest in the 'special-natural'. Further, that as part of your research for it, you studied the 'Fiosaichean'.

Cameron, I implore you to put disbelief aside for a moment when I tell you that you, yourself, are of the line of the Fiosaichean! Believe me please, because without doubt I know this to be true, as I, myself, am also of such lineage. If you struggle to accept this fact, then, at the very least, please acknowledge that you have only scratched the very surface of your psychic, para-normal and wider 'special-natural' skills and capabilities.

As you know from your research, it is only in the rarest of cases that an exceptional individual is born inheriting the timeless gifts of the line of the Fiosai-chean. Although, I refer to the 'line' and allude to inheritance, I do not, of course, refer to a birth descent within a family (an exception being a child conceived by the congress of two Fiosaiche), rather a progression through history of individuals with such unique powers, appearing at most infrequent intervals, like extraordinary stars in the expanse of the galaxy.

In similarity to myself Cameron, you are such a rare and exceptional individual.

Indeed, it is because I am one of the Fiosaichean that I know so much about you – the psychic and 'special-natural' gifts, the abilities, the powers, have permitted me to do so. As a Fiosaiche you have at the very least the same - and I believe even greater - gifts to those of myself. The fact that you are such a powerful Fiosa-iche has led you to be chosen to undertake the important task to which I refer.

If we can go back for a moment to the notion of 'time' not being what it seems. You need to be aware that you are presently living near to what I shall describe as a crossroads in time, a very important juncture indeed.

This fact prompts my making of this request of you at your current date in 2022, along with its urgency. You and you alone, Cameron, have the ability necessary to successfully perform the assignment, details of which I shall share details with you shortly.

Critical in relation to this task, is a book, a very important, historic one, and further, its keepers in your present-day.

Back in what you will know of as the 'dark ages', within Dál Riata - the ancient kingdom of Scotland - a text known as the *Facal an Fiosaiche* manuscript (the Word of the Seer) was written. Inscribed upon vellum in a particular form of the Ogham alphabet and illuminated with Pictish art, the script is believed to be from the 6th century, pre-dating the Book of Kells by some three hundred years. It is essentially a book of dark magic, reputedly scribed by a Fiosaiche who sadly used their special gifts to seed and promulgate evil.

The book had been referenced in carvings upon on a small number of Pictish stones, but its existence was not fully confirmed until it was uncovered in Kilmartin Glen, Argyll, by the 16th Century landowner, Cecil Whitham-Fotheringay. Further to its loss in a gambling wager, the script then fell into the hands of a clergyman by the name of John Kellie, then minister of the small parish of Spenton, Hadintunshire.

You will be certainly wondering why, with all your historical research, you had not come across references to the existence of such an important artefact as the *Facal an Fiosaiche* manuscript? Well, that is by design, rather than accident. The holders in your present day (and their predecessors) having done all they could over many years to erase any reference to it within historical annuals, records and otherwise. This even included, in the late 19th century, the destruction of the aforementioned remaining Pictish stones, along with University archives at St Andrews relating to its examination in 1568. Such action was taken to consolidate their power of possession over the book and reduce the likelihood that it would ever be taken from them, by theft or other means. ... More about them in a moment.

Further to his possession of the book (or perhaps more aptly, it's possession of him) the reverend Kellie managed to decipher key parts of its cryptic writings, including dark magic. He then became involved in certain nefarious activities, including murder for which he was apprehended and executed (with his remains being burnt to ashes). Thereupon, nothing was known of the dark-age tome and its whereabouts until in 1889, when it came up for auction at Bannerman & Goudelock, a then specialist auctioneers in

Edinburgh. The date of the auction was 28th February that year. Although, permit me to rephrase that, for reasons I shall explain shortly – the date of the auction <u>is</u> 28th February 1889. The seller's anonymity was maintained however, it is likely to have been descendants of whoever had inherited Kellie's estate back in 1570 (something I have been unable to verify).

The identity of the purchaser, however, I do know. Not an individual but an Edinburgh gentlemen's group going by the name of the 'Noble Order of Eidyn'. The present-day incarnation of this society, which remain in possession of the artefact, is one that I believe you have already crossed paths with Cameron. All records of the 1889 auction were subsequently destroyed in a fire at Bannerman & Goudelock's premises in the late 1890's (which I have no doubt that the Order had a hand in starting). That is save as for a solitary auction program which had been obtained from the auction house archives prior to such destruction.

Please further attempt to put aside lack of credence for a moment if you can - I appreciate that this asks a lot after what I have already divulged to you.

Once more, I would be grateful if you could reflect upon the idea that 'time' is not what it seems. In fact, time may operate on several dimensions - these are 'planes', or 'thoroughfares' of time as I refer to them.

As incredible it may seem to you now, I come from the future of one plane – one possible plane. A future which has been desecrated by greed and profligate disregard for our planet's natural resources – where Mother Nature's generous bounty has been plundered to the huge detriment of the human race. From the thoroughfare of time that I hail from, I can look back and see that the move of ownership of the manuscript to the Noble Order of Eidyn set in force a chain of events that shaped world history and the human race - setting a destructive and catastrophic path for our world's climate and environment.

A path forward that would have almost certainly been avoided had the gentlemen's group not taken possession of the sinister text. However, it is also a trajectory, Cameron, that need not be so, as the route may be altered! I shall shortly explain further what I mean by this.

The manuscript in the wrong hands - ones that can uncover its dark mysteries and decipher its secrets - can be used a tool of evil, to satiate greed and wreak havoc. John Kellie, the minister of God, turned murder, being an example; the Noble Order of Eidyn being another.

As you may know, in your present day, the gentlemen's group comprise a sizeable group of the finest professionals, businesspersons and 'high-society' figures of the city and beyond. Back in 1889, this was not quite the case, rather they were a far smaller and aspiring group of such individuals. Nevertheless, on purchase of the manuscript, the members of the Order used their expertise and academic connections to uncover a number of its mysteries, decoding certain passages of its obscure wording as well as symbolism (albeit, despite such expertise, not to the extent that the reverend Kellie had managed to achieve prior to his untimely demise).

It was sufficient, however, that in the years that followed, they were able to perform many spells and the like laid out within the pages. In fact, in doing so, they were able to harness aspects of its malign sorcery which allowed them and their kin to rise to the very tops of their professional fields, to win business deals, predict share movements, and more broadly, to satiate all manner of whims and desires as is possible to imagine. It is this greed, and use of the aged manuscript to gratify, that ultimately leads to the aforementioned catastrophe for the world.

Ceremonial aspects of invocations as directed by the book's Ogham text, reputedly require the exacting of levies or dues in order for the spell to be properly performed. In the preacher man's case, this was murder, amongst other requirements. In certain instances, it may necessitate the apprehension and killing of an individual meeting particular specifications. For example, a young, virginal female who is reaching her first menstrual cycle, someone of a particular race, a person who in some way has dealt misfortune to or challenged a keeper of the antique tome (or an individual who is a senior representative of an organisation or association which has caused such misfortune or challenge). In other cases, levies may separately or additionally require the grisly acquisition of human body parts or organs – such as the head, the eyes, the liver, the heart and/or the genitalia, for example - in whole form, or utilised in some manner as part of a potion or otherwise to accompany the sorcery.

Hence, the carrying out of certain depraved acts is necessary for proper performance of the wicked enchantments of the book. The Order can spend many months carefully preparing and accumulating such gruesome artefacts, as required, in advance of actually performing a spell (which is generally at an invocation ceremony). At the same time, seeking to avoid unnecessary suspicion being cast in their direction.

Note that the members of Order consider the disgraced reverend John Kellie to be their spiritual founder. He, above all other individuals, is credited by them for most fully deciphering and understanding the manuscript's particularly impenetrable form of Ogham script.

Full membership of the gentlemen's group is primarily reserved solely for the first-born sons of members on a primogeniture basis; that is in line with principles applying to hereditary peerages in the House of Lords and, for centuries, the royal line of succession to the British throne. However, in certain cases, important and influential persons hitherto with no connection to the Order, may be invited to join, either as a full member or as a trusted associate. Strong links are reputed to exist to the 'dark state' of the British establishment and the House of Saxe-Coburg-Gotha.

Please be aware that in order to cloak its despicable activities, the Order operates publicly as a 'Charity Limited by Guarantee' in the UK, over which designated members exert executive control. Associated not-for-profit organisations have long been set up in numerous countries abroad for similar purposes. As part of its public face, various community and civic endeavors are carried out via such charitable organisations, including the funding and support of good causes. All of this fostering much positive public relations for the Order as a benevolent and generous institution, akin to organisations such as the Red Cross and the Salvation Army perhaps. I am sure that will already be aware of this public persona of the gent's association Cameron, at least more locally.

During the latter part of the 20th century and early 2000's, the Order, with growing international connections (particularly within Israel, Saudi Arabia, UAE, Russia, China and the USA) and always on the lookout for money making opportunities, took on a major funding role for a then fledging technology called 'micromagnetic fracking' - a process to harvest 'oil shale'. Branded as an environmentally friendly alternative to tradition fracking technology, the truth was very different. The carbon emissions growth from such process, in particular that of methane, as it was subsequently launched on a large-scale basis (from around 2025, although in operation earlier in a more limited - but still damaging - capacity), was exponential.

As the rollout out accelerated apace, the consequent impact on global warming and pollution was immense – at a scale hitherto thought unimaginable over such a short and finite period. The explosion in use of such technology during the late 2020's and 2030's was as a direct result and consequence of investment and support provided by the Order to the micromagnetic fracking sector. At its height, the industry was operating in over 90 countries worldwide.

On the back of profits accumulated, at the expense of the fragile bounty of Mother Nature and our precious environment, the members of the 'Noble Order' continued to amass and expand their financial wealth.

It was, of course, only through the evil magic of the *Facal an Fíosaíche* manuscript that the group was able to exert political, business and other influence necessary to allow such rapid expansion in micromagnetic fracking.

Due principally to this, by 2030 a 'tipping point' had been reached. A cascade of abrupt shifts in the planet's climate ensued at a truly alarming rate - a speed that the truly independent climatologists had forecast would occur with the roll out of the technology. As Rome (literally) started to burn, the industry continued to significantly expand with the undiminished efforts and support of gentlemen's group, along with its payrolled pet 'scientists' and corrupt officials.

That was up until 2038 when the United Nations finally intervened with a panicked, but all too late, global ban on micromagnetic fracking. By that stage, the world was experiencing temperature warming of around 5°C above pre-industrial levels. Side by side with this, sea levels had risen by 1.5 meters, the polar ice regions had all but vanished and extreme weather events had become habitual. Wildlife, agriculture, fishing and aquaculture habitats had been devastated, with the food chain in collapse. Floods, famines, disease, and pestilence haunted the world like the grim reaper's shadow, never to be evaded - the loss of human life incalculable, going forwards into the future.

At this point, I looked up from the weathered parchment pages - I needed a moment to collect my thoughts. It really was too much to take in and there were still several sheets left. Quaffing the remainder of the pint of Tennents, now flat, I noted that next to it on the small, oval table, sat a double whisky which must have arrived at some point when I had been immersed in the letter.

Shaking my head in disbelief at what I had just read, I gazed towards Aoife. She smiled softly in response and with an expression of understanding, before urging me to continue. My hands shaking like those of a jakie, I lifted the small glass of amber fluid to my mouth and necked it in a oner; then, taking a deep breath, looked down once again at the antique paper leaves before me and resumed reading …

So, Cameron, we come to your required task – your fate, your destiny, if I may again be so dramatic.

A rare attribute of the Fiosaichean is the ability to traverse the aforementioned planes and thoroughfares of time. Yes, it is true - and you too sir, have that special gift.

Incredible and unbelievable as this sounds, please have faith as I know it to be true. We Fiosaichean are the chosen few who may navigate the planes of time.

If you doubt me then please consider for a moment the gifted physicist, Albert Einstein who, in a letter to family members shortly before his death wrote, "*... hat die Scheidung zwischen Vergangenheit, Gegenwart und Zukunft nur die Bedeutung einer, wenn auch hartnäckigen, Illusion.*" This translates into English as , "*... the distinction between past, present and future has only the meaning of an illusion, albeit a persistent one.*"

Einstein through science and logic, with his study of relativity, grasped something that had hitherto eluded virtually all others, except the Fiosaichean – that, indeed, 'time' was not what it seemed.

We Fiosaichean are able to navigate around the false distinction between periods and epochs of time. We can place ourselves firmly in the reality of time. What is generally thought of as the past, present and future, we can really, truly and actually place our feet within - to walk, see, feel, hear, smell and taste . And, sometimes, with great care and caution, we may even alter the course of time - in terms of the form and shape of the future!

I said before that fate demanded a task of you. The broader reality is that this is actually our Mother Earth reaching out to you... that is no exaggeration. I hear her cries, I feel her pain, and, as one of the Fiosaichean, I am merely a conduit, a special voice, a written word, seeking to relay and explain on her behalf what you simply <u>must</u> attempt to undertake.

You may have recently experienced individuals with psychic gifts (albeit very much more limited than our own) reaching out to you, including coming up to you in public and similarly urging you to complete a task - they are the 'comasach', her mortal messengers.

What is requested of you Cameron, is to traverse back from your present day - your 'home epoch' (*àm dachaigh*) - to 28th February 1889 and attend the aforementioned auction at Bannerman & Goudelock, 23 Broughton Place, Edinburgh. At the early evening event - commencing at 6.00 pm - you are to place the winning bid for the purchase of the *Facal an Fiosaiche* manuscript, thereby denying it from falling into the hands of the Noble Order of Eidyn or indeed any other mortal soul.

Once in possession of the accursed volume, you are to destroy it directly and personally by setting it alight so that it burns - every single part and page - into ashes. Despite the manuscript with its cryptic Ogham text having such malevolent abilities, it is made from normal, combustible material – calf skin vellum, with a rough hide cover - and may be disposed of once and for all in such manner. Thereupon, you are to collect the ashes and disperse them - an ideal place being within the sea off Portobello sands.

Through such deed you will create a ripple through time. The consequences of which will be the altering of the otherwise inevitable future of tragedy, suffering and despair in the world of which I earlier sought to paint a graphic picture. With your actions, you will have saved our Mother Earth from imploding with a cruel and ignominious demise; you will have stopped evil being promulgated by the gentlemen's group through the wicked sorcery of the *Facal an Fiosaiche*.

I hear you asking, would there be unintended conse-quences triggered by such interference with the course of events of the past and the undulations possibly cre-ated? Well, I must be frank and say that there may be. However, any such consequences are surely insig-nificant in comparison with the good for humanity by ridding it of the dark powers of the *Facal an Fiosaiche* manuscript as harnessed under the greedy and murderous hands of the Noble Order of Eidyn. When traversing time, your day-to-day interactions and comings and goings are highly unlikely to have more than a minimal and inconsequential impact.

That said, you need to exercise caution – unnecessary and undue interference, inadvertent or deliberate, has the potential to cause more than insignificant waves in the time continuum. Hence, a word of warning in relation to any intentional meddling, please avoid and resist any such temptation to carry out unless properly and fully justified.

Clearly, deliberate interference is what we seek in relation to destroying the vile text. Indeed, we would be wish to cause not just a ripple in the time continuum, but rather a wave of tsunami proportions! But one that would be a force for good, for Mother Earth and humanity. Of course, the significant and devastating environmental impact of the Order in its use of the dark book does not truly and significantly manifest until after 2022, your home epoch, albeit some climate impact will already be evident in that year and before (you may have already noticed unusual changes to your climate patterns and weather).

Perhaps the next crucial question to address Cameron is how we Fiosaichean, in a practical sense, traverse time?

In answering, it is important for you to know that the ability of our kind to cross the thoroughfares of time is subject to certain limitations and requirements.

Firstly, it is essential for you to appreciate, that despite our special gifts, we Fiosaichean are mere mortals - the toll on the body and mind of travelling the planes of time is considerable. Hence, this ability should be exercised sparingly and on infrequent occasions. These particular powers of a Fiosaiche can become spent, leaving the individual unable to repeat time-travel or at the least, require respite and recuperation (which can be of a long and indeterminate duration) between attempts. I have myself suffered from such exhaustion of abilities, of which I shall tell you more about in due course.

The second limitation is that, generally, a Fiosaiche is only able to journey back in time once to any particular time juncture or event. Hence, they are unable to return on multiple occasions, such as to seek to correct a mistake made or grasp an opportunity missed before. The mysterious operation of the time continuum and its thoroughfares will typically thwart any effort to do so. Perhaps so as to avoid the incongruity of a traveller encountering themselves on a different traverse which may cause schisms in the very foundations of such continuum. For the same reasons, a Fiosaiche is advised not to seek out their former or latter self in differing time period.

Thirdly, the transfer between time dimensions may only take place at an intersection of spirit or ley lines (àite-tarsainn). This is the juncture – a particular physical location - at which the earth's natural spirit energy is at its highest and may allow a form of space-time synthesis. It presents the opportunity for a Fiosaiche – and only a Fiosaiche, of course - to a step from one thoroughfare of time and on to another. Imagine these thoroughfares, if you like, as multiple moving escalators with various steps and going in differing directions - you are able to take your foot from a step on your current escalator - your home epoch - and onto that of an another - the 'destination epoch' (àm ceann-uidhe) - alighting at such point. Where you travel to the past and make changes, such as we have already discussed, such ripples and undulations may alter the direction of the escalators. Hence, when you travel back to your home epoch - taking the step back on the original escalator - and get off, certain aspects will have changed due to the aforementioned ripples and undulations. As said before, such changes are generally minor, save as where a deliberate intervention has been made to influence otherwise.

Fourthly, a Fiosaiche who wishes to traverse time, must generally have upon their person two 'objects' (*nithean*). One which is closely associated with the exact date and location that they wish to travel to, the destination epoch, and another with such association to their home epoch (assuming that the individual intends to return there).

It is important that the particular object or article, in both cases, is linked to the general whereabouts of the aforementioned ley line intersection, such as the town, city or particular geographic area. Further, it should ideally have the date that is sought to cross to written or otherwise imprinted upon it (note that in certain cases, a digital imprint may suffice). Typical examples include newspapers, transport tickets, event programs and the like which have such association.

Be aware that without such appropriate object, it is still possible to time-traverse, however, the location and date can be wildly out of sync with that intended. Indeed, travel forward in time, at least in the first instance, may be practised in this manner, but carries such risk and, more broadly, the peril of the unknown in terms of the circumstances that you may face upon arrival (hence, I would advise great care in relation to any such attempt).

There is a fifth and final limitation which applies, at the least, to myself - I shall say more upon that shortly.

So, Cameron, from what I have said, you will appreciate that thorough and adequate preparation for crossing the planes of time is essential. As part, you should seek to appear as unobtrusive as possible in the destination epoch, making every effort to blend in. Further, to have the practical necessities, such as money of the day, for subsistence.

Another important point to note is that when you arrive at the chosen destination epoch, the time of day will be exactly as that from which you travelled. Yet, no matter how long you end up spending in that time epoch - be it hours, days or months - when you return to your home epoch, generally only a short period of time will have elapsed from when you first departed. This can be as little as a matter of minutes or, perhaps, a few hours; in my experience, it is never more than the duration of one day, but this does mean that in certain cases you may find yourself arriving back a day later than the imprinted date or association of the object facilitating your return.

As indicated above, I have journeyed through time and on many occasions. So, I am sure that it will not surprise you Cameron to hear that I have myself already tried and failed on a number of occasions to acquire and destroy the mystical script, including at the 1989 Bannerman and Goudelock auction itself.

I have no doubt that you will be questioning why, with me having such experience and being one of the Fiosa-ichean, that I seem unwilling to personally try once again to destroy the manuscript, rather I am asking you to undertake? The simple truth is that I no longer believe that I am able to do so.

After the exhaustive and unsuccessful efforts to attain and destroy it, I had the growing awareness of two things. Firstly, that my powers of time-traverse were waning; and secondly, that for whatever reason, I was not going to be the person - the Fiosaiche - who was going to be able to do away with the aged volume, at least directly. Specifically in relation to purchase at the 1889 auction, in any case, of course, I had failed in my attempt; a further effort by me being essentially precluded by the 'second limitation' to which I referred. My conclusion was that perhaps the time continuum was railing against alteration, at least by myself (a Fiosaiche whose home epoch had already been so radically altered by the dark forces of the script). Hence, I reached the belief that, for me, this was a 'fifth limitation' of time-traverse - that I was prohibited from altering the thoroughfares of time by destroying the abhorrent book.

It was at that juncture that you first came into my thoughts Cameron via dreams and visions. As part, that such restriction - the fifth limitation - did not however apply to you. Further, as you were such an individual - such a Fiosaiche - I understood that I needed to contact you and present you with a request, along with a plan, to gain possession of the aged text.

I judged that the 1889 auction would provide you with the best opportunity to do so, as well as it being a pivotal juncture in time, with possession of the vile volume otherwise moving to that of the Order. Hence, I decided that I must locate an original copy of the auction program as the necessary 'object' to facilitate - most exactly - your time-traverse to 1889. I promptly sought to travel to 1892 (utilising an old Edinburgh tramcars docket of that year which I had managed to locate as the article to facilitate my traverse) in order to gain a copy within the archives of Bannerman and Goudelock. However, on seeking to traverse, to my alarm, I found that my time-travel powers were spent. That was in 2056.

Indeed, my abilities were not to return for many long years. In fact, it has taken me until now - 2082 in my home epoch - to make this long-anticipated trip back to 1892 to procure the auction program for you. Thankfully, I have successfully managed to do so within the auction house archives prior to other copies being destroyed in the aforementioned unexplained fire at the premises in the late 1890's.

In terms of making contact with you, I ascertained that I had to pick the optimum moment to pass on this precious 'object', along with what is stated in this letter. My dreams and visions led me to understand that in 2021 and 2022 you were starting to appreciate your 'special-natural' gifts more fully. Hence, I concluded that the best time to get in touch would be in your 33rd year in 2022, at a date to allow your powers to develop as fully as possible (giving the optimum chance of success in accomplishing the required assignment), however, before the key crossroads in time, which I earlier referred to, were reached. As indicated, this important juncture in time is shortly to be reached in your home epoch. It is critical that you undertake the requested task prior to this being met - and, rather, to stop it being met. More relating to this in a moment.

Against this background, I have decided that, rather than endeavouring to time-traverse myself to 2022 in order to speak to you directly and outline your task, it is far safer for me to lodge this letter with such details, along with necessary enclosures, with a solicitors' firm instructed to pass on to you when the appointed time in 2022 is reached. Currently, as I write, I feel my powers of time-traverse are weak and could fail me. There is no saying whether I would be able to traverse from here in 1892 to 2022 in order to speak to you. That with such waning abilities, I might even find myself inadvertently travelling to the wrong time epoch and becoming lodged there.

Hence, I consider the risk is too great and that such an attempt might mean that you are never provided with details of the vital task that fate, our Mother Earth, requires of you.

So, prior to seeking to return to my home epoch from this day, Wednesday 15th March 1892, I am leaving this letter, along with an instruction missive at Gilfeather & McLean LLP. This is a solicitors firm which I believe that I can trust as they have no discernable link with the Noble Order of Eidyn over the years as far as I have been able to ascertain. Further, it is a firm that I am aware continues to be in existence to 2022 and beyond.

Needless to say, on my initial enquiry, the senior partner, the affable Mr Tavish Gilfeather, was most surprised at my intended instruction for delivery of a letter, some one hundred and thirty years hence, to a man that would not be born for nearly a century! It was greeted by some disbelief and even amusement by him; that I must be some sort of deluded, eccentric, a crazy lady no doubt. That was until I proffered a substantial upfront payment relating to the fee, along with future expenses, and at a level that his firm could simply not refuse. At the time of writing, Mr Gilfeather keenly awaits this signed and sealed letter for lodging within his firm's safe, together with my instruction missive; and he even more eagerly antici-pates provision of such promised funds to the firm's bank account. In my experience Cameron, not least from traversing the thoroughfares of time, there are three things in life that are certain - death, taxes, and the professional diligence of Edinburgh's legal frater-nity in complying with a paid for instruction (well, at least those not in the pocket of the Noble Order in any case).

For your information, I obtained the requisite monies as a random bundle of worthless notes from a dock-side junk stall in my home epoch as part of prepara-tion for my trip back to 1892. I had not fully appreciated the considerable value of the currency in this time period until I had arrived. As such, the sum is also intended to cover the amount required for your visit to 1889, including the auction purchase. Based upon my research, it should be more than sufficient to outbid the Order of that time, along with meeting any incidental costs resultant to your time-traverse.

If matters have progressed according to my letter of instruction to Gilfeather & McLean, you will cur-rently be in the in the company of one of their most trusted and discreet representatives. My upfront payment, of course, includes provision for their service and support to you. It is up to you how much of what I have said in this communique is shared in confidence with them as an attorney bound by the Law Society of Scotland's strict professional code. As part of their role, he or she is immediately available to provide you indirect assistance in your task, such as with practical preparation. From deposited within my sealed instruction letter, they should have in their possession to pass on to you the aforementioned monies along with the Bannerman & Goudelock auction program for Thursday, 28th February 1889. Needless to say, although the law firm's representative is there to support you, it is only you, Cameron, that is equipped with the necessary skills and aptitudes to complete the vital task assigned.

I appreciate that all this is a huge amount for you to take in, however, please bear with me. May I continue to outline the practicalities of the job that is asked of you...

You will recall that I outlined the necessity of an intersection of spirit or ley lines as the physical location allowing a Fiosaiche to traverse time. Such an 'àite-tarsainn' point exists in Edinburgh in the Holyrood Park lands. Most specifically, at the site of St

Anthony's Chapel overlooking St Margaret's loch and the ruins of Holyrood Abbey. You may be aware that the so called, Salisbury Crags, adjacent to the Chapel, are in fact the ancient 'Rocks of Dead' - Creagan nam Marbh – so named due to spiritual and mystic forces at play in the area. You shall harness those forces to assist your passage through time. For information, the locations of such spirit or ley lines intersections throughout the world are generally discoverable via research of the applicable primordial and indigenous cultures and religions – that, alongside, harnessing the psychic vision of a Fiosaiche.

In order to traverse the thoroughfares of time, you must not only be at the applicable intersection point, but you need to reach a particular state of being - mental, physical and, most importantly, spiritual - permitting you to step from one epoch or time plane and onto another.

As I indicated earlier, my mind's eye told me that in 2022 you were already undertaking 'psychic medium readings'. Further, I know that this has included communicating with those who have passed. Once in location at St Anthony's Chapel, you must use similar techniques of contemplation, meditation and reflection in order to reach the state of being to which I refer. Seek to focus upon the time period – the required epoch - and, more specifically the exact date that you wish to traverse to. This includes a visualisation of the calendar date and images of that time period.

In relation to the crucial 'object' of the destination epoch that you are aiming to traverse to, it is very important to, i) hold or position it close to your heart (in your hand, breast pocket or within an adjacent pouch or bag, for example) and, ii) focus your thoughts upon it, in particular the date written/imprinted which matches the time period which you wish to traverse to. Using the article as a tool of time-traverse in such manner tends to exclude any inadvertent interference from other items upon your person. In case you are concerned, may I reassure you that the use of an object from the home epoch for return traverse remains unaffected by any ripples created within a traverse to the past, even though certain aspects of the home epoch may have been altered. Again, it is the association of the object with the date and location that is crucial. To use my analogy of before, you will take your step back on the same escalator within the thoroughfares of time, albeit its direction may have been altered.

By following the aforementioned, you will gradually - all going well - reach the necessary ephemeral state for time-traverse. Trust me, you will know the moment of transition when it arrives due to the intensity of the sensation throughout your whole body and mind. Thereupon, breathe deeply, notice the unfamiliar smells; listen closely and hear the differing sounds; feel the invariably changed temperature, weather and atmosphere upon your being; then, slowly, ever so slowly, open your eyes once again... and behold!

My instructions to Gilfeather & McLean were that you should be provided this letter at noon of 25th October 2022. As indicated above, I felt from my visions and dreams that this would be the optimum moment to contact you with the vital request. Should your initial attempt or attempts to travel back in time prove unsuccessful (this is all very new and strange to you, of course), then this should allow you the opportunity of a few days to master the skills necessary to enter the required state for successful transition.

However, as I have already indicated, matters are time critical. You must not delay your time-traverse more than a few days. This is vital, as after Monday 31st October 2022, the significant crossroads in time I referred to before would have been reached. Events fully set in motion at this point, would be of such nature as likely beyond prevention or alteration by a time traversing Fiosaiche residing thereafter. I shall not trouble you here with further details. In any case, attaining the dark manuscript at the 1889 auction and destroying it, as requested, would ensure that such time crossroads were no longer relevant or a threat.

Please take the necessary leap of faith Cameron - Mother Earth is depending on you!

Yours aye,

Sgàthach

CHAPTER 13

Servant of the Kirk, 16th Century

F urther to the Scottish Reformation, the reverend John
Kellie was the first Protestant minister of Spenton Kirk
and the surrounding parish, commencing the appointment
in 1567.

He relished this position of authority, although would have preferred a more prominent parish rather than that of small, sleepy
Spenton in Hadintunshire. There was also the issue of the meagre stipend the church afforded its rural parish clergy for their
duties - something he had broached with the high-heid yins of
the wider Kirk, but to no avail. Unlike many of his peers, he
was not the kin of a titled family, nor the son of a wealthy physician or advocate, rather he had to survive purely upon such
payment.

Despite his proclaimed religious observance, Kellie was fond
of gambling; over-fond, in fact and he had amassed substantial
debts as a result. Having to support his wife, Margaret, added
to the burden upon his already severely strained finances.

It had been fortuitous though that in December 1569, the clergyman had the opportunity to enter a wager with well-kent
drunk, fornicator and profligate nobleman, *Laird o Pairlament*
Cecil Whitham-Fotheringay. With hereditary lands in the

Lothians as well as in Argyll and the West, Whitham-Fotheringay had substantial funds at his disposal to frivolously whittle away upon wagering. Monies that Kellie was more than happy to relieve the haughty debaucher of. In this case, however, the stake that Whitham-Fotheringay put forward for the series of games of dice was not Pund Scottis, rather an artefact, a highly usual and aged manuscript. It bore a hide cover and had the most exquisitely marked symbols upon its vellum pages within.

The reverend had felt instantly drawn to the item, perhaps due to his concealed interest in mysticism. This was particularly the case when, in advance of the wager, the boor aristocrat allowed him to hold and inspect the artefact - a feeling of some euphoria came instantly upon him. This was an item Kellie knew that he must win from the evening's gambling. There was something far greater than the mere monetary value he felt; something related to the spiritual, even orphic arts perhaps? The preacher man did not know how or why but he had the intuitive feeling that taking possession of the queer text would bring him great wealth, along with other favors. As for his own stake, he put up a solid gold chalice - part of the Kirk's precious pre-reformation collection - that he had craftily managed to purloin whilst on a trip to St Giles to meet his parsimonious superiors.

Whitham-Fotheringay explained the provenance of the manuscript to the churchman, at least in terms of what he was able to confirm. The *Laird* had been in the process of clearing his Argyle lands of crofting peasant dwellers and tenant farmers to make way for a new and experimental process of sheep farming which promised, in his opinion, to be more profitable. He believed that he was way ahead of his time amongst the Scot's landed gentry in such use of the land and that in the long years hence they would eventually follow suit, and on a widespread scale, rather than ridicule him as they currently did, saying, "*sheep cannae pay yeh taxes!*" It might take them a couple of hundred years, but they would eventually see the light, he surmised scathingly. At the same time, he was building a tower house upon the land. This would be a peaceful summer retreat from the distractions of whoring and gambling in Edinburgh's impious underbelly. In relation to its erection, he had engaged a troop of the now homeless and desperate displaced peasants to dislodge various ancient standing stones which, due to their location, had provided an awkward blockage to his desired carriage route to the entrance of the new tower abode. There had been one particularly large stone which the men had been reluctant to attempt to shift; not because of its considerable bulk, but due to the fact that it bore strange carvings and symbols, including that of a sea-horse beast. According to myth and superstition in Argyll, any person who inflicted harm or damage upon a so-inscribed slab would be subject to ill fortune and death. Such were their fears and reluctance, that the foreman had had to take his *sgian-dubh* to the one of the wretches before they submitted, winding ships ropes around the stone's girth - the ends of which were then tethered to two sturdy, Lanarkshire, draft-horses. It had been a battle to dislodge the huge monolith, nonetheless. Much of it had lain beneath the earth, clearly accounting for the fact that it had survived upright for a reputed, one thousand years, at the least. The hides of the giant cuddies had needed to be whipped until they were soaked with blood before it even started to shift. Ropes were broken and replaced numerous times during the process.

"*Aye, it wis near dusk whin eventually the beast o' a slab wis upendit, landing on one o' the glaikit cheuchters ahm telt,*" Whitham-Fotheringay explained to the Kirk minister with a smile of gay merriment.

The toppling of the stone, he explained, had exposed a hidden chamber hollowed out from its base. Cracked open by the force of the stone's removal, this secret compartment revealed a reliquary casket - wooden, but covered with silver and copper-alloy. The foreman had ridden overnight to Garvald Castle, the nobleman's Hadintunshire residence, to present the curious item to him.

On receipt, the Scots peer had promptly ordered the joints and lock of the casket to be knocked out with a blacksmith's slaegan hammer, hoping to find gold and jewels inside. He had been disappointed however, when upon opening it revealed merely an aged tome of peculiar appearance. Frustrated at what he considered was a worthless book of bizarre scribblings, he immediately cast it aside towards the inglenook, thinking that at least it would be of some use upon feeding the hearth that evening.

But a chance luncheon that day with an antiquarian acquaintance, Robert Dougall of Kilconquhar, had prompted him, just in time, to rescue the volume. After explaining to his companion the nature of the strange item, along with the unusual circumstances of its find, Dougall advised an evaluation of the script to be undertaken by one of his colleagues, a Regent Callum Bain, member of the Senatus Academicus at St Andrews, as well as Regent of Theology at St Leonard's College.

"*It could fetch yeh a bonnie gold Ryal or twa,*" the archaist concluded. In fact, after Bain had the opportunity later to inspect the manuscript, his opinion was that it could reach several gold Ryals in excess of that were it put to sale in right quarters.

Hence, Whitham-Fotheringay sought to assure the reverend that the old tome held sound monetary value, whilst not quite appreciating that his gambling adversary's interests were uncommonly focused otherwise. At the same time, the aristocrat was well attracted to the stake put forward by his clergyman confidant in relation to the wager. He knew, however, not to make too many enquiries of Kellie as to the provenance of the gold chalice. It was no concern to him in any case. He felt it was at least an equivalent stake - thinking that he would have the vessel melted down into an ingot to sell or otherwise fashion jewelry and trinkets out of. The latter, as currency, would surely keep his various courtesans eager to satisfy his desires, he concluded… well, at least for a reasonable period.

This was not to be for the licentious nobleman, however. Rather, the preacher man left Garvald Castle that evening, a little unsteady on his horse after a belly full of wine and whisky, but with both the chalice and the manuscript in his saddlebag - the roll of the dice, again and again, coming in his favour, as if fate had been on his side and determined.

Upon taking its possession of the curious artefact, the Spenton parish minister spent many long hours endeavouring to decipher the markings upon its vellum pages. As part, he consulted with Regent Bain who had previously analysed the book, along with his equivalents in Theology and Divinity at the universities of Glasgow and Aberdeen. At the same time, he himself studied writings within the *In Lebor Ogaim*, a 14th century Irish treatise on the Ogham alphabet. Such learning and analysis led him to conclude that the manuscript held a particularly cryptic and deliberately impenetrable form of the scribing system.

Making an excuse to temporarily release himself from what he viewed as his tedious, rural Kirk duties, he then took a trip to the west coast, to Kilmartin Glen. There he spoke to a number of the last few remaining peasant dwellers (now with mandated shepherding duties rather than those of cotters, of course) regarding the myths and legends of the standing stones and the inscribed symbols which they bore. The common folks intrigued him with their tales, including that of the ancient kingdom of *Dál Riata*. This prompted the reverend to visit the remnants of Dunadd Fort, its reputed capital, setting up camp there overnight. He also took the opportunity to visit the final few marked stones in the glen which had escaped Whitham-Fotheringay's ropes and draft-horses, sketching down with a vine of charcoal upon parchment the images and markings present upon them for ongoing analysis.

During the period of examination of the script and ongoing research, Kellie had also been a regular visitor to the gothic vaults under Yester Castle at Gifford, a few miles west of his Kirk at Spenton. The building had lain empty since the owner, Lord John Hay, had hastily vacated in the early 1560s, feeling an uncanny presence around the place and witnessing a number of strange happenings within its walls. At such time the nobleman had ordered the building of an alternative residence at the other border of his lands. In the meantime, and during the years of building, he preferred to lodge in one of the humble cottage dwellings on his estate, rather than to spend even one further night in the castle, no matter his social standing and the talk it provoked within Edinburgh society. This allowed the clergyman to visit the vacant and unloved edifice and its vaults unnoticed and unhindered. It was here that he felt the presence of an evil but kindred spirit. Initially, he had thought that he may have been daydreaming or that it was perhaps resultant to too many nights consuming whisky and sack, but he felt a vivid connection with the 13th Hugo de Giffard, another previous resident of the castle. Beyond the grave, the church officer felt that de Giffard was attempting to communicate to him method and instructions on how to decipher the cryptic Ogham text of the manuscript! Certain key nuggets of information were seemingly being transferred to Kellie's willing and receptive mind. Although, a little sceptical at first, he soon realised that these insights were indeed of huge value in the analysis of the puzzling script.

This mysterious commune with de Giffard, along his wider and fastidious study, eventually allowed the preacher man to create a crude key to the previously unfathomable text of the aged tome.

By this point however, he was not a well man. During his frequent visits to St Giles on Kirk business since his appointment at Spenton, he had been unfortunate to have contracted syphilis from congress with a young doxy in Edinburgh's Grassmarket after an evening's carousing at a local ale house. Despite her comely visage, he had suspected at the time that she may have been ridden with the pox due to the fetid stench that arose from her oyster as she'd parted her thighs and beckoned him towards her. At the time, due to his intoxication, the representative of God's Kirk had not been deterred and proceeded to bury his head deep between her fleshy hurdies to sup at her table, before turning the polluted grisette over and fully satisfying himself via her dung breach.

At a further gambling evening with Whitham-Fotheringay, he was to tell the *Laird* of the efforts he had taken to cure his malady,

"*Aye ha bin subject tae the unpleasantness o' mercury treatmit. A mixture a the chemicil an' grease, the resultin foul substance administered topically, thrice daily, to syphilitic ulcerations on ma mooth, anus, an' pintle. They aw burn at the chewin noxiousness o' the vile application. But, Sir, they are tae no avail ithir than tae increase ma malady wi' sweats, salivation as if aye wir a hound with diuresis."*

The syphilis had impact not just upon Kellie's body, but his mind. By June 1570 he was suffering from considerable mental instability.

This, along with his obsession for deciphering the mysterious script of the antique volume, seemed to prompt him to give increasingly manic and fervent sermons at Spenton Kirk. At such time, poor Margaret endured numerous beatings at the hands of her husband with his ever more frequent fits of rage. It was as if, she felt, that he had become possessed.

By the end of August 1570, after working numerous days and nights using his rudimentary deciphering key, the churchman believed that he had uncovered at least one full spell, possibly two, within the cryptic Ogham markings. As part, the invocation wording appeared to give instructions that he undertake certain acts and procure certain offerings in order to fully perform - including, human sacrifice and particular body parts as components of required potions and for other ceremonial purposes.

Upon his next visit to St Giles and after consuming a fair quantity of whisky, this culminated in him seeking the consort of a young dandy. Such youthful gentlemen and more aged companions were known to frequent a particular ale house on the eastern edge of the Nor loch. Kellie plied the brightly dressed aberrant with damson wine, thereupon, with the promise of a half-merk, asking that he join him under the Mary's Wynd bridge to a quiet spot where they would not be disturbed. The dandy had been a little hesitant at first due to the puss-filled and weeping ulcers evident upon the reverend's lips whence in the tavern - concerned that they may be due to the pox - however, the offer of the silver coin (more than thrice his usual charge of two shillings) was more than sufficient inducement. In the shadows and with the foul stench of the Nor wafting in his nostrils, Kellie ordered the slight young man to remain standing upright. The minister of the Kirk then bent to his knees and unbuckled the youth's troos, pulling them down along with the undergarments. Then, with some disgust, took the malefactor's expanding pintle - which had sprang out - in hand; thereafter, fashioning a back and forward motion. The reverend cursed that he was reduced to such depravity, but the manuscript's spell demanded it of him, and he knew that he must obey.

The epicene wretch was clearly enjoying the encounter, he considered, placing his womanly hands upon Kellie's head and motioning towards the clergyman's mouth. But the Spenton minister knew what he had to do and with abhorrence, took the degenerate waif's stiff pintle between his lips, moving its length from there to the back of his throat, in and out, in and out. Thereupon to his disbelief and revulsion he found a rising sensation in his own tadger, feeling it harden within his breeches. The dandy was now making pants and squeals like one of the adolescent hoors that Kellie was oft to partake of within the dark closes and hidden recesses of the High street and Grassmarket. Taking him somewhat by surprise, the young man's seed suddenly exploded into his gullet, whereupon he found himself willingly and greedily swallowing the slimy load. Just as the laddie-lassie was beginning to soften and disengage, the preacher man took his moment and bit hard. At the same time, he took a dirk from under his cloak and abruptly detached the dandy's pintle from its base, 'baws an' aw'.

Kellie felt further repulsed as the miserable weasel fell away, crying out like a wee bairn. The reverend, still a well-built and substantial man despite the effects of his malady, then took his boot and with some pleasure smashed the miscreant's soft facial features with full force to halt the sobs, not least that they might attract unwanted attention. This elicited a crack of bone and skull and thereupon, silence.

Spitting the bloody and slimy seed covered lump of shriveled flesh into his hand, he then carefully deposited it within a leather purse under his church officer's cape. Furtively making off from under the bridge, he was satisfied that he was now in possession of an essential ingredient for the potion required for performance of the manuscript's spell. At the same time, however, he was alarmed to sense that his own seed had been spilt within his breeches further to the clandestine encounter. Departing the scene, he reflected that he had one more act to perform to satisfy the mystical book's spell requirements.

On the morning of 31st October of 1570, Kellie's devout and god-fearing wife was upon her knees praying in the bedroom of the Kirk Manse. Whilst the bells for prayer service rang at Spenton Kirk, the churchman snuck up from behind her with a towel and wrapped it tightly around her neck. Despite being a diminutive lady, Margaret struggled valiantly. With her husband's powerful force, however, she was unable to halt the asphyxiation and was soon strangled to death. As his wife lay motionless on the floor before him like a marionette puppet dropped from height, the preacher man smiled, pleased that not only had he achieved another necessary component of the deciphered spell instructions, but that he had, at the same time, rid himself of the financial burden of the pious crone.

Licking his pustule ridden lips, a delicious thought entered his mind - he would take the hag up the rear vennel, something that she had never allowed him to do, saying it was the way of beasts in the fields and ungodly. On occasion he had tried to force her, especially after an evening supping whisky and sack, but it was troublesome to stop her escaping from the position required for such penetrative action. In these instances, he would generally take her on top via the oyster canal - much more straightforward - again, this was something she had rarely permitted by consent, despite the fact that she had never been able to become with-child. Smiling, he knew that there would be no escape for her this time! Just as he was pulling down his breeks from under his clergyman's robe, repetitive pops of flatulence emitted from the corpse and a waft of foul air engaged his nostrils. Kellie summised that the sphincter had already disengaged, and that the greedy heifer must have had full bowels. Not allowing her to escape a final indignity, he swiftly moved round, knelt and grabbed her head by the top of the hair. With her sad eyes still open, he took great pleasure looking down into them as he forced the full length of his pintle into her mouth and halfway down her gullet. Charged up by the intoxicating nature of the previous moments, after just a few thrusts the officer of the Kirk had deposited his ministerial seed within pitiful Margaret for the last time.

The next part of his plan then swung into action - to make the murder appear to all and sundry as a suicide. He took a rope that he had earlier that day hidden under the bed, made a noose and slipped it over Margaret's limp neck. Thereupon he moved her to the entrance hall of the Manse, hoisting her lifeless frame from a hook in the ceiling.

Straightening his garments, he thereupon proceeded right-eously from the Manse to the Kirk to deliver his morning sermon, greeting members of his flock with a virtuous smile as they made their way to the service. In advance of leaving the Manse, however, he had been careful to lock its front door from inside, leaving the key in the back of the keyhole and then exiting through a side window, jamming it shut thereafter.

After delivery of a fervent but more than usually eloquent sermon on sin, damnation and strict observance of the ten commandments, he invited parishioners to join him back at the Manse for dandelion tea. He told them that Margaret had been feeling low in spirits that day - a recurring problem of late - hence, explaining her absence from the Kirk service. That their visit would act as a tonic to lift his dear wife's mood.

Upon arrival at the Manse, there was some consternation and concern as the front door appeared to be locked from within. Further, Margaret could not be summoned despite repeated knocks and calls. It was uncommon in rural Spenton to lock one's door, certainly during the day and, particularly on the Sabbath. With the reverend's approval, a couple of the congregation - burly farm laborers - managed to force the door open. Parishioners were thereupon greeted by the horrifying sight of Margaret, the god-fearing and dutiful wife, dangling dead from a hook, neck askew and with her tortured face looking towards them like that of a ghoul. Kellie then in theatric style, sunk to his knees in mock surprise and despair, holding his hands to his head wailing in crushed tones, *"what has she done... what has she done?... let the Lord forgive her in his mercy!"* All but a few of the shocked Kirk-goers immediately fled the gruesome scene in terror.

The fact was that the devout wife had become a barrier to the clergyman's evil ambitions. In any case her murder (as a human sacrifice), along with attainment of the dandy's severed pintle, had been integral to performance of the spell that Kellie had managed to decrypt. The successful incantation and invocation, he believed, would ordain and deliver his remarriage to another local nobleman's daughter, a comely lassie some 19 years his junior, with whom the preacher man had become besotted. At the same time, it promised to bestow upon him great wealth and riches.

Once he had managed to successfully perform this first dark magic, his intention was shortly after to plan and prepare to execute the second spell which he believed he had, as near as possible, fully deciphered. In relation to this, again, the antique text instructed as part that he must take human life, as well as attain body parts for the invocation ceremony and as constituent ingredients to a potion. This time it would require the heart of a person who, through their own actions or those of others - including an organisation or association that the individual represented - had brought misfortune upon or challenged the then keeper of the mystic book (of course, this being Kellie himself at that juncture) in some way. Further, it required a potion to be concocted directly from the body of young virgin female who was approaching her first menstruation; in addition, the life blood of a recently born child. This second spell would bestow on him something far greater than the first - the gift of '*beatha shìorraidh*' - of eternal life.

Kellie's twisted ambitions, however, were never realised. In fact, despite his heinous acts to facilitate the dark magic of the manuscript, he was never able to attempt to perform the first spell, never mind the intended second.

Unbeknown to the reverend, his superiors at the Kirk had become suspicious of him earlier in the year, after a number of thefts of valuable church artefacts coinciding with the Spenton minister's visits to St Giles. There had also been reports of his presence in and around the notorious gambling and drinking dens of the Grassmarket and High Street, as well as the hoor houses of such indecorous locations. Further, more recently, he had been spied entering a reputed dandy bar of the Nor loch area of the burgh. Kellie's deteriorating physical and mental state was also evident to them, with the ulcerated sores upon his lips and face, along with testimony from Spenton of his delivery of ever more manic sermons. This, they surmised, indicated a malady consistent with the after-effects of consorting with the wretched souls that wandered the nether regions of the toun and would perform an ungodly act for a mere bawbee or a few swigs of heather ale. Concerns were also present that the Kirk officer had an unhealthy interest in dark mysticism - a parishioner recounting having heard him uttering a strange incantation one evening as they had ventured past Spenton Manse.

Shortly after the demise of unfortunate Margaret, further suspicion was raised when the physician attending to her corpse reported to the Elders within the Presbytery that a man's seed appeared to have been deposited along the length of the woman's gullet. Further, that in his opinion, this must have been implanted there after death, rather than before, as it had neither been discharged by the mouth nor ingested. Shocked, the Elders questioned, regardless of such ungodly circumstances, how could the woman have possibly been hanging dead and thereafter - whilst still suspended by a noose tight upon her neck - be impregnated in the gub and strangulated throat with a man's effluence? No, no... they concluded that she must have been dead prior to the hanging, having certainly been murdered. And afore being hoisted, lifeless, upon the makeshift gallows, this daughter of the Kirk must have been defiled in such an unholy manner. This was the work of the Deil himself through one of his weak mortal servants, they unanimously agreed.

An order was promptly put out by the Kirk to detain Kellie pending questioning by Court members. This was followed through by locally appointed men, giving the minister of Spenton the indignity of having his neck fastening in the jougs at the entrance to his very own parish church whilst awaiting the arrival of his religious superiors from Edinburgh. He cursed the Kirk for such humiliation in front of his flock. Upon the arrival of members of the Presbytery and before they had the chance to interrogate him, in a manic rage, he saved them the trouble - blaspheming at them vilely, pledging his allegiance to satan and gleefully confessing to the murder of poor Margaret.

In early December 1570, the hitherto servant of God was subject to trial in the capital and convicted of '*slaughter with precogitat malice*' along with, '*cum mortuis et tale suscipiant felatio necrophilia*'. Soon after, he was hanged (a fitting sanction, of course). This was carried out in public at the Leith Walk Shrubhill gallows; his body promptly burnt thereafter. On being led to the gallows he shouted to the assembled crowd, once again cursing the Kirk and threatening that he would make them pay, including their most senior official, from beyond the grave. Once again, he sought to pledge his allegiance to satan, but this last utterance was cut short as the noose was tightened around his neck.

Despite his ashes having been ordered to be scattered within the local sewer [this was instead of upon hallowed ground, such as at Spenton Kirk which would have been the usual resting place for a minister of the parish], the remains had mysteriously disappeared, hence not allowing such action to be taken. A story later circulated that they had been collected by a robed onlooker to the execution prior to fully extinguishing; further, that this was an individual sympathetic to John Kellie who had admired his clear interest in the occult. The exact location or placement of his ashes thereafter was unknown, save as to this person and any others he or she had chosen to confide in.

CHAPTER 14

Leap of Faith

Clutching the letter in my trembling hands, I felt totally be-mused by what I had read. Trying to shake myself from a stunned daze, I looked up from the parchment pages and towards Aoife. She gazed back at me smiling, I could not help but think that she bore an expression that a nurse might give a patient suffering from mental delusions.

With a rather shaky voice, I enquired, *"I am not sure how much you know of the nature of what I have just read Aoife? The claims the author - the oddly named 'Sgàthach' - makes are completely crazy and surely can-not be true?"*

"I understand from a colleague that her name is pronounced like, 'Skah-hakh' and that it's a Gaelic name predominately in use in the Highlands. As I said to you before, I do not know the exact content of her letter to you, just some summary details from the instruction communication given alongside it which she - our client - chose to divulge to my firm all those years ago. The details were indeed rather strange, in line with the wider nature and circumstances of this matter," Aoife replied.

"Well trust me, it is more than a little strange!" I exclaimed uneasily.

Observing my anxious state, the lady lawyer once again placed her hand upon my shoulder reassuringly and said, *"Look, I know how weird all this is, but do please know that I am here to support you. Indeed, that is part of the client instruction. You are not alone to face this Cameron."*

I certainly needed some reassurance. She then went on to suggest that the both of us relocated from the Espy to my house - as long as I were comfortable with that - as it would be easier to discuss matters in private there. She was right, of course. Fearing possible further encounters with the 'starers' - the *comasach* as the 130-year-old letter had sought to describe them - along with the fact that the glasses were now empty, I agreed.

Back in my kitchen, still in somewhat of a daze, I put some coffee on hoping that the caffeine would help me to focus and better consider what to do in relation to the communique and its contents.

Rightly or wrongly, I decided to share it in its entirety with Aoife. I really felt that I could not cope knowing the details all on my own. In any case, I pondered, what was the worst she could do having read it? - not much. She was there to provide support to me after all, and the author had indicated that it was for me to decide what I divulged to the law firm's representative.

What followed as we drank our mugs of hot coffee (followed by several refills and a packet and a half of biscuits), was a good two or three hours of discussion and consideration of the bizarre contents of Sgàthach's letter. As part, I sought confirmation from Aoife that this was not some sort of crazy and elaborate practical joke that folks were playing on me through her. I half expected that friends of mine were suddenly going to appear, jumping and laughing from the bedroom, shouting, *"surprise, sucker."* In fact, I really hoped that it was some daft ruse (even if on one level it was alluring to think that I may be of the 'Fiosaichean'), although I sensed in my gut that it was not. Despite the outlandish nature of what was written, I instinctively felt the veracity of the letter and had a sense of foreboding regarding the situation that I now found myself in. At the same time, I was trying to dismiss such feeling and convince myself that it was all patent nonsense.

It was difficult to read my legal companion, but I was surely trying. After she had gone through Sgàthach's missive in full, it was not clear to me whether or not she believed the claims. In any case, as a diligent professional, it was evident that she would bravely carry out her instructions, including support of me, in whatever form or shape that might take. At the same time, I could detect a certain excitement in her eyes and demeanour from it all - this, of course, must have been one of the most extraordinary client assignments ever… probably in the history of the Scottish legal system!

Needless to say, we had only just met, and I knew that I really should not flatter myself or get carried away, but I felt that there was a little bit of a mutual spark developing between us - a certain affinity if you like. That was positive, I reflected, as I surely needed a friend, a confidant, and not just a solicitor at the current time. Déjà, who had jumped up on the table during discussions to introduce herself, also seemed to have warmed to Aoife, rubbing her wee head against our attractive visitor's hands as they held the coffee mug, looking for claps.

After the lengthy consideration, we resolved to follow the instructions within the letter - or at least to make an attempt at time-traverse - on the basis that if they were false (as was surely highly likely) then nothing would actually happen; hence, that there really wasn't anything to lose and no harm to be caused by trying. My guest assured me - or perhaps, more accurately, herself - that no breach of the law appeared to be involved in any such endeavour. At the same time, in the unlikely event that the claims in Sgàthach's dispatch were valid and true, then I had an important job to do, a very important one indeed!

In line with such thinking, we agreed that we would suspend any disbelief for the time-being and prepare for the latter scenario, albeit we really expected the former to transpire. As part of this approach, we decided that all our discussion, research and preparation from then on would be on the basis that the time-traverse WOULD happen, never mind our obvious scepticism. This seemed a logical way forward, or at least as logical as we could manage within such bizarre circumstances. By not long after 3 pm, a basic plan had been hatched and we were both already busy preparing, researching and making ready for it to happen, as follows:

The next morning, we would meet early doors. I would collect Aoife from near her digs in Meadowbank and we would head to a warehouse on Roseburn Street which contained costumes and props for theatre companies. Becoming ever more enthusiastic, she had already rung up and arranged an appointment for us in anticipation, claiming to be a representative of a new amateur dramatics group in the Lothians. Out of their stock, I would seek to get kitted out in attire properly befitting a gentleman attending an Edinburgh auction in 1889; we were doing research on the internet as to exactly what that might consist of.

According to initial findings, my existing leather case seemed to fit the period - I had known it had been 'vintage', but not that vintage - so we would use that to carry the various items that I needed to take with me. These included, firstly, the monetary notes of the day which Aoife had received, enclosed within Sgàthach's initial client instruction letter; secondly, the important 'object' which had also accompanied the instruction letter (the Bannerman & Goudelock auction program for 28th February 1889) to assist me to travel to the 'destination epoch'; and, of course, the other essential object - of my 'home epoch' - to allow me to return time-traverse to Edinburgh, October 2022 (for such purpose, I had suggested that directly prior to any attempt to cross the thoroughfares of time, I would buy a newspaper, one sold in Edinburgh with the day's date upon it - we agreed that it should fit the bill in line with Sgàthach's written account).

With me fully suited and booted, my leather case packed, and once the research and preparation were concluded, our aim was that on Saturday 29th October a first effort at time-traverse to 1889 would be made.

Clearly, it was not the best or most watertight plan in the world, but in the truly weird and surreal circumstances we found ourselves in, we were relatively pleased with it.

In order to concentrate on matters in hand, I made my excuses for pre-booked psychic medium readings and other work commitments for the rest of the week and even into middle of the next one, rearranging where possible. My legal friend assured me that she was already available from her firm, with permission to spend such period as was necessary to support me as per the historic client instruction.

For the remainder of the afternoon and into the evening we undertook further research, principally online, relating to the destination time period, including, for example: the auction process of old; customs of the late 19th century; the then sitting government; news, events and popular music of the day; as well as gentlemen's etiquette and language nuances which I might expect should I actually reach the destination epoch.

At one point I had made some soup and sandwiches to keep us going, however, by around 9 pm, it was clear that we were both thoroughly exhausted. My lady visitor asked if I could call her a taxi. When it arrived, I could not help but admit to myself that I felt a little sad at seeing her go.

The following day, Thursday, after collecting Aoife as planned, we went to the theatre store and, based on our (although, mostly her) costume research, hired the following:

- thick wool, grey flannel suit, complete with waistcoat and three-quarter length jacket
- set of braces
- white, wing-collared shirt
- dark maroon silk tie (which I particularly liked)
- heavy full-length black wool overcoat
- black boots which fitted under the flare of the suit trousers
- silk scarf in purple and dark red paisley pattern (which apparently had been quite dapper at the time according to the research)
- calf-kin leather gloves
- faux gold pocket-watch with T bar chain
- top hat, black
- silver-topped, ebony cane

When we came back to Straiton Place and I laid out the items of period apparel on the bed in the spare room, Déjà immediately jumped up, inquisitively sniffing over them. They did pong a bit, no doubt having been used in numerous sweaty theatre productions over the years and most, I guessed, were originals from the era, likely not having had a real wash since then or ever.

I decided that I would wear a plain, dark pair of my own socks and boxers, not expecting to have to strip down in front of anyone in the destination epoch. In my leather case I put an extra shirt and change of underwear - hopefully there would be no requirement for an overnight stay, but best to be prepared, I guessed.

Another item we were fortunate to spot just as we were leaving the Roseburn store was a leather sheath wallet of the era. In to this Aoife deposited the cash of the day - the sum of £700 of the 19th century tender which had been sealed with her firm's client instruction letter. This was equivalent to more than £90,000 today according to our internet research. Of course, Sgàthach had indicated that this would be more than sufficient a sum to outbid all others at the auction, including the Order (who at that time it seemed were not particularly flush with funds), plus deal with incidental expenses. £300 of the old money was in £1, £5, £10 and £20 notes, and the rest in just four £100 notes. All bills were rather large in size in comparison with today's notes. Further, each were embossed on the front left with two unicorns of Scotland holding between them a shield bearing the Lion Rampant; above and below were Bank of Scotland medallions. I reflected that I had never held a current day £100 note, never mind one from the 19th century, equivalent to £13k in today's money. It seemed crazy that you could make a cash purchase at auction with such a huge sum, but then again, of course, they didn't have the debit and credit cards of today. I would need to be careful not to get mugged should my visit to that era actually take place (and, with all this preparation, I was starting to truly believe that it would). Although, my most precious possession, would not be the cash, of course, but the object of my home epoch - the newspaper that I would buy in advance.

Our research and preparation over the rest of the day at Straiton Place went pretty well. As we had found previously, there was quite a lot of useful historical material and resources online to help. This included a 'Bartholemew's' map of Edinburgh of the period indicating the street layout; I managed to print this out in sections on my wee home inkjet printer. Once again, later in the evening, Aoife headed home in a taxi. Perhaps I was imaging it, but I sensed that, like myself, she was a little reluctant at her leaving.

And she truly was brilliant - like a duck to water researching and preparing me for my (possible) adventure. Akin to a theatre or film production manager perhaps. Maybe it was something to do with her professional training, I thought. It was true that I had become quite taken with this petite legal eagle and her quiet, confident manner. It was like I had known her for years, rather than barely a couple of days, and I really enjoyed having her around.

The next day, Friday 28th October, Aoife arrived back at my bungalow around noon. We then did a dress rehearsal, with me putting on all the garments we had picked up from the costume store the day before. She was busy, like a proud-but-fussy mum of a primary one pupil on their first day at school, adjusting the wing-collar on my shirt, straightening my silk tie and dusting down the heavy overcoat on my back. Then she was in fits of giggles as I theatrically paraded up and down the hall, donning the black, silk covered top hat after firstly giving a bow, twirling the ebony cane and flamboyantly throwing the fine, paisley pattern scarf around my neck. I enjoyed making (and seeing) her smile.

Déjà was evidently pleased to have our lady visitor back once more, sitting like a wee sphinx right next to her on the arm of the sofa and purring whilst she did further research on her laptop. The wee puss was probably bored to tears of my own company and was likely enjoying having the perfumed scent of a beautiful woman in the house as much as I was, I mused with a grin.

As we worked on into the evening, we agreed that with our background research and planning going well we were almost ready to attempt my time-traverse the following day. To keep us going, I ordered some Thai food (which Aoife said was a favourite of hers) for delivery and opened up a decent bottle of Californian Zinfandel which I had bought on my recent trip to Asda. Taking a glass, she sipped at it a little hesitantly at first and I guessed that she was not that used to red wine. She seemed to enjoy it all the same. Along with the wine, to help create a relaxing vibe as we continued our work, I played at low volume the mellow prog-rock tones of Pink Floyd's 'Dark Side of the Moon' on my record player (a few months previously I had been fortunate to pick up the original vinyl album for a reasonable price at a bric-a-brac market on the esplanade).

As it got quite late, whilst she continued to work in the front room, I made up the bed in the spare room - just in case - after putting the fusty 19th century garments in the wardrobe. As I poured the last of the wine, I offered for her to stay over there, saying that it would allow us to make an early start on final preparations in the morning. I have to say I was a little surprised (but delighted) when she said *"yes"*, rather expecting that I would be asked to order her a cab home once again. It was good that she had felt comfortable enough to stay, I reflected, as for all intents and purposes I was still pretty much a stranger to her … and, obviously a man.

On the Saturday morning, I got up before I could hear my guest stirring in the spare room, pulled on a pair of jogging pants and went to the kitchen to put a pot of coffee on. Just then she poked her head round the door, saying jokingly, "G*ood morning, how is Mr Guthrie, my debonaire 19th century gentlemen, doing today?*" She was wearing an old, baggy tee shirt of mine which I had lent her for the night, presumably over her knickers. Not that I could really see, as little more than her head was visible as she keeked into the room sideways. I guessed that she did not want me checking out her legs and ass (… which, of course, I would have done, given half the chance) or at least coming across that she did. My lady lodger certainly looked cute despite her morning-time disheveled hair.

After a light breakfast, we decided that after a final run through of our research and my putting on the necessary theatre store attire, we would head to Holyrood Park, aiming to arrive around 1 pm. Aoife asked if we could "*fly by*" her flat first on the way so that she could have a "*quick shower and change.*"

Recalling Sgàthach' s letter (… and again, trying to suspend disbelief as I did), the text had, of course, outlined that on arrival at the destination epoch, the time of day would be exactly the same as that from which I had travelled. As the auction was not until 6 pm in the evening of 28th February 1889, we concluded that getting to the Park around 1 pm would leave plenty of time for me to practice the time-traverse techniques in situ at St Anthony's Chapel. Looking at the old street map, we figured that it would only take me forty-five minutes to an hour, maximum, to walk from there (the supposed time dimension crossing-point) to the auction house premises on Broughton Place, even when clad in the cumbersome and uncomfortable gentlemen's period apparel. There was, of course, no need to cut things fine timewise. Reminding myself once more that Aoife and I had agreed to progress on the basis that the time-traverse WOULD happen, I considered also that on arrival in 1889 I would want the opportunity to have a proper look around and savour the crazy and bizarre experience. After all, I would be one of the very few in humankind to have ever experienced such a trip back in time, me being of the Fiosaichean (if indeed that were true?).

Letting my mind fleet off in fancy, I imagined how incredible and exciting it would be to walk around amongst my Auld Reekie predecessors. It would be like stepping into an old, black and white still photograph and then, suddenly, having everything animated in full color and 3D, with actual, physical 19th century life and living breathing people all around me! To see the sights, hear the sounds and smell the smells of this long bygone age would be quite something - as if arriving in a far-off foreign land, but one that was both familiar and very unfamiliar at the same time.

Déjà gave me a suspicious look as we headed out the door, as if to say, where the hell are you off to with my nice new mistress? Although perhaps she was simply incredulous at how daft

I looked all dressed up in the theatre store clothing (… although I had not yet donned the top hat in case it were knocked off by the door frame). I left a couple of days of food and fresh water in the wee soul's bowls… just as a precaution.

In actuality, we did not get to Holyrood Park until nearer 2 pm. I should have guessed that Aoife's idea of "*fly by*" would be quite different from mine. After something like nearly an hour waiting outside her flat, she had breezed back into Syd with a virtuous smile, freshly showered and bringing a very pleasant, fragrant and feminine scent with her. We still had plenty of time, of course, and it was only a couple of minutes from where she lived, just off of Whyte Place, to the Park.

In any case, waiting for her outside had given me the opportunity to pop into the local newsagents to get a copy of a newspaper with the day's date on it - of course, one of the two crucial objects I dare not forget (the other being the 1889 Bannerman and Goudelock auction program - already firmly lodged within the inside pocket of my leather case). As I'd went into the shop in my odd-looking gear, the shopkeeper, of Scots-Asian heritage had asked with a grin, "*Are aff tae anywhere special the day, dressed like that pal?*" I replied with a chuckle, *Aye, you could say that.*" On inspecting the newspaper shelves, it seemed like they only had copies of the 'The News Express' and 'The Mail Daily' left. Part-joking to myself, I wondered whether if I were to take one of these rags with me to 1889, would I be in danger of returning to 2022 as a petty, right-wing bigot? Thankfully, however, just as I was about to sully my hands by picking up one of those titles, I'd spotted a copy of 'The Nation' hidden underneath (deliberately, no doubt, by a reader of one of the aforementioned papers) and proceeded to take it to the till, the newsagent continuing to smirk at me as I did.

I was glad to finally get to Holyrood Park as it had been quite awkward sitting in the warm car and driving in the whole gent's get-up of the era (obviously without wearing the top hat!). Casual dress in jeans etc. was what I was used to, and the formal, heavy garments and boots were rather uncomfortable and con-straining. We parked up at the wee car park not far after the Meadowbank entrance and at the head of St Margaret's loch. I handed Aoife my keys, including for the car and my Straiton Place abode (which were on a 'Hearts Cup Champions 2012' key fob) saying that she had better keep them for me as they would look a little out of place in 1889. Further, that she could always wait in the car for me if I were to take longer than ex-pected. Similarly, I gave her my mobile phone. I was thinking, in line with what Sgàthach had advised, that it was better to leave such items in case I really did travel back in time - alt-hough, clearly, I was still struggling with that notion. It was just as well that I felt that I could trust my new acquaintance.

Putting the strap of my leather case over my shoulder and hold-ing the topper, we headed past the loch and up a steep path on the left-hand side. There were a few joggers, dog walkers and tourists around, but on this rather dull and windy day it was otherwise pretty quiet. No starers/*comasach* were evident either, thankfully; in fact, I had not experienced any further encounters with such individuals since agreeing to attempt the time-trav-erse in line with aged letter's request. Perhaps they could sense that fact that I had agreed to attempt the assigned task to attain and destroy the dark manuscript and were no longer psychically driven to approach me? Mind you I had hardly been out the house all week since meeting Aoife at the Espy, other than to the theatre store.

The young lawyer effortlessly skipped up the sharp incline to St Anthony's Chapel. As for me, it was quite a bit more of a struggle, what with the cumbersome clothing and being buffeted by the wind. It was also not helped by the fact that despite the blowy conditions there was an oppressiveness in the air, incongruous to the time of year.

The Chapel, of course, was in fact a ruin, and with really only its front stone façade left in place along with part of the wall on the south-western side. Approaching it, with its window openings and gaping doorway, it came across a bit like a shocked face looking over the modern-day city with disapproval and disdain.

Thankfully, it was deserted. With the Crags to my left and Arthur's Seat in the background, I positioned myself just outside of its entrance doorway. Standing there, I took in the fine view over the loch and to its surrounding area, including the Parade ground, the ruins of Holyrood Abbey, the Palace of Holyrood House, the Scottish Parliament and, of course, the white armadillo tent-like roof structure of 'Our Dynamic Earth'. Further afield I could see tenement blocks, church spires and other buildings, young and old, making up the eclectic architectural mosaic of the capital. In the distance, despite the clouds and mist in the air, I could spy the blue-grey Forth and over to a rather hazy Fife. How different would this scene be in 1889? I wondered.

Finally, I was in situ at what Sgàthach had said was an intersection of spirit or ley lines - the '*àite-tarsainn*' - the place from which I could traverse back in time, if indeed she were correct. Close to the left-hand side of my chest, and hence my heart, I embraced my leather case. Of course, within its inside pocket was the essential object from the Edinburgh of 28th February 1889 - that version of the city which I sought to traverse to.

Aoife, standing about two meters away to my left and clearly observing that I was ready, gave me a warm smile. I reciprocated and then closed my eyes, seeking to meditate, using techniques similar to those which I had now used frequently for my psychic medium reading sessions and in line with Sgàthach's advice. As part, focusing on my breathing, I sought to rid my mind of cluttered thoughts and then to visualise the Edinburgh of 1889 which my companion and I had been so closely studying from photographs and research over recent days.

Withing a few minutes of such focus and technique, I reached a state of inner calmness. However, I had to conclude that I was not experiencing anything like the intense feeling that Sgàthach had referred to in her letter as an indication of time-traverse. Persevering, I stood there meditating like this for some fifteen minutes. Gradually, my arms were becoming weary clutching the case to my chest. Further, I was getting a little bit uncomfortable standing upright in the same position. At this point, trying to keep the faith, I wondered, had I transitioned? Perhaps I had done, I questioned, despite the lack of sensation referred to in the strange missive? Gingerly, I opened my eyes. But, on doing so, I was greeted by the sight of Aoife just as before. Not an unpleasant sight, of course, although not one that I had hoped to see on this particular occasion. Looking a bit curiously at me, I thought that maybe she was wondering whether that was me back from 1889, having already accomplished my task. Of course, I had not gone anywhere.

Needless to say, we were both disappointed. Taking a break, we chatted and had a wee walk around the grassy area at the back of the Chapel which sought to lighten the atmosphere. We agreed that I should try again. However, despite my best efforts, the next time I could not even get myself into a meditative state, never mind into anything deeper. Two further attempts later, I shook my head and reluctantly had to admit that we were going to have to call it a day.

"Yes, I think best that you go home and rest Cameron. We can try again tomorrow, of course. There is still the opportunity for that," Aoife responded in a fairly upbeat manner, evidently trying to reassure me. Of course, the failed efforts were disheartening and only sought to make me further doubt the veracity of the contents of the communique from Gilfeather & McLean's client of yesteryear. It was surely all a hoax after all and would never happen, I could not help but think.

Back at the car, the lady lawyer said that there was no need to give her a lift as she would walk the short distance to her flat. Further, that she did not think there was any real requirement to do any more research that day, rather it was better just to relax. I agreed, however, I could not help but feel a little bit disappointed as it would have been nice to have had her back at Straiton Place again. How funny it was that only a few days ago I had been cursing her presence at my door, I reflected. I'd had made such an effort to avoid her. Now, here was me wishing she that she were coming back home with me. We were not a couple, of course - I knew that - but there was an undeniable closeness between us, a bond of some manner even. We both sensed it, I was sure of that. I could see it in her rather mesmorising amber eyes, as well as her expression when she looked at me - there no hiding it. Before departing we agreed that I would collect her at 1 pm the next day, Sunday, at her flat and we would return to the Chapel to give it a further - and final - shot.

CHAPTER 15

Up the Duff in Dunpender

J ason and Megan were both Dunpender born and bred. The town, on the coast in East Lothian, about twenty-five miles south of Edinburgh, had originally been a fishing village, however, it had grown exponentially in recent years with new housing developments spurred by the easy journey to Edinburgh via the A1 and by train.

They had met at the high school and started dating after having a snog at the annual end of term party and barbeque on the fine sandy beach adjacent to the town. Love had blossomed over a bottle of Scrumpy Jack and toasted marshmallows. On leaving school, Jason had been lucky enough to secure an apprenticeship with a local electrical contractors. Equally, Megan had been fortunate to promptly find a job as a nursery assistant at one of the private childcare providers in the town. At the same time, she supplemented her income by doing baby sitting on nights and at the weekend - with Dunpender principally being a commuter town, there was no shortage of working parents seeking such support.

After dating for only around a year, both having work income and being sick of staying with their respective sets of parents, the pair decided to look for a place of their own place in one of the new estates on the outskirts of the town. In late 2019, they found a lovely two-bed, mid-terrace house in the newly built Black Agnes development at the back of the railway line. With the help of a Scottish Government scheme for first time buyers, this was affordable not just to rent, but to buy on their joint earnings. To say that they were thrilled at being able to purchase their own place, would be fair understatement.

It was, of course, a big step moving in together and out of their family homes. A departure from childhood, and the relative freedom of responsibility, to the world of mortgage payments, utility and other household bills. But it is true to say that they loved it, settling into their comfortable wee nest like the love-birds that they were, with no parents or siblings to get in their way. One thing was missing, however. Not marriage, as neither were particularly religious nor saw it as a necessity for a couple. Rather, what they felt was missing was a baby.

To have a child would make them complete, they agreed. Not just a couple, but a family, a real family. Megan could not help but be a little envious of a number of her girlfriends in the town, whom, despite still only being in their teenage years, were already pregnant or had little ones.

Those feelings grew over the next two years as, despite trying to conceive through regular unprotected sex, Megan failed to fall pregnant. After the first year of disappointment, she looked into ways of hopefully encouraging conception, talking it over with her mum Tricia and doing her own research at the same time. Firstly, she learned more about her fertility pattern, buying a wee book online, 'How to Chart Your Menstrual Cycle'. This explained that over her cycle of 28 days, she was actually only fertile on the day that one of her ovaries released an egg -

ovulation - and the 5 days in advance of that. So, really only a short time. Having sex within that brief window was key. So, at Megan's insistence, the pair concentrated their lovemaking on these crucial days. Jason was not allowed one night off 'from the job' during such periods, even when he arrived home exhausted after a twelve-hour shift rewiring a house the city or such like, and with an early morning start the next day.

At the same time, she looked at their diet, reading that eating more fruit and veg could help with fertility. So, they started buying and preparing more, even organic when they could afford it and it were available at the local Dunpender shops, such as the 'Crunchy Apple'.

Stopping smoking was another measure Megan sought for them to attempt. She managed it herself, but to be honest, had a bit of a job persuading her man. He kept telling her he had given up and that he wanted a baby as much as her. But quite often when he got back from work, she could smell the smoke off him, and he would generally be chewing minty gum as he arrived in the door in the evenings. Jason would blame the smell on his work mates who he said were all heavy smokers, with fags hanging out of their mouths' half the day - that much Megan knew to be true.

She also cut down on her boozy nights with the girls - the occasions where they would meet up at one of the local bars or one of their pads for a blether and a few drinks. When they all gathered in such manner, it seemed like nothing had really moved on between them since high school and they easily lapsed back into the close companionship of such days, dishing out and dissecting the local gossip. The big change, however, was that by this time all of them, apart from Megan, now had kids. These nights were fun, but the alcohol was harming her chances of falling pregnant, so she believed.

Jason, for his part, was fond of a good bevy with his mates, such as Baz and the crew. Generally, on Fridays, if they had enough spare cash, they would get a slab of beer and some weed between them and disappear into the Lochside woods to consume against the heat and convivial ambience of a makeshift campfire. At the same time, chatting about favorite music, football and who had managed to get their end away recently and with whom. He gradually started to skip such nights, not just to please Megan, but because he felt the absence of a baby was starting to damage their hither-to close relationship. He really did love her, but a lot of pressure was coming from the baby situation and more and more frequently she would irritable and demanding of him. It was true that after a fill of beer and weed, he was not much use in 'getting it up'. If skipping some of the lads' nights would help, he resolved that he would do it.

After all these months of trying to get pregnant and without any success, Megan began suggesting that he go to the GP and get a 'semen analysis' undertaken, thinking that he may be 'shooting blanks'. Jason, a bit put out by the inference, insisted that she was barking up the wrong tree there, feeling that the request was a little bit insulting of his manhood. *"Ahm as fertile as an Arab stallion and could get any lassie in Dunpender up the duff any time ah' wanted,"* he would defensively reply whenever she brought the topic up.

Needless to say, Megan was none too happy with such a response, not least that he had failed to get her 'up the duff' for coming up two years now! Nevertheless, her partner eventually bowed to pressure and went ahead with the test. After which, in fact, he was pretty much proved right, registering in the results a very healthy sperm count, with negligible sperm dysfunction. Jason picked up the note from the doc's surgery detailing this and marched home proudly, with his chest puffed out as he presented it to Megan. On reading the note - that her man was indeed something of an Arab stallion in the potency department - she had burst into tears. Not that she was disappointed with Jason's result, of course not, but rather as it had now been confirmed that the problem must lie with her and her alone, no matter what they said at the gynae clinic. After that news she would lie awake in bed at night worrying that Jason would eventually leave her for one of the other lassies in town - there was always the ones that would openly flirt with him to wind her up - a girl that was normal and who could bear him a child.

She decided to seek out further medical investigation. Despite their relatively young age, after various tests, the pair were accepted by NHS Scotland for a first cycle of 'in vitro fertilisation' (IVF) treatment. This involved various steps including Megan taking special medication and hormone injections. Further, after removal of a number of her eggs, to have them fertilised in a laboratory with Jason's sperm. The process was aimed at creating a 'viable embryo', the doctor said, which would at the appropriate time be transferred back inside her - implanted within her 'uterus'. They were both amazed and grateful to have science and medicine help them to conceive in such manner. At the same time, they were wary of not getting their hopes up too high, having heard that the success rate on the first cycle was only about 50%, even for a woman of her age.

About a week after the embryo transfer, Megan started taking home pregnancy tests. This was despite her having been told by the IVF nurse and in the explanatory leaflets to leave it until at least couple of weeks had passed as any such test may give false results. She simply could not wait however; such was her excitement and anticipation.

Early on the Sunday morning, exactly ten days after the embryo transfer, Jason was awoken by his cherished lady sat next to him on the bed, greeting her eyes out. She had just returned from the bathroom and was holding a plastic stick to his face. Even with his bleary eyes, two faint blue lines were visible upon it. "*I'm pregnant… I'm pregnant Jase!*" Megan cried, with tears rolling down her cheeks. He could not help but start to greet himself at this wonderful news. Hugging her close and kissing her head gently, he rocked her lovingly as she sobbed with joy and relief into his chest.

CHAPTER 16

A Dapper Gent in Auld Reekie

The following morning, Sunday 30th October, it was a similar routine. Parking Syd up by Aoife's flat just before 1 pm, once again I popped into the newsagents and picked up a paper - this time the 'The Nation on Sunday' - to replace that of the previous day. The shopkeeper looking at me as if to say, do you really wear that get-up every day? Back at Syd, I lodged it safely within the body of my leather case.

She was again late emerging from her flat, just half an hour or so. It was a pleasant enough day, although once more oddly humid for the time of year. Hence as I waited, I stood outside the car in my 19th century garb - far more comfortable than sitting inside - leaning against a lamppost and leafing through the pages of the newspaper. I was pleased to see her when she eventually appeared, of course, and as our eyes instantly met got the impression that the feeling was mutual. As she approached Syd, I opened the passenger door with a smile and, with an extended arm, melodramatically said, "*Our time machine awaits, madam.*"

"*Oh, why, thank you Mr Guthrie, kind sir,*" Aoife replied, smiling back, looking a little flushed.

"H.G. Wells' time-traveller had it easy. Imagine how good it would be to simply set a dial on Syd so that the pair of us were transported back to 1889," I added.

Of course, that was not the way it worked in reality (or at least according to Sgàthach), I reflected regretfully. Further, my time-traverse - if it ever did happen, which I continued to sincerely doubt - had to be a solo mission, unfortunately, and without Aoife.

On arriving at Holyrood Park, we parked up a further time at the wee car park at the head of the loch. Thankfully, unlike the previous day, there was an absence of wind. A few more people were out and about, but no one appeared to be up at the Chapel itself.

For a second time, we ascended the steep path to the left of the loch. Despite the calm conditions, it was still a struggle due to the closeness of the atmosphere and the antiquated clobber upon me. At the Chapel, I positioned myself as before, but this time, choosing to crouch down rather than stand, resting my back against the large stone jambs at the side of the door opening and once more clutching my leather case close to my heart. This felt a more comfortable position to seek to enter the necessary meditative state. After fixing the shiny, black topper to my head, Aoife and I exchanged smiles and I then proceeded in the manner Sgàthach had advised in her mysterious missive.

Closing my eyes, I breathed in and out, slowly and fully. At the same time, I tried to empty mind of thoughts, before moving my focus to the Edinburgh of the 1889 era. In my mind's eye I sought to recall the photographic images of the gentlemen and ladies of that time period which Aoife and I had looked at online during our research.

Hugging my leather case even more tightly to my chest, I visualised the auction program within its inside pocket. In particular, the front cover, which stated:

'A Cordial Invitation is extended to Ladies and Gentlemen for the
Auction of Curiosities and Antiquities of North British Historical
Origin
Bannerman & Goudelock Auctioneers,
23 Broughton Place,
Edinburgh
[Official Auctioneers to HM The Queen and The Gentry]
Thursday, 28th February 1889
Proceedings commencing at 6 pm with a toast to Her Royal Majesty Victoria Saxe-Coburg-Gotha
of the United Kingdom of Great Britain and Ireland
Program of proceedings herein'

In stark contrast to my attempt the previous day, almost immediately, a rather queer sensation started to ripple through me. Firstly, and gradually, from the tips of my toes, then to the rest of my feet and ankles, my calves, knees, along my thighs, through my pelvis and up to my chest - my heart fluttering somewhat in response. At the same time, from my fingernails to the backs of my hands with a kind-of shimmering effect - where I could feel the blue veins tickling under vibration. Then, the sensation progressed up my arms, along my shoulders and to my neck, face and head, right through to a pleasant tingling upon my scalp and hair. It was almost like I had stepped into a warm bath and was easing my full body down into its luxuriant and comforting waters.

It was then that, suddenly, I experienced an intensely pleasurable sensation, with a rush of blood to my head and palpable feeling of release of tension from my body and muscles. Trembling and dizzy by this stage, and with a silver shingle of stars appearing before my shut eyes, I was not quite aware whether I was still crouched upon the ground, standing or even suspended in mid-air! This state of being seemed to last somewhere between thirty seconds to one minute, although it was difficult to tell as time seemed meaningless within the rapturous embrace of the extraordinary sensation. As it eventually subsided, I strangely felt both relieved and disappointed. Remembering Sgàthach's advice, I proceeded to take some deep breaths.

My nostrils sensed a misty and wet atmosphere. Further, I could feel a strong, chilly breeze in my face. As I inhaled and filled my lungs, I could detect a yeasty, beery smell hanging in the air. The closeness of atmosphere of only moments before was no longer present. Focusing also on what I could hear, in the not too far-away distance, I could detect an array of sounds being carried on the wind. None of this was present and familiar only a minute or so earlier. Taking another deep breath, I wondered, had I actually traversed time?

With some, perhaps fearful, hesitation, I made to open my eyes slowly and gradually. In alignment with my other senses, it was indeed a cold, damp and grey Edinburgh day - very different to that which I had only just been present within. Looking around for Aoife, she was nowhere to be seen. Scanning the skyline, I was shocked to realise that this was definitely not 2022!

For a start, the unmistakable Scottish Parliament building was absent. As was the suspended dome of 'Our Dynamic Earth' - it had vanished from sight. My heart was racing - I truly and actually HAD traversed time. Sgàthach had been telling the truth all along… "JEEEZZUS THIS REALLY IS EDIN-BURGH IN 1889," I thought to myself near hyperventilating. I was doing all I could to suppress myself from shouting out loud in dumfounded surprise and elation.

Trying to suspend any lingering disbelief, I gingerly contemplated what lay ahead of me. The prospect was truly thrilling, and I was intoxicated with the allure of it all. Once down from the Chapel, I would be walking the thoroughfares of the Auld Reekie of this era! Later in the day I would be arriving at the auction house and mingling with the well-to-do denizens of the 19th century city. The ladies wearing their elegant - if conservative apparel - crowned with splendid hats. The gentlemen, clothed in splendid tailor-made suits, including waistcoats and accompanying gold pocket watches on chains, and carrying fine canes - all rounded off with dignified and rather majestic top hats, indicating a certain social standing within the metropolis. At this thought, I put my hand up to my head to check that my own topper had remained in place through my time-traverse and was relieved to find that it had. I was one of these dapper gentlemen, I considered, not being able to help a certain sense of smug satisfaction come over me. Nervously straightening my fine maroon, silk tie, I felt giddy, almost drunk, on the thoughts of the day ahead and the experience that lay before me, in the romance of 1880s Edina.

Making my way cautiously but eagerly down the hill towards the western end of the loch, the various echoes and reverberations being carried on the intermittent gusts of wind grew louder and more discernable. Looking towards the Palace below, I could see in the distance a large throng of people gathered at the far end of Parade ground. The sounds were from these 19th century city inhabitants, speaking, joking and laughing. Perhaps there was even musical accompaniment such as from an ensemble, I could not quite yet discern.

I had to pinch myself when considering these would be living, breathing people of the 1880s. As I got closer, I could make out that quite a few of the individuals were carrying poles of some sort. Further, there were bright colors in and amongst the busy crowd, far removed from the black and white inanimate period photographic images which Aoife and I had studiously surveyed in our online research. Maybe it was a fete or some sort of celebration for the reigning Monarch, Queen Victoria? I pondered with mounting excitement - the gathering was taking place adjacent to the Royal Palace of Holyroodhouse after all. Possibly, even the great lady herself was in attendance, alongside her Prime Minister, Robert Gascoyne-Cecil, 3rd Marquess of Salisbury? I was no monarchist, but, wow, would that not be something unbelievably special - what a unique thrill and experience to witness, I mused dreamily. And what I was observing as I made my way down from the Chapel was surely Her Majesty's loyal Scot's subjects setting up festive maypoles and flying flags of her Great British and Irish Union? Such a shame Aoife was not with me to share and experience this most wonderful day, to witness the spectacle, I could not help but reflect.

The wind turned again in my direction, bringing with it more sounds, even louder as I was closer still, of the celebratory cheers and cries. But also, rather incongruously, a mechanical-type noise? Perhaps it was that of a fair ground ride of the age, I speculated, but I was not yet close enough to confirm.

My long, heavy coat, tailored suit, stiff leather boots and top hat, suddenly felt very comfortable and reassuring upon me. With my paisley-patterned gentlemen's silk scarf billowing in the breeze, gold watch chain swinging from side to side and ebony cane in hand, I felt every bit the sophisticated and debonair 1880s gent. Once again inhaling deeply the 19th century air, this time to calm myself a little, I felt both exhilarated and anxious at the same time - I had travelled back in time over 130 years after all!

As I took the damp, musty, air into my lungs, thinking of what lay before me, I wondered for a moment why there was no trace of smoke within it? There was certainly a brewery type aroma, but not one from chimneys. Looking towards the city skyline, I could make out the chimney pots of the tenements, however, there was no smoke visible rising from any of them, as far as I could see, even though it was a fairly chilly February day. That was surprising, I reflected, not least as the nickname 'Auld Reekie' had been given as a moniker to the Edinburgh of this era – it was Scots for 'Old Smokey', as the sooty clouds from open coal and peat fires had reputedly hung over the city like an unwelcome and noxious fug. Perhaps, it was due to the fact it was a rather windy day, I contemplated, the gusts clearing the air?

However, as I got nearer and closer still to the throng, I was prompted to stop with a start. The mechanical noise had now become clearer with the wind in a steady direction towards me. It was the unmistakable boom and echo of an electronic speaker system into which a man was bellowing. And now it was visible that what people were carrying were not festive maypoles and celebratory flags for Queen Victoria and her glorious Union at all, rather they were actually makeshifts signs and banners of all different colours, with messages plastered upon them. From what I could make out they were emblazoned with slogans, including, 'No Poll Tax', 'Fuck the Tories' and 'Cole

Not Dole'. It was then that I had the dawning and shocking realisation that although I had indeed travelled back in time and was in Edinburgh, I had not traversed back to the romantic 1880's after all... rather I had set foot in another eighties, the 1980s!

"Oh, for fucks sake, I'm in Thatcher's bloody Britain!" I exclaimed in despair, thinking to myself, christ Cameron, how did you manage such a complete time-travel fuck up?

The slogans I recognised from my interest in Scottish modern history – and I judged that the 1980s was definitely the time period I presently found myself within. I had been aware that the Margaret Thatcher Tory-led government of the era had decimated traditional Scottish industry, including coal mining. Further, they had done this whilst siphoning off our North Sea oil wealth, yet simultaneously telling us we were poor and reliant upon the largesse of our southern neighbour to survive (something the 'Mc Crone report', of course, had blown apart, yet successive Tory and Labour governments had deliberately buried it from public view and knowledge). Around the end of that decade, I recalled, there had been particular public angst against the use of the Scottish public as guinea pigs for the introduction of the hated 'poll tax', prior to a UK-wide roll out. So, the gathering of folks here I was sure had to be a political demonstration of some sort against Tory rule from London and imposition of the poll tax and it was likely to be some time in the late 1980s, although, I could not be sure exactly of the year.

As I walked along Queens Road towards the gathered crowd and the Palace, I could see a group of four young guys coming in the opposite direction, heading towards the Meadowbank exit to the Park. From what I could see they appeared to be laughing at and mocking those attending the demo. As the gap between me and them narrowed and they were quite close by, I was able to observe that they were all decked out in smart-casual wear. Two of them in pastel coloured 'Fred Perry' polo shirts, another wearing a checkered shirt sporting a prominent 'Ben Sherman' logo. These were all buttoned up to the top and accompanied by smart jeans and new looking 'FILA' and 'Adidas' trainers. The last of the four had a 'Sergio Tacchini' branded track suit on; it was multi-coloured and made of an implausibly shiny material. He was shod in equally garish 'La-coste' logoed trainers. One of the Fred Perry boys had a prominent 'Hibernian FC' tattoo on his forearm. Taking turns at swigging from large, blue-colored plastic bottle (with Dia-mond, something or other, written on its side), the group of late-teens/early-twenty somethings were clearly the worse for its contents.

It did not require my keen psychic senses to detect potential trouble here, so I promptly averted my gaze and put my head down in an effort to avoid any incendiary eye-contact. Making to continue past them, I hoped that they had not noticed me.

Mr Sergio Tacchini, however, was quick to dash that wish, re-marking to his mates in slurred tones, *"Hey, have yeh seen the state ah this cunt? Whit the fuck is ey wearing? Christ sakes ... Lads take a deek at the clown."*

I was now conscious that I did look rather ridiculous in my pe-riod theatre store outfit ... but that coming from someone dressed like him, really? In the shock of the last fifteen minutes or so realising that I had travelled back in time, but to the wrong era, I had not had the presence of mind to appreciate that my outfit was rather incongruous to the 1980s. Belatedly, I now concluded that I must take off my top hat and stop swinging the silver tipped ebony cane like some debonaire 1880s gent as I made my way along the pavement.

Howls of laughers came from the wee group of boy-men in derision; they were doubling up from it. "*Fuck's sake. Must be one ah they festival, theatre cunts,*" contributed one of the Fred Perrys. "*Or one ay they new romantic ponces,*" Ben Sherman added.

A second later, before I had had the chance to take it off myself, my top hat off had been flicked off my head from behind by one of the group. Caught in the wind, it blew a few meters away. They went running after it laughing, like a pack of braying hyenas.

Jeez, the last thing I wanted was a needless confrontation, I reflected - not least due to the potential the 'ripple effect' outlined in Sgàthach's writing - so I resolved to ignore and continued walking towards the Palace end of the Parade ground. A minute or so later, I looked back round towards the group and saw them disappearing towards the Meadowbank exit, my topper being thrown between them like a silk-covered frisbee.

At the same time, I took a glance towards the wee car park by the loch. It was there in exactly the same position as in 2022, but I felt rather unsettled by the absence of the sight of Syd which, for me, had only recently been parked there, patiently awaiting my return.

Approaching the political protest, alongside the plethora of flags and banners with political slogans, there were a few folks selling the paper, 'Socialist Worker', as well as those carrying grotesque effigies of Maggie Thatcher, which I assumed would be set alight at some point during the proceedings.

The volume of sound system was at a level quite uncomfortable on the ear, not helped by the rather forceful oratory of the guy up on the stage shouting into the microphone in heavy Glaswegian tones. I recognised him from the Scottish political scene of the 2020s, but a much younger version and with an almost a full head of hair - Terry Donovan or something like that, I could not quite recall. It was difficult to make out exactly what he was saying, not merely due to his bellowing, but the poor-quality speaker set-up - typical of the day I imagined.

There were a group of other individuals milling around at the side of the stage in a cordoned off area. I guessed that they were in the line up to speak. Again, I recognised a number of them despite their more youthful looks, such as, her that had been 'Mary Doll' in the vintage comedy show, along with various other dramas on the telly, and the Proclaimers blokes (looking more gangly, ginger and speccy than ever). Amongst these individuals, I noticed also a shy but determined looking young lady. Petite with a short-bobbed style mop of brown hair, she was perhaps 19 or 20 years old and wearing dark, student-style clothes of the day. She looked very familiar although I couldn't quite place her.

It would have been brilliant to have been able to stay and listen (or, at least, try to listen) to the speeches, but 'time', of course, was not a luxury I had. That was despite my having the ability, it would seem, to travel in it! As much as it would have been intriguing and fascinating to have had a wee tour around 1980's Edinburgh, contemplating my next step, I decided that I must turn around and head back up to St Anthony's Chapel to try, once again, to traverse to my originally intended landing of the 19th century city. Of course, having now fully realised the veracity of Sgàthach's communique, I appreciated that I really

DID have a job to do, and that it was crucial for me to get on with it.

The top hat was gone, of course; however, I reckoned I could buy one when I arrived in 1889 with the money in my leather case, still safely in my possession. Sgàthach had, after all, indicated that there was more than enough than required to win the bid at auction. Struggling up the hill to the ruined Chapel once again, I repositioned myself at the outside of the door opening, leaning back against the stone. On this occasion, however, I decided to take the Bannerman & Goudelock auction program out of my case and held it tightly in my hands, close to my heart - I would implore it to send me to the correct destination epoch! Closing my eyes, I tried to clear my thoughts - once more I focused on 28th February 1889 and the wording on the front of the auction program, seeking to attain the necessary meditative state.

Fully expecting to experience the rush of feelings that had come upon me earlier, I was disappointed, as on this attempt I felt nothing, absolutely nothing. It was exactly like previous day, Saturday, in my 'home epoch', when I had first tried and failed to time-traverse.

Pausing for a while, I paced around the Chapel, trying not to panic and to regain composure. After about ten minutes, I endeavored once more and failed. And then, again, and again... but it was useless. With a queasy feeling of unease growing in my stomach, I realised that there was no way I was going to be able to time-traverse further that day. Maybe I was doing something wrong or, perhaps, like Sgàthach had indicated, I just needed a break - to recharge my Fiosaiche powers (if that is what they truly were, as it now seemed)? Stuffing the auction program into the breast pocket of my heavy coat, with some reluctance, I accepted that it was going to have to be, at least, an overnight stay in 1980s Edinburgh.

Needless to say, I did not want to stay all night in the cold and wind on the hill, so I began to make my way back down towards the demo and the old town. However, before doing so, I temporarily disposed of my gentleman's cane (stashing in some thick, long grass adjacent to the ruined Chapel, to be picked up when I returned the next day). Of course, it was just another hindrance to my blending in within the current time period; the rest of my gear, I needed.

Deciding to bypass the demo and make my way up to the High Street, the Royal Mile, I started to think about getting somewhere safe and dry to kip later on, along with food to keep me going. I guessed that I was as well to make the best of things for the night and come back the following day and make another effort to reach the correct period - with any luck, my ability to do so would have returned... I hoped, I really hoped so.

As I passed by the Palace, along the snaking bend in the road towards the Canongate, I reflected how bizarre it was not to be greeted by the sight of the Scottish Parliament. Yes, things were different, although when greeted by the sight of Canongate Tolbooth housing the 'Peoples' Story Museum', along with 'Huntly House' on the opposite side of the road, it was like I was being reacquainted with long, lost friends. Mind you, even though it was reassuring, it was also disconcerting at the same time.

Ruminating upon my predicament, I decided that one of the first things I must do was establish exactly when in the 1980s it was, in terms of the date. Spotting a newsagent's shop on the other side of the road, I crossed to find a newspaper that would provide this clarity. As I approached the rack at the doorway, 'Belfast Child' by Simple Minds blared out from the shop's radio inside. Picking up a copy of the 'North Britishman', I gasped when under its title on the front page I could see stated, 'Tuesday, 28th February 1989' - for fuck's sake… my time traversing had misfired by exactly 100 years to the day!

It was, of course, quite staggering that Sgàthach had actually been telling the truth about time-travel and me possessing the special powers of the Fiosaichean, however, how could she have been so wrong about the 'object' allowing me to reach 1889? I asked myself, more than a little perplexed. I had followed her instructions exactly as she had laid them out - the Bannerman & Goudelock auction program of 28th February 1889 had been safely tucked in the inside pocket of my leather case, which in turn had been held close to my heart; I had focused my mind on it as she had said I should do whilst seeking to gain the necessary meditative state. … So how the hell did I end up in 1989, 100 years out, instead?

Suddenly, a light bulb illuminated in my head. Hastily grabbing at my leather case, I delved with my hand deep down into the inside side pocket and yes, felt that something was lodged within. Taking hold of it with my fingertips, I pulled out what was there. Of course, it was the football program - the one from the Hearts v Bayern Munich game. When I had collected it from the odd-ball guy in Edina Place the previous Monday night, I had placed it in my leather case for safe keeping. But, with all the drama occurring since then, had simply forgot to take it back out. Glancing impatiently at the cover to confirm my thoughts, it stated, '*Hearts v Bayern Munich, First leg UEFA*

Cup Quarter-Final 1988-89, Tynecastle Park'. Of course, the 88/89 season and the match had been played in 1989.

Within its hiding place, the footie program had obviously been as close to my heart or perhaps even closer than the 1889 auction program lodged within the same inside pocket. With great Cameron Guthrie aplomb, I had managed to confuse and fuck-up the ancient space-time continuum with a bloody Heart of Midlothian match program … Jeez, well done son! I thought in self-mockery, shaking my head in disbelief at my carelessness.

Another lightbulb then abruptly sparked from within me. With my blood pumping, I reached again for the copy of the 'North Britishman' from the newsagent's rack again and turned it over to the back page. The headline proclaimed, 'Hearts up against German giants' and underneath there was punditry opening with, 'Tonight's game …' Breathing fast, I turned once more to look at the match program in my other hand, studying it more closely this time. I gasped in disbelief to read the full text, including the last line giving the exact date and time.

'Hearts v Bayern Munich
First leg UEFA Cup Quarter-Final 1988-89
Tynecastle Park
28th February 1989 at 7.30 pm'

For fuck's sake, I was in Edinburgh, it was 28th February 1989, and the game was being played THAT BLOODY NIGHT at 7.30 pm… yeh gods! I surely could not pass up the opportunity to attend this legendary match?

CHAPTER 17

Animal Sanctuary, mid-October 2022

Unbeknown to all but the most senior office bearers of the Noble Order of Eidyn, their Gillane Manse contained a number of secret chambers within its substantial subterranean cellar. Security access to which was strictly limited to the Paterial Secretary and the Grand Pater of the brotherhood, along with any individual they chose, at their discretion, to grant special (and generally temporary) permission to enter.

The most sophisticated door entry system, using retinal scan and associated technology, provided assurance that no-one, other than those authorised could gain access to this basement and its secret undercroft areas. There were four such chambers in total.

The first, was a climatically controlled conservation vault in which the *Facal an Fiosaiche* manuscript resided. With dimensions of around sixteen meters square, the hallowed book sat in regal fashion atop a plinth positioned in the centre. A steady and optimum range of temperature and atmospheric moisture conditions were maintained under the climate control system for preservation of the precious text. In addition, a thick ceramic glass protective and fire-proof casing enveloped the revered tome, mirroring within the wider, regulated environmental settings. This chamber contained additional security measures such that it would be a far simpler feat to gain unauthorised access to the ancient Honours of Scotland and the Stone of Destiny in the Crown Room at Edinburgh Castle.

The second chamber, which Farquhar Sutherland and Alister Forbes-Fleming affectionately called the 'zoo', contained a number of cages with animals that had use in the ingredients necessary to perform incantations as dictated by the antiquated book's Ogham text (or, at least to the extent to which the Order had managed to decipher).

For example, one such cage contained, 'Yogi' an Asiatic black bear, which the Order had purchased as a cub via a corrupt official at the Royal Zoological Society of Scotland. In the eight years the animal had been in the captivity of the Order, its growth had been curtailed due to the fact its movements had been deliberately restricted within cages no bigger than the dimensions of the tortured beast's body. This allowed for ready extraction of Yogi's bile via a catheter through the animal's abdomen and into its gallbladder. Bile, with its high levels of ursodeoxycholic acid, appeared commonly as a necessary ingredient for performance of dark sorcery. Other animals - live, or just about living specimens - included, for example, bats, monkeys, a various assortment of rodents, snakes, cats and dogs.

Although, the existence of the 'zoo' cellar area was not definitively known to the wider Order membership, rumor had it, that it existed. Speculation extended to talk that, in addition to the animal specimens, the undercroft also contained caged humans - those people abducted from time to time from the streets of Edinburgh and surrounds. Where a human body part or section, such as an eye or a kidney, a severed testicle or slice of labia, were required for performance of a particular spell, such individuals would provide ready access - at least that was what was speculated. Hence, avoiding a rushed kidnapping or murder with the risk that that inevitably entailed. Sutherland and Forbes-Fleming neither confirmed nor denied such rumor.

At the same time, this chamber contained a freezer the purpose of which was to preserve essential organs and body parts, often from victims meeting particular and exacting requirements, procured for the performance of especially important invocations. This similarly allowed prior preparation and avoided a hurried and perilous procurement immediately in advance of ceremonial proceedings. The area was also kitted out with a large surgery and butchery table, together with leather containment straps so that no beast (nor human) could escape the grisly procedures to be undertaken.

Ernest, a retired oral surgeon from Auchtermuchty had been appointed as guardian of the 'zoo'. A task to which he had taken to with relish, very much enjoying the special access to the caged specimens that this privilege afforded him. When requested by his brotherhood superiors to procure a body part or section for their ritualistic purposes, the beady eyes on his gaunt face would light up and he would lick his shriveled lips in eager anticipation.

The third chamber was the 'kitchen', for use in relation to preparation for the performance of hexes and the like, including the making up of required tinctures and potions. This was not dissimilar to a commercial catering area, with a large range cooker, a number of deep stainless-steel sinks, along with the various accoutrements normally associated with the preparation of food (such as, knives, cooking implements, pots, pans, pestle and mortar etc.). It also housed a large walk-in storeroom containing shelves and drawers filled with jars and sachets of various dried herbs and plants, along with bottles of various chemicals and solutions - all of which could be called upon as component or facilitative parts in the carrying out of malign magic.

The fourth and final chamber was the 'war room' as the Paterial Secretary and the Grand Pater grandly referred to it. As youths, both had been in their respective Edinburgh private schools' 'Combined Cadet Forces', and although neither had thereafter served in the Her Majesty's forces, they shared a passion for the pretence that they had done so. In keeping with this, the room was laid out in the fashion of a military situation room. In practice, it served as a research and planning hub for the Order's nefarious activities.

As part it was equipped with the latest IT equipment to explore such actions, potential and actual. The walls were hung with large digital display screens. These presented all pages of the sacred volume, dully scanned, alongside known translations of applicable sections of the Ogham text further to analysis and research undertaken to-date.

Over recent days, the two premium office holders of the Noble Order of Eidyn had spent considerable time in the 'war room' busy planning for a very special and significant ceremony and incantation to be held shortly, one that they believed would herald a new, golden era for the Order.

CHAPTER 18

The Diggers

It was strange to think that this year - 1989 - was the year of my birth, although I would not be born for another three and a half months. Currently, my pregnant mother would be staying with my dad in our upper villa in Carrick Knowe Crescent.

My goodness, how I missed them since they were taken from me in that awful car accident in 2009, I reflected sorrowfully, my eyes welling up. Of course, they would not presently realise that sad fate ahead of them, as few of us do in relation to when and how we will depart from this mortal existence. I thought for a moment that I should perhaps visit them? Not knock on the door, of course... rather, observe them from a distance, such as when they were heading out to the shops – maybe on a wee trip to buy baby clothes and similar items for their imminent arrival? I mused. Mum's pregnant tummy would probably be getting pretty visible at this stage, I thought. Or should I actually go straight up to their door, I pondered, and take the opportunity to alert them not to travel by car on the future day of their demise?

However, no sooner than such thoughts had entered my head, I dismissed them. I had, of course, been explicitly warned by

Sgàthach against any unnecessary and deliberate interference with the time continuum - and to avoid and resist any such temptation to do so. Further, in reference to the 'second limitation' she had indicated that a Fiosaiche coming into contact with their former self could perhaps spark some sort of space-time calamity. Okay, I was only in my mum's womb at the current time, but I judged that it was not worth the risk.

My attending the Hearts v Bayern Munich game, however, was surely an altogether different matter, I surmised.

I recalled that my dad had gone to the match with my grandfather, also taking my cousin Douglas, who must have been around six or seven years old at the time. Over the years as I grew up, they had often talked about it at family gatherings. Dougie, as a teenager, was fond of saying to me how amazing it had been to be at that game, rubbing it in that I'd never had the chance to attend. You can imagine how that felt to a child.

But here I was in 1989, I reflected, unbelievable as it seemed. It was the day of that very match and I had the rarest and most inexplicable of opportunities to go… to join the crowds of Hearts fans at Tynecastle Park and witness that beautiful game unfold. In a flash of decisiveness, I resolved that I was going to grasp the thistle and go!

The fact that I had no ticket, no money (at least of legal tender in 1989) and was dressed like an eejit did not factor into that mental decision-making process, of course. Neither was the fact that my most pressing priorities were (or should have been) to find somewhere to stay for the night and food for later.

In contemplation of how to square this circle, I meandered slowly up the High Street from the newsagents in the direction of John Knox's house. On the left, not far after crossing St. Mary's Street and passing the entrance to the 'World's End Close' I noticed a curious little shop, 'Goodfellows'. It had a quaint appearance with crisscross sash bars on the windows and a 'ye-olde' type sign jutting out from a pole above the door advertising that it was a specialist in historic coinage and collectables.

On seeing this, I immediately thought that perhaps I could trade-in part of the 1889 wad? - reflecting again that Sgàthach's missive had indicated that there was more than enough within to cover the cost of purchasing the manuscript at auction, plus incidental costs (one of which, of course, was a new top hat). I considered, that in the circumstances of her writing, she would surely have erred on the side of being over-generous, providing a fair bit more than I was ever likely to need? And, in any case, it was surely up to me to decide what came into the category of 'incidental costs'? Perhaps a few of the notes from the antiquated dosh, duly traded into the current day tender, would be sufficient to cover the cost of a match ticket from a tout (they would surely be about outside the ground before kick-off, just like in 2022)? Maybe even, a hot meal from a café, along with cheap digs in a hostel for the night as well? Although, of course, I would be fully prepared to sacrifice that latter two for the former.

One way of finding out, I thought, as I pushed the door to enter the wee shop. As I did so, there was the ding-a-ling of a little bell. Behind a counter stood a diminutive chap, sixty-something, with half-rim glasses perched upon the end of his nose and wiry tufts of grey hair at either side of a bald dome of a head. He gave me a suspicious look and asked in a standard-posh, southern English accent, "*May I help you?*"

"Yes, hopefully. I am not sure if this is an unusual request or not. It's just that I saw the sign on your door and was wondering if you purchased 19th century bank notes? If so, what might you offer per pound?" I enquired politely, smiling.

In a slightly superior tone and manner, he responded, *"Well, as the sign says, we deal in historic coinage and collectables. 'Collectables' does, indeed, include currency from all periods of the Scottish realm, as well as those of further afield. In all cases, whether we would wish to purchase and, if so, what we might possibly be able to pay depends principally upon the condition of each note - the denomination, serial number and the year. In relation to 19th century Scottish notes, as you may be aware, particularly relevant is whether said note was issued before or after the Banknote (Scotland) Act of 1845."*

After rummaging around in my case, trying not to reveal to the curious wee fella the exact size of the wad and quantity of 1800s currency held within, I eased out a small selection of notes, including one each of, £1, £5, £10 and £20 denominations. I decided not to take out a £100 note as would likely be the rarest and I might be in danger of profligately bartering away too much of the auction monies.

Taking some time to examine each with a small circular eye glass, he said he would only be interested in the £10 and £20 notes - taking into account his aforementioned criteria, the others were apparently of negligible worth on the vintage currency scene. After a little haggling, including me play-acting walking out the shop door until he (thankfully) called me back in and upped his offer, we agreed on £60 (1980s tender) for the applicable notes.

Further to the research that Aoife and I had undertaken, I did have some idea of the value of the 19th century notes in 2022, however, I really had no clue in this time period. Hence, I was unsure as to whether or not I was being ripped off; with my obviously naivety about the antique currency trade and after his eagerness to call me back into the shop, I suspected that I probably was. But it really did not matter. I knew that I had been very fortunate to come across this shop - it would have been begging or stealing otherwise, and I did not want to end up in a 1980s Edinburgh cop-shop, that was for sure.

£60 in the present-day notes, I 'guesstimated' (perhaps with a little wishful thinking) would be sufficient cover the cost of a match ticket, plus leave change for food and even a bed for the night in modest lodgings. Possibly, it would even stretch to a pre-match pint or two if I were lucky? - that would be icing on the already heavily glazed cake. The two 1889 notes sold did not leave too much of a dent in the auction monies. Although, in the back of my mind I could not help but think how much of a disaster it would be for me to successfully get to the 1889 auction and find out that I was slightly short to make the winning bid, and all due to my determination (and selfishness) to go to the Hearts v Bayern match. Imagine me having to own up to Aoife on that score, I thought with a grimace … never mind the bigger picture as graphicly outlined in Sgàthach's letter.

The match was not until 7.30 pm and looking down towards the famous clock jutting out from Canongate Tolbooth I could see that it was not quite yet 4 pm, so I was in no desperate rush. Hence, I decided to make my way to Gorgie by foot - I wanted to drink in the atmosphere of 1980's Embra.

Before I left the High Street, however, I could not help but pop into the 'Other Record Shop' which I spied not far from the junction of Blackfriars Street. This was a music retailer I re-called that some of the older vinyl afficionados at the record marts talked wistfully of. Of course, in 2022, despite being the download age, there had been somewhat of a renaissance in vi-nyl. I was one of the converts, of course. Sure, there were one or two specialist wee, walk-in shops, in addition to the odd mart, but this was place was something else! A true treasure trove.

As I entered the store, I could immediately see that it was not just a retailer, but also a cool hangout for the city's youths and musos, with an eclectic assortment of clientele from punks, heavy metalers and goths, to mods and new romantics - judging by their respective dress - all trying to outdo each other with their style and avantgarde pretentions. In fact, it was more like a bar or a club than a shop, with folks chatting, smoking - yes, smoking - and drinking coffee from a machine.

'New' stock appeared to be located on the ground floor, plenty of vinyl, but also cassette tapes and CDs; the latter, of course, in take-over mode at the current time. Towards the back was a bank of huge cabinet-sized computer gaming machines. As I made my way upstairs to investigate further, 'Goodbye Mr Mackenzie' by the band of same name began blasting out. Shirley Manson's formidable backing vocals unmistakable. The upper floor a had a vast supply of second-hand records (includ-ing LPs, 12 and 7-inch singles, and EP's) with yet more gaming machines, some of which were like little coffee-tables with seats either side and ashtrays atop (all overflowing with butts). I was rather surprised when a group of goths huddled in the corner smoking gave me a nod, as if in recognition. Returning the ges-ture, I surmised that my 19th century full-length, black overcoat and heavy boots, along with the silk scarf in purple and dark red, must have earmarked me as a kindred spirit.

To be a little less conspicuous, I started browsing through the racks and tubs of second-hand discs. Needless to say, I could have spent hours in there and traded the entire sixty quid of 1980's cash on vinyl to play on my reclaimed record player back in the Straiton Place of my 'home epoch'. After what seemed like only a short while looking through the collection, I noticed a clock on the wall indicating that it was near 5 pm. It was hard to believe, however, I had already spent something like an hour inside the shop. Einstein had clearly been correct, time was indeed an illusion, I thought smiling to myself. Reluctantly, I sought to leave the store, with the heavy bass and jingly-jangly guitar tones of 'Jesse Garon and the Desperadoes" 'Grand Hotel' (… I knew my old vinyl, of course) ushering me out of the exit and back onto the High Street. The shouty vocals line, *"… WHAT THE HELL IS HAPPENING, WHAT THE HELL IS GOING ON?"* made me reflect upon my current circumstances and seemed quite an appropriate accompanying track.

Heading past St Giles, onto George IV Bridge and then down Victoria Street, I made my way to the Grassmarket. As I proceeded through and up onto the West Port, I chuckled to myself observing the same rough-looking 'Western Bar' as was in 2022, standing there unabashed as always, complete with threatening looking bouncers at the door and, chatting to them and smoking, a scantily clad, hard-faced strip girl. Moving on and emerging onto Fountainbridge, it was interesting to see that the area had not yet been turned in the soulless office complex desert of my time. It still had traditional tenement buildings, community pubs, even if a bit down at heel. Sadly, all too soon, to be demolished.

With a pang of hunger in my belly I was delighted to come across Brattisani's Fish & Chip shop on Morrison Street, a favoured venue many years ago after matches at Tynecastle. I broke into one of the Goodfellow's £5 notes on a haggis supper loaded with salt and sauce, all washed down with a can of sugary-sweet Irn Bru - some things never change! I was also prompted to recall visiting their Newington branch as boy with pals after trips to the Commie pool, all having worked up healthy appetites for our pokes of chips. Both branches had sadly shut down at some point in the early 2000s. As I made my way through Dalry, I experienced again the yeasty, nutty aroma that I had detected earlier in Holyrood Park. This smell was also something reminiscent from my youth and, I guessed, emanated from either the Fountain Brewery or the North British Distillery, both nearby. The former, I recalled, had been shut down in 2004 and the latter had been ordered by the Council to take measures over the years to filter out the odour which came from the distilling process. A loss to the city, I reflected, as smells are deeply evocative of place and another reason, perhaps, why the Edinburgh of the past had gained the moniker of Auld Reekie. I took a deep breath, filling my lungs with this fleeting moment of olfactionary nostalgia and it warmed me from my head to my toes.

By this stage there were now a good number of Hearts' fans on the streets making their way to the match, many of whom were wearing the 'Novafone' sponsored strip of the 1988-89 season. They were exchanging good natured banter with the odd group of Bayern Munich fans. There was no time to find accommodation prior to the match, so I decided to make my way to 'The Athletic Arms' on Angle Park Terrace - aka 'The Diggers' - for a pre-match beer, thinking that my 1980s cash reserves could stretch to that. I imagined that there might be the odd ticket tout circulating inside, so a potential win-win. The pub had gained its nickname as was situated between two graveyards and, historically, had been a popular watering hole for the thirsty Edinburgh Corporation grave diggers between excavations. At the same time, it was a legendary pub for Heart's fans prior to home matches. I did not know exactly how long it had been there, probably at least a hundred years, so it would be standing in 1989, I was sure.

And indeed, it was. As I approached its corner entrance it was near 6 pm, after the end of the working day, and it was clear that it was already choc-a-bloc with parched Jambos. I was equally dry in the throat as I made my way inside. The interior of the bar looked pretty much the same as in 2022, but as I edged my way in between the jocular groups, I was struck by the thick fug of cigarette smoke which, of course, I was unaccustomed to (a pub smoking ban having been in place since before I was even legally allowed to drink alcohol). The barman, smartly kitted out in a white jacket and red dicky bow, looked towards me. I smiled realising he was a much earlier vintage of old Danny who continued to serve behind the bar in my home epoch! Professional as always, he nodded as I raised up a finger indicating just one pint was required, and then started to pull a 'McEwan's 80 Shilling' ale via a tall fount - there essentially being only one drink in this establishment, at least in the 1980's. Dials on the wall rotated demonstrating that pulling and pouring were in progress and by the time I had edged my way through to the bar counter, the ruddy nectar was sat their waiting for me, with creamy head ready to be broken. I put out my hand with the unfamiliar assortment of shrapnel and £1 notes left in my pocket after breaking the fiver at Brattisani's and let Danny pick the correct sum out, saying that I had forgot to bring my glasses. I half expected him to recognise me, but of course, that was not possible. My god, I savored that pint, taking in its warm roasted flavours, along with its fine aroma. All the better for being amongst the throng of braw companions of a day before I was born - the great and the good of Edina's fathers, grandfathers, uncles, brothers and sons. Not many women frequenting the place in those days, at least on match days - a bastion of equality of the sexes, the Diggers was not.

Nudging my way around the bar, I found a wee spot to stand next to a pillar where I could observe, pretty much anonymously, the scene before me. Without the top hat and cane and having taken off my scarf and tie (albeit maroon), I did not stick out too badly despite the lack of wearing a Heart's top or the like. The fellow punters were, in any case, busy enjoying their beer and banter with pre-match buzz and chutzpah. I felt like an imposter - which, of course, I was - but a hugely privileged one, and as if I had walked onto a film set and become immersed in the alternative reality that was laid out.

It was then that I got a pang of anxiety. What if my dad and granddad would appear in the bar? What would I do? Of course, with young Douglas in tow they would not be popping in here pre-match, I reassured myself. It was, however, possible that I could see them en-route to the match or in the ground itself. If so, I would need to adhere to my passive voyeurism; again, it was not my role here to interfere. That was other than intervening when it was properly and fully justified, such as obtaining and destroying the evil manuscript - a task, of course, that I was utterly failing at due to my inadvertent jaunt to Thatcher's Britain!

There was just time, I thought, to get another quick pint in before the crowd in the bar started to dissipate, the good folks drifting off towards the stadium. After settling up with Danny for that, I did a quick money check and there was just over £55 left out of the sixty quid I had started out with. Not bad considering I'd had a haggis supper and bought two pints. Surely that would be sufficient, at least for a match ticket? I thought to myself hopefully.

As for such ticket, no touts had been apparent in the bar. After swiftly quaffing the ale and a visit to the gents (an earlier vintage of the same dire piss-trough), I headed off and down towards Gorgie Road, thinking that it was probably also better looking for a ticket nearer kick-off time as the touts would be more anxious to get rid of them and at a reduced price. Approaching McLeod Street, I could see the glare of the lights and hear the crackle of the pre-match audio. My heart was thumping with the anticipation as I continued on to the Wheatfield Street entrance and turnstiles.

Amongst the sea of maroon and chorus of Edinburgh vocal tones, I could make out the words, *"Match tickets, Match tickets,"* in a nasally Liverpudlian accent. Jostling my way through the match-goers towards the general direction of the speaker, I eventually reached the tout, mullet-haired and standing on the step of a tenement doorway. Donned in a shiny track suit reminiscent of Mr Sergio Tacchini in the Park earlier in the day, I told him that I was after just one ticket.

"Awrite, that'll be sixtee quid mate."

£16 was pretty good, I thought, and proceeded to take out a £20 note, indicating that I had no change. Shaking his head impatiently in response, he said, *"It's two score more mate."*

Jeez, £60! I reflected ruefully that I should never have had those pints and chippie - imagine missing the opportunity of attending this iconic game for that?

He was not for negotiating though, despite my best efforts. Moving away I scouted around for other ticket sellers. After trying my luck with a couple more, with the same scouse accents and dodgy threads, it was clear that £60 was their uniform, agreed rate. "*Fuck's sake*," I said to myself with anxiety building.

Minutes ebbed away and my spirts dropped as the last smattering of fans disappeared through the turnstiles and up towards the Wheatfield Stand. It was not long before kick-off. I could see the touts were now huddled together, keenly counting their notes as if they had emerged from an elicit gambling den having fleeced the other players. Presumably, they would shortly be heading down the road and back over the border. However, just as they were divvying up the proceeds, one of them noticed that I was still hanging around and shouted over, "*Hey kidder. Yous still after a ticket?*"

He said £45 and I did not haggle - no time for that - I gladly handed over the sum. Grabbing my pass to the match, I then rushed towards the turnstiles, like a child heading to open their presents on Christmas morning.

As I made my way through, I saw that the stub was for the old, Archibald Leitch designed 'Main Stand', demolished in 2017. Racing round and up the steps (not an easy feat wearing the heavy 19th century boots and wider apparel), I noticed a Heart's scarf that someone must have accidentally dropped on their way in – 'that will do nicely', I thought to myself as I picked it up and hooked it around my neck. Entering the terracing (which, in itself, was a new experience for me), my eyes scanned in some disbelief around a very different looking Tynecastle Park - that of prior to the mid-90s and later redevelopment. At the same time, I was enveloped by the melody 'Hey Jude', accompanied by a chorus of thousands - not exactly as penned by Paul McCartney - of, "*Na Na Na nananana… nananana… Jam Tarts*", along with a moving sea all-around of white and maroon scarfs, looped and being twirled in the air. Needless to say, I croakily joined in, taking my new-found scarf in hand and circling over-head .

As the singing died down, a crackly sound began to emit from the ground's speaker system, a bit like when I put an LP on my old record deck and lowered the needle just before the first track. A lump came to my throat, as it broke into accordion music which was then shortly accompanied by the homely timbre of Hector Nicol. At the same time, all around the ground (save as from the bewildered looking Bayern fans in the 'Roseburn Stand'), and gieing it laldy, came the following mass duo with wee Hecky …

> "*Away up in Gorgie at Tynecastle Park*
> *There's a wee fitba team that will aye makes its mark*
> *They've won all the honours fir footballing arts*
> *And there's nae other team to compare wi' the Hearts*"

… and then on to the chorus, just as I had not so long-ago heard Alec of Magdalene singing from beyond the grave …

> "*H-E-A - - R-T-S*
> *If you cannae spell it then here's whit it says …*
> *Hearts, Hearts, glorious Hearts*
> *It's down at Tynecastle they bide*
> *The talk of the toun are the boys in Maroon*

And Auld Reekie supports them with pride
This is my story this is my song
Follow the Hearts and you can't go wrong
For some say the Celtic and Rangers are grand
but the boys in maroon are the best in the land"

After the remaining verses, I really did have tears in my eyes. To think that my dad and grandfather were right here in the ground singing along with me - both of whom in 2022 were long dead. Not forgetting my cousin Dougie as a child. No doubt Alec was there in fine voice to. The singing - their singing - with joy and pride, rang in my ears, giving me goosebumps all over.

Cheers then promptly proceeded to take over as the teams emerged from the tunnel and on to the pitch. Moments later matters moved swiftly towards kick-off as the Ref carried the ball to the center circle, alongside the respective team captains, Dave McPherson for Hearts and Klaus Augenthaler for Bayern. That night the pitch was a bit of a quagmire. Not what the Bayern players - many of whom played for the West German national team at the time - were used to. The visiting team were on the top of the Bundesliga that season, but as the game sparked into action against the doughty surroundings of 1989 Tynecastle Park, you could see which group of players was really up for it.

Of course, I was the only spectator to know what the ultimate result of the match would be, but, of course, that in no way diminished the excitement and thrill for me.

The gifted German elite were somewhat cowed early on as Mike Galloway and Neil Berry charged towards them, putting the boot in. Tempers flared, however, after Kenny Black lunged in on Reuter - the visitors reacting with a brutal challenge on John Colquhoun. The game was in danger of getting out of hand. The Ref soon had to assert his authority by showing a yellow card to Alan McLaren for keeping his foot high after going for fifty-fifty ball. The tension was written all over the face of the then Heart's manager, Alex MacDonald, who I could see pacing on the edge of the dug-out as if he were outside a maternity unit where his wife was in labour with their first child.

At half-time, nerves were certainly on tenterhooks amongst the Jambo fan base. Popping out to take a piss, it seemed that every supporter was nervously sucking on a doup, clouds of smoke billowing around at the back of the stands on the chilly and breezy February evening air. Nevertheless, there was clearly widespread satisfaction at the way that Hearts had physically taken the game to the German giants, at least from what I could overhear from the generally positive chat. I took a wee covert look around for dad, grandad and Douglas, but to no avail.

Not long after the start of the second half, Craig Levein pushed a long pass out to Galloway, who in turn sprayed the ball across goal. It was out of reach of Iain Ferguson, but Eammon Bannon took a hit which rebounded off one of the Bayern defenders. The atmosphere was electric, and the capacity crowd roared approval with hopes rising. Not long after, Ferguson had a fine free-kick effort saved by Aumann, the German's goalie, which sought to ramp up the fervor in the home support by some additional notches.

Not even two minutes later, the scene I had watched on YouTube over and over again played out right there before my very own eyes - in reality, and for the first time. Just outside of the penalty box, Kenny Black was brought down by a Bayern defender and a free kick was awarded. Tosh McKinlay and Fergie sidled up in front of the German wall leaving them guessing as to what set-play they were about conjure. McKinlay then deftly rolled the ball towards the feet of Fergusson, who at the same time swung his right leg like a sledgehammer, sweetly catching it with the side-instep of his boot and cannoning it towards the left-hand side of goal. Aumann hurled himself to towards it, stretching as wide as his body and fingertips would allow… but he had no chance and the crowd witnessed it flying past him, thumping into the back of the net!

Delirium and wild celebration erupted throughout the Park. All around me on the terracing and stands was a joint frenzy of flaying and jumping, as if the home support were one big maroon beast and greater than the sum of its parts.

Thereafter, the Jambos did not relent and took the game to their visibly rattled German visitors, despite for a few hairy moments for the fans when Bayern were on the threatening counterattack. Of course, there was no real tension for me as I knew that Bayern would not score - not unless my mere presence had created some crazy change in the time continuum (… I could not help but feel a little anxiety for a moment at that thought). But towards the end of the game, it was Hearts that had the better chance to score and make it 2-0 with Dave McPherson finding himself in the penalty box with the ball. But, as the script went, it was not to be, and he skied it over the bar.

As the final whistle sounded to a cacophony of singing and chanting, the European heavyweights had been humbled after a night that would become stuff of folklore and legend in west Edinburgh and beyond.

My mind in a frame of stunned surrealism, after some time savoring the celebrations, I decided to make my way out of the stadium, resolving to find somewhere to half-decent to kip for the night if my remaining funds would stretch. Recalling that Grove Street, just off Haymarket had long been a popular spot for cheap B&Bs, I made my way in that direction hoping that despite the fact it was now coming up for 10 pm, I might still find one taking in guests.

There was now a misty rain along with wind. I was so grateful for the heavy 19th century wool overcoat which I pulled closely around me, hooking the collar up. Of course, I still had my leather case with me, on a strap which was now biting into my shoulder. Weary, after one of the most strange but exhilarating days of my life, I was really needing to find a place to rest. The first couple of B&Bs I tried, ignored the bell. At the next, I was greeted by the surly coupon of the landlady at the front window pointing to a no vacancies sign which had hitherto been obscured by the drab curtain, then tapping her finger at her wrist, presumably to indicate it was too late in the evening to be knocking at her door. Approaching the top of the street and the junction with Fountainbridge, I noticed on the right-hand side a rather peculiar tenement façade illuminated under the orange glow of the streetlamps. It had a certain gothic quality unusual amongst its peers, not just in Grove Street, but in the city more widely. Above a stone canopy, a sign announced that it was the '*The Artisan Hotel*', with smaller lettering underneath saying, '*superior lodging-house for working men*'. Probably within my budget, I was thinking.

And it looked as if it was still open as I could see the lights on beyond the partially glazed front door. On pushing it to enter, I was greeted by a dilapidated hallway and the sight of a rather severe looking, older middle-aged man at a counter. He promptly glanced towards me, then at the clock on the wall behind him, before saying, *"You've just made it chief. Nae wan admitted eftir 10.30 pm, ken."*

Clearly observing the Hearts scarf still around my neck, he added, *"But ye'll need tae take thon scerf aff as nae fitba colours allowed … you've no been here afore huv yeh?"*

As he said this, I could see the red, white and blue insignia of Rangers Football Club tattooed on his left forearm, and on the other, a military badge of some sort with *'Nemo Me Impune Lacessit'* written underneath - indicating, presumably, that he was an ex-serviceman. On his lapel, was a name badge stating, 'Billy Grant, Corps of Commissionaires'

A bed for the night plus breakfast was £9, he explained. This, I was delighted to hear, as knew that I had just enough to cover the charge, thereafter, leaving around £1 cash spare from £60 I had received earlier in the day from the wee guy at Goodfellows.

After providing him the necessary upfront payment, he led me down a poorly lit, narrow corridor towards a dormitory room from which an assortment of coughs and throaty voices emanated. At the same time, he listed a set of "house-rules" and that breakfast was at 6.30 am to 7.30 am the next morning, with the requirement to leave the 'hotel' by 8 am.

As we entered the hall-sized room, there were perhaps fifty or sixty slim, metal-framed single beds arranged side by side, cheek by jowl, like graves in a cemetery. A hodge-podge of gents chatted and coughed around them, some playing cards, others getting ready for bed and coming and going from an adjacent bathroom area. The room had an aroma reminiscent of wet dog, together with a liberal dashing of the contents of an ashtray. But that was of no matter as I knew that, at that time of night and with my meagre cash reserves, I had been very lucky to get a place to rest for the night at all. I was out of the rain and cold wind, so was certainly not complaining.

My good fortune was further confirmed when I was led to probably the only vacant bed left in the place. Getting here early and out of the cold seemed to have been the modus operandi for my fellow guests of the Artisan Hotel, likewise grateful for this place of shelter. Amongst them were a wide assortment of men of all ages, many of whom looked rather desperate, with worn and troubled faces. The need for such a place of refuge in 1989 was perhaps a stark reminder of the impact of Thatcher's Britain upon Scotland and the people. Now, in the latter years of her premiership, Maggie's supposed 'economic miracle' was not in much evidence here, that was for sure! The hostel was presumably operated and funded from charitable donations, rather than via the 'caring arms' of the British state - I felt sure of that. I wondered whether there was somewhere similar in the city for women in like-need?

It was good to note that my 1889 clothing did not really stand out as anything unusual amongst the other occupants of the lodging-house as most appeared to be clad in an assortment of jumble type trousers and jackets, probably handed out by charities, rather than anything akin to the fashionable gear of the day. No one would be remotely interested in what I was wearing in any case, I surmised - they clearly had far more important and pressing matters on their minds.

After a quick wash, I took to my bed, deciding to use my leather case as a pillow. This was really to keep it and the contents safe whilst I hopefully managed to get some kip. The actual pillow was stained and a bit greasy to the touch, so my case was a better option all round, I judged. In order to dry out my big overcoat, which was damp from the misty rain, I did what the other men were doing and draped it over the metal frame at end of the bed - lifting the bottom feet over the last inch or two of the coat's fabric, so that the material was sandwiched to the floor and, hence, presumably the coat made more difficult to snatch. There was nothing valuable in it in any case, I reflected. In similar fashion, I placed the top two feet of the frame inside each of my heavy boots, respectively. Otherwise, I slept fully clothed.

Despite a chorus of coughs and snores through the night, I managed to get a few hours well-needed sleep. In the morning a shrill bell went off early doors and, after a trip bathroom and putting on my boots, I joined the other guests in the 'mess hall' which was situated further down the dingy corridor off the entrance to dorm. Needless to say, I brought with me my leather case, with its precious contents safely inside. The room had a number of long tables stacked with crockery and spoons. Metal ashtrays advertising the names of different brands of beers were dotted intermittently down each. Observing the others, I took up a mug, bowl and spoon, then went to a queue at a serving area. At my turn, I was given a healthy dollop of porridge, along with some steaming hot tea. At an adjacent table, there was sugar and milk to add as desired.

Joining a group of guys at a table, I listened to chat and banter regarding where they would be going and what they would be doing in the day ahead, before returning to the Artisan in the evening in the hope of securing a bed for the night. A popular destination appeared to be a welfare center on the Cowgate that served a lunch free of charge. Another was Edinburgh Central Library on George IV Bridge where, it would seem, you could have a sly snooze for an hour or two out of the rain and cold at one of the tables as long as you put a newspaper or book in front of you. I recalled the lettering carved in stone above the entrance stating, 'Let there be light', a motto adopted by libraries which had initially been set up and funded by Scots/ American industrialist and philanthropist Andrew Carnegie. I considered that it should read in addition, 'Let there be Shelter' and that Carnegie might well have approved.

It was clear that the vast majority of these fellas were simply down on their luck, or rather casualties of a British political system under which they were deemed expendable fodder. They were hitherto miners, factory workers, shipbuilders, engineers and the like, who had lost their livelihoods due to the damage wrought upon Scotland by the imposition of industrial and economic policies of the then London Westminster government - a 'Tory' government that the people of Scotland had never voted for, rather had emphatically rejected. Such as were the 'broad shoulders' of the union, ha! Rather, shoulders that barged decent, ordinary working men and women out of the way and into the gutter as made their way to over-indulge at the feeding trough. Including to my home epoch of 2022, the Conservative party had not won a national election in Scotland since the 1950s. However, it was not merely the Tories and their governments - the other London based parties, such as 'Labour' and the 'Liberal Democrats', likewise supported a union and constitutional system where Scotland was an unequal partner, so that her people could always be out-voted, and their wishes overridden (a House of Commons where 85% of the 600-odd members' seats were allocated to just one constituent nation of the UK). At the same time, these political parties had consistently sent unelected politicians to a corrupt 'House of Lords' - the second chamber of the UK parliament - to my knowledge with over 900 members, consisting principally of failed politicians, cash-for-honours stooges and 'hereditary Peers'. In my home epoch, there were more than 90 of the latter category and with titles generally passed via a male line of succession (the 'Noble Order of Eidyn' adopting the same 'primogeniture' basis for full membership, according to Sgàthach's letter). In this parliamentary system - that was an anathema to democracy - the number of such hereditary peers numbered roughly equivalent to the entire compliment of elected Members of Parliament for Wales, Northern Ireland and Scotland put together!

As we finished our porridge and tea, most of the gents were immediately rolling fags and sparking up. Sat opposite me, Kenny - as he introduced himself - explained that one of the house-rules was, "*food afore fags.*" That perhaps accounted for the speed at which many of the diners had walloped down their breakfast - it was not merely due to hunger pangs. Clouds of smoke filled the air as overnight nicotine withdrawals were satiated. I guessed that Kenny was probably in his mid-30s, but with furrowed brow and dark circles around his eyes perhaps prematurely ageing him. He told me how he had lost his job along with around 1,800 thousand others when Leyland Trucks in Bathgate had gone under. With a family to support, he then found himself struggling to pay the bills, eventually leading to them being evicted from their semi in Boghall. At this point, he explained ruefully, that his wife and kids moved in with her mum, but there just had not been enough room for him in addition. With no opportunities of work locally, he came to Edinburgh in the hope of finding something, but no jobs were to be had - and that was coming up for three years ago now. During the period to-date, he outlined how he had spent long spells sleeping rough on the city's streets. Further, that when he had been fortunate enough to have scraped together enough cash from begging (the outside of Haymarket station being his most favored pitch, when he could get it), he would treat himself to a night in hostel-type accommodation such as this (if a place were available, of course).

I admired Kenny's pride and spirit in the face of the adversity. But it was difficult to see how, in 1989 Britain, he could lift himself out of the circumstances he currently found himself in; that resolve would surely and eventually be crushed. I reflected that similar personal tragedies had been - and were being - played out by the other temporary boarders at the 'hotel'. As I scanned the mess hall, with the gents chatting and smoking - the generations of fathers, grandfathers, brothers, sons and uncles - I reflected upon the sad waste of skills and talents, and of crumpled hopes and dreams. For a moment, I wondered, had I actually travelled back to the 1800s, rather than 1989, such was the obvious poverty and hopelessness of so many in the Edinburgh of this day? I suspected that the gents I had met were simply the tip of the iceberg.

This reminded me that I really needed to get moving and back up to Holyrood Park. This unexpected sojourn to 1989 had been quite an experience, not least for the opportunity to attend the Hearts v Bayern match, however, I had work to do, serious and important work - I had a manuscript to buy at an 1889 auction... and then to destroy!

Looking around, I suddenly realised that I was the only person in the mess hall who had not brought their outdoor coat or jacket in with them from the dormitory room. There must have been a reason for that, of course. Feeling a little panic rising within me, I sought to reassure myself that there had been nothing of value in the coat, rather it was all in my leather case which sat safely in between my feet on the linoleum flooring under the breakfast table. But a sickening feeling promptly came over me as I had the photographic recollection of stuffing the Bannerman & Goudelock auction program within the breast pocket of my overcoat the previous day at St Anthony's chapel - that I had done so immediately after my failed attempts to traverse time from 1989 and acceptance of the need for an overnight stay in 1980's Edina.

Abruptly leaving the breakfast table, heart pounding and clutching tightly my leather case, I rushed back into the dorm room only to find that my coat was no longer draped over the metal bedframe... it was gone! A big, warm overcoat like that, I belatedly reflected, would be a much sought-after item for those at the Artisan, who, to a man, would likely have to spend most or all of the day outdoors and subject to the frequently harsh Edinburgh weather.

"*You fukin' eejit,*" I could not help saying out load, cursing myself for such stupidity. Firstly, I had conspired against myself to arrive in 1989 instead of 1889, 100 years adrift. Now, I had only gone and lost the precious object - the one that Sgàthach had waited 26 years to risk a time-traverse to procure for me, the one that had been carefully held in a solicitor's firm's safe for many generations awaiting its secure passage to me. The object that was necessary and essential to allow me to traverse time back to the exact day of the 1889 auction and complete the vital task which I had been assigned. Shaking my head and sighing, I tried to console myself with the fact that, at least, I still had my leather case - I had never let that get out of my sorry sight. Inside, of course, lay the other vital 'object', the copy of 'The Nation on Sunday' from Aoife's local paper shop of the previous day in 2022. Oh, and I still had my boots to thankfully, as I had a lot of walking to do. There was nothing for it now, I had to get back to speak to the lady lawyer in my home epoch and, together with her, plan what the hell to do next!

How great it would have been to return proudly proclaiming to Aoife 'mission accomplished'… Cameron, the hero. But, instead, I would have to own up to the complete dog's breakfast I had made of it all. We would need to get our heads together and work out another way for me to get to 1889 despite the lack of the auction program. Perhaps, a museum or antiquities shop could provide an appropriate article closely associated with Edinburgh and the auction date? I contemplated wishfully. There would be little time though as Sgàthach, I recalled, had said in her letter to me that it was 'vital' to undertake the assigned task without delay, as after Monday 31st October 2022 a 'critical time juncture' would have been reached. Further, that after then it would likely be too late, even for one of the Fiosaichean, to stop the awful events she had foretold unravelling upon the world.

I then remembered with a little relief (which was at least something) that she had indicated that a return traverse to my home epoch would generally involve arrival only a short period after having first left, perhaps even just minutes. Hopefully, that would indeed be the case which would then allow Aoife and I the rest of the Sunday to come up with a new plan.

It was nearly 8 am and "*turf oot time*" at the Artisan as Billy Grant had described it the previous evening and folks were preparing themselves to face the elements. Before leaving, I had a quick scout around the mess hall in the forlorn hope that the overcoat thief would be as brazen as to still be there, standing smoking, whilst admiring his new cold weather apparel. But no, they were clearly long gone. Saying goodbye to Kenny, exchanging a companionly g-lock handshake, I gave him the last of my change so that he could afford to take shelter in a café for an hour or two over a cup of tea, explaining at the same time that I had a wee bit more than I needed for the day and, in any case, was due to collect and cash a benefits giro cheque later in the day. He thanked me gratefully, saying that he hoped to catch me later when the 'hotel' re-opened at 6 pm - advising me to queue outside from no later than 4.30 pm to have the best chance of getting a bed for the night. Nothing to do with Kenny, of course, but I certainly hoped not to be there. As I departed and stepped out onto the wet pavement of Grove Street, taking in the yeasty aroma of the brewery hanging in the air, I contemplated, rather pessimistically, what would become of him and the others that I had met at the Artisan lodgings.

Outside, it was one of those baltic Edinburgh days of old that chilled you to the bone and with the loss of my big coat, I was instantly feeling it. Officially nearly Spring, but that fooled no one, the city was definitely still in the grip of winter. That said, there was something noticeably purer and more natural to the outside environment than in 2022, I reflected - at the same time recalling with unease comments in Sgàthach's letter about how we were heading for climate catastrophe unless I successfully achieved my assigned task.

A brisk walk to Holyrood Park would help warm me up - at least I hoped. Buffeted by the wind, I headed off at a fair pace, making my way through Fountainbridge to Tollcross, then up Lauriston place. Passing the McEwan Hall, I then headed down past the back of the National Museum of Scotland towards the Bridges. As I walked, my hands were buried deep in the pockets of my suit trousers in an effort to keep them as warm as possible. Unexpectedly, my part-numb fingers felt in the bottom of one, a couple of coins which, evidently, I had missed when putting my change together to pass to Kenny. Quite pleased by this find, before I continued further towards the Park, I resolved to see if I could find a café and whether the coins were enough to stretch to a coffee to help warm me up. As I crossed South Bridge, I spotted up the road a bit, opposite Nicolson Square, 'Larry's Luncheonette', and made my way there.

In this fried breakfast establishment, the plastic seats (joined to the plastic tables), appeared to be filled mostly with an assortment of trendy teen and early twenty-somethings in wee huddles who looked as if they had been on the randan all night, clubbing. Before heading home against the tide of the morning commuters it appeared that they were lacing their stomachs with greasy bacon, sausage, black-pud, eggs etc. No doubt as sustenance for the rest of the day spent in bed and to aid recuperation from the night's excesses, I surmised. A few older dudes, such as had been in the boarding-house, were also dotted around, sitting solitary and gazing contemplatively as they puffed on their rollies and nursed mugs with steaming contents.

Thankfully, the coins were just sufficient to purchase a take-away coffee. Although, admittedly, it was pretty dire - scalding hot instant in a plastic cup so thin that it seemed to be part-melting whilst it burned my hands. But as it cooled down a little, to be fair, it served pretty well as a hand warmer and reviving drink. Moving on, I headed down Drummond place, on to the Pleasance, and thereupon Holyrood Road and past the Dumbiedykes scheme.

Along the route, of course, I noted many differences from 2022; not least the absence of odd weather out of step with the seasons which seemed to be a regular and increasingly common feature in my home epoch. However, it was when I reached the lower part of the Holyrood Road, that the differences became particularly stark, and not just with the absence of 'Our Dynamic Earth' and the Scottish Parliament as I had observed the previous day. Derelict brewery buildings were all around. The future site of our rather impressive Parly building, hosting a run-down and ugly industrial premises; from this building hung a weather-worn sign proclaiming it was the 'Headquarters of Scottish and Newcastle Brewery'.

The lack of the parliament struck me to symbolise the general appearance and aura of 1989 Edinburgh as rather down at heel and desolate - lacking soul, if you like. Yes, I had felt nostalgia, not least at Tynecastle Park the previous evening, and with the old community vibe of Fountainbridge, but there was a palpable lack of confidence and self-worth about the place and its people. All I had ever really known, from ten years of age and into adulthood, had been a Scotland with reborn self-governance, the Scottish Parliament re-opening in 1999. That was, of course, subject to the strict parameters of devolution imposed by the London Westminster Parliament. Despite the limitations of devolved government, in comparison with Edinburgh of 1989, with my unique perspective it was evident how such self-governance had allowed and facilitated a blossoming of self-confidence and esteem. The city of 2022 certainly had further to go, but it felt like it was on an unstoppable journey - agitating to be the elegant and proud capital of an independent European nation once again. A city of which its residents were rightly proud to be a part.

The transformation of Edinburgh, largely for the better re-minded me of the importance of completing my mission to destroy the *Facal an Fiosaiche* manuscript and, hence, to stop an even worse fate befalling the place and its inhabitants… a truly chilling prospect. Not just important for Edinburgh, or Scot-land, of course, but for the wider world as graphically outlined by Sgàthach.

Moving from this post-industrial decay towards the Park, it was both welcome and reassuring to see the familiar and graceful presence of the Palace of Holyroodhouse - the grand old lady - with the timeless landscape of Salisbury Crags and Arthur's Seat as her backdrop. The latter like a slice of the Scottish Highlands within the midst of the city, reminding the urbanites that Scot-land had far more to it than just the central belt,

It was a relief to get back up to St Anthony's Chapel. I had the shakes with the cold, and the strap on my leather case was kill-ing my neck and shoulders. On such a damp, chilly day there was no one around apart from some dog walkers by the loch that lay below. After collecting my ebony cane from the long grass in which I had temporarily disposed of it the previous day, I proceeded to take out from my leather case the copy of 'The Nation on Sunday', dated Sunday 30th October 2022. Holding it close to my heart, I prayed that it would allow a return to that day, and to my (usually) quiet life; to my bungalow in Porto-bello, to Déjà and, of course, to Aoife whom I felt that I had formed a special bond with despite our short acquaintance. Yes, I still needed to make a traverse back to the day of the auction in 1889, but without the Bannerman & Goudelock program that was not really possible at the moment, at least with any precision. That was a problem that Aoife and I would discuss and resolve - I felt sure - once I had returned.

Kneeling in the same spot as before, I took a deep breath, once more sensing the nutty, yeasty tang in the air. As the bitter breeze licked around me, I took one - hopefully last - look at the panorama of 1980s Edina, then shut my eyes. After seeking to clear my thoughts, I proceeded to focus - upon the newspaper that I held close to my heart and of the city and time period that I considered home.

CHAPTER 19

Hush Little Baby Don't Say a Word, Saturday 29th October 2022

"Ally bally, ally bally bee,

Sittin' on yer mammy's knee,
Greetin' for a wee bawbee,
Tae buy some Coulter's candy.

Poor wee Jeanie's gettin' awfy thin,
A rickle o' banes covered ower wi' skin,
Noo she's gettin' a wee double chin,
Wi' sookin' Coulter's Candy."

Wee baby Mia looked up with her bright blue eyes and gave Jason the most adorably cute smile as he sang to her, whilst gently rocking her in the pram at the front of their house in Black Agnes Court. The idea had been to get her off to sleep, but it seemed to be having the opposite effect.

"That's me ready now Jase," Megan called from the hall, looking intently in the mirror and applying the final touches of lippy.

"About bloody time, eh!" Jason replied in mock annoyance.

As they made the short walk to Dunpender High Street, despite the rather windy conditions Mia finally dozed off with the comforting motion of the pram. Being the Saturday before Halloween, the local shops were busy with kids and their parents getting various items for the big day, including the ghost, ghoul, witch, demon etc. fancy-dress items. Easy to carve pumpkins were nowadays favored for the kids' lanterns, in place of the hard neeps of their parents' and grandparents' generations (… with many a scarred finger demonstrating that this was indeed welcome progress).

The Americanisation of the celebrations also meant that the term 'guising', had been replaced with that of 'trick or treating'. At the same time, today's children expected goodies in return for simply turning up at their neighbours' doors and yelling, "*trick or treat.*" They would stand there in the shadows looking glaikit and nonplussed if the recital of a poem, song or joke were expected in advance of such provision. And whether it was inflation or the Americanisation, they would be no less than affronted by the offer of some fruit or biscuits for their efforts; rather, they expected a decent haul of sweets or a few quid at the very least!

On their trip out, Megan wanted to get her 9-year-old niece, Grace, a spooky-themed make-up set in advance of the primary school Halloween party on Monday evening, as well as any 'trick or treating' of the neighbours and family before that.

As she and Jason pushed the pram along, Megan could not help but check upon Mia every couple of minutes to see that she was safe and snug inside, poking the sides of the fleece blankets around her to ensure that they were properly in place. On peeking in, she could see the soft whisps of light ginger-blonde hair that adorned her beautiful daughter's wee head, as well as her cherub-like face snuggling in next to the pink bunny that adoring granny, Tricia, had bought.

Mia had only just turned 10 weeks old and was an absolute joy, the light of her parents' lives, bringing the couple back closer together after a difficult period. Once again, they were like the lovebirds that they had been before all the frustration and anxiety of two years of negative pregnancy test results. What a fantastic baby she was too. After her bath and feed in the evening, she would usually drop off to sleep right away and remain in the land of nod right through the night until around 7am the next morning. Megan and Jason could not quite believe their luck as had been warned that they would be totally sleep deprived once their infant daughter had arrived.

Dunpender being a small town, there were plenty of people on the long, flat High Street that the couple knew and who would stop to say hello and, of course, coo into the pram.

"*Aww isn't she just gorgeous hen. I can see baith yersel an' Trish in her bonnie wee face. Ahm fair delighted fir yous,*" Mrs Logan, a bingo pal of Tricia's clucked.

Megan swelled with pride at each such encounter. Especially when she met friends from back in the day at school. Passing the 'Pick for a Pound' shop, she thought that she would pop in as knew that they were generally well-stocked at this time of year with items such as she was after for Grace. Leaving Jason outside with wee Mia safely tucked up in her pram, she did just that. Indeed, Megan found that there was a good selection of Halloween-themed make-up kits, containing black, white and red greasepaint, wee plastic bottles with fake blood, little sponges, brushes and the like. She was spoilt for choice, in fact, and stood there with her shopping basket mulling over the different options on display.

Outside, Jason rocked Mia's pram devotedly, his wee angel still fast asleep inside. As he did so, from the corner of his eye he thought that he saw Baz, one of his old buddies from the Cat's Row scheme where he had grown up appearing from one of the side-vennels off the High Street. Turning round to get a better look, releasing the pram handle momentarily as he did, he confirmed that, indeed, it was Baz.

At the same moment, his old mate clocked Jason and approached to say hello, "*Hey, how' its gaun bud? Nae seen yeh in months. Me an' the crew are missin' yeh oan Friday nights doon the Lochside woods.*"

The two of them did the obligatory fist-bump greeting.

"*Ahm sound son, sound. Been kinda busy it's true,*" Jason replied, before asking "… *where are yeh off tae?*"

"*The bookies, ken. Got a wee tip on the 12.30 pm at Musselburgh.*" Baz then cupped his hand to his mouth, leaned in towards Jason, all secretive, and in a low voice, saying, "*Nag's name is 'The Reeper' if yeh fancy geeing it a wee tickle yersel' … kindae appropriate name fir Halloween, eh!*"

"*Yer tips are aboot as much fuckin use as yer clapped oot, auld van bud,*" Jason responded with a grin. "*Ah remember the last time yeh gied me one ay yer tips, I lost a score. Anyways, I got anothir mooth tae feed these days, ken. Cannae afford tae be throwing ma money away on gambling when thirs nappies an' god know aw what tae buy for the weein.*"

At this Jason turned back round to gesture to the pram, with his sleeping beauty within.

Looking in disbelief, there was an empty space on the pavement where the pram had only a few seconds before stood. Jason's chest heaved and stomach churned in horror as Mia's pram was nowhere to be seen! Scanning up and down the pavements of the High Street, he just could not see it anywhere.

Thinking to himself that he must calm down, he considered that Megan must have surely come out and wheeled the pram inside the shop on seeing him, through the window, blethering with his pal. That must be it, he thought trying to reassure himself. At this, he immediately darted inside the retail premises only to witness Megan standing at the till paying for items that the shopkeeper was popping into a bag, but with no pram next to her - "*FUCK*," he shouted by reflex.

At this, the new mum promptly turned to see him standing there just inside the doorway. From the blind fear evident in her partner's eyes, Megan sensed that something was wrong, very wrong, and screamed, "WHERE'S MIA?"

In full blown panic now, Jason rushed outside to confront a somewhat bewildered Baz, "*Did yeh see any cunt head off wi' the pram... OOR MIA'S IN IT.*"

Baz rather shocked, stuttered in response, "*Uum... aye.., some gadge wi' ah big-long, purply kindae coat an' hood, couldnae see eys puss, like. Thought it wiz mibbae one ay they hippie dudes fae Belhaven wi' eys kid.*"

"*WHERE DID THE CUNT HEAD?*", Jason barked back directly.

"Think ey wheeled the pram doon there," replied Baz shakily, lifting a finger and pointing towards the nearby vennel that led to the Co-op car park.

As Jason tore off down the narrow lane, Baz called limply after him, *"Ahm sorry pal... ah didnae ken the kid wiz yours, ... didnae even know your burd had popped yin."*

Megan who had at once dropped her shopping, was now outside of the store wailing in horror at the absence of her darling Mia. Dropping to her knees, she started pulling at her hair in shock and anguish.

As the distressed dad steamed into the car park from the vennel, he could see an expensive looking shiny black Range Rover type car approaching the exit on to Tranent Road. The driver's face was not visible due to a hood of some sort obscuring. Coming from the direction of the boot was the unmistakable sound of his baby daughter greeting. Jason bolted towards the car, but just as he reached it with his fingertips - nearly touching what he thought was a latch to open the boot - there was a screech of tyres on tarmac and the vehicle abruptly swung out onto the main road. As it then sped off towards the town boundary, he ran in hopeless pursuit.

Megan and Jason were never to see their darling wee Mia ever again.

CHAPTER 20

Passage to Porty

G asping slightly after being overcome by the strange but not unpleasant ripple of intense sensations that hopefully meant that I had traversed back to Sunday 30th October 2022, I reflected upon how the experience, again lasting no more than thirty seconds to one minute, was perhaps akin to an extreme form of autonomous sensory meridian response. Hesitant to open my eyes in case I remained stuck in the 1980s, firstly, I inhaled deeply, filling my lungs from my nostrils with the surrounding air. With some relief, I sensed not the faintest whiff of the nutty, yeasty aroma of only moments before, rather just a hint of the sea from the Forth. At the same time, I could detect a much milder day around me - although the closeness in the atmosphere was back, just as it had been when I'd first made my time-traverse. Surely this meant that I had been successful and returned to what Sgàthach had described as my 'home epoch', I asked myself in anticipation?

Opening my eyes, I looked towards the direction of the Scottish Parliament building, considering it a barometer for my time-travel progress. Yes! ... I could witness it proudly standing there once again, sighing in relief at the sight. The Edinburgh without its Parliament had seemed to be missing an integral part of its being and purpose. At the same time, just along from it,

I could also see the white armadillo-like dome of 'Our Dynamic Earth'. Jeez, it felt so good to be back amongst these familiar, old friends.

On then looking round in the hope of seeing Aoife's smiling face to greet my return, I was a little bit disappointed to find that she was not there. Considering that she may have been resting, I scanned round the perimeter of Chapel ruin thinking that on this decent enough day she may be sat somewhere on the grass… but no, she was not.

Peering down towards the car park however, I was heartened to spy Syd waiting there patiently and loyally for me, a bit like a metal version of a golden retriever - I was definitely back in my home epoch, thank goodness. Wasting no further moments, I made my way back down the hill from the Chapel. It seemed to me that it was only slightly later in the day from when I had first traversed, so my guess was that I had only been away for short time, maybe just half an hour to an hour maximum.

As I approached the car, I could see a snoozing Aoife on the passenger seat. I imagined that she must have thought I was going to take a lot longer than I had done to reappear, so had decided that it would be more comfortable to wait and rest there. Looking through the window at her dozing, I smiled. Hesitating for a moment before rapping lightly on the window to arouse her so that she could let me in, I was thinking to myself what a welcome sight she was and also, how beautiful. Stirring, she gazed up at me looking a bit surprised. At the same time, she seemed pleased to see me as broke into a warm smile before unlocking the driver's door from the wee nib by the window - something that more modern cars, of course, no longer seemed to have.

As I deposited, with some relief, my leather case, along with the ebony cane on the back seat and proceeded to get in, Aoife could not help but say, half-teasing, half-serious, *"Goodness me Cameron, what a state you are in."* Pinching her nose, she added, *"And what's that awful smell? Have you been holed up on a doss house or something?"* I smiled wryly at this. She also remarked upon the absence of my overcoat and top hat, to which I responded that there was a long story to tell once we were back in Porty.

As we pulled up at my wee house in Straiton Place, I noticed Syd's retro analog clock indicating that it was just after 1.30 pm. That had to be wrong, I concluded - the clock had never been the best timekeeper and must be running slow. It had even been later than that - around 2 pm - when I'd made the initial time-traverse, so, by my calculations, it was now surely past 3 pm, at the very least? That really had to be the case, even if I'd promptly returned from 2022 only minutes after having first traversed - what, taking into account the time it had taken me to walk back to the car from the Chapel, as well as to drive home.

Exhausted, I had never been so glad to open my front door and see the place. At one point, when I'd been forced to spend the night in 1989, I had wondered if I may ever set my eyes upon it again (the 2022 version, at least). After my time-travel debacle I could have done with just curling up in bed to rest and lick my wounds. But, of course, there was no time for that as Aoife and I had planning to do in order to get things back on track.

It is just as well Sgàthach were not present here in 2022, I reflected, as she would be none too chuffed with me to say the least!

Aoife sensing my fatigue, sought to chivvy me up, telling me to go straight away and change out of the - now rather dowdy looking - 19th century gents' apparel and have a shower, saying that I would feel better for it. Although with the fact that I smelled so bad, it would surely mean that she would feel better for it to. The thought of immersing myself in hot water after being chilled to bone all morning was a very appealing one. As I went to the bathroom to follow her advice, Aoife disappeared into the kitchen, saying that she would put a pot of coffee on. As I got the shower running and, with relief, finally got out of the uncomfortable wool, flannel suit, I could hear her opening and shutting kitchen cupboards and then the click of the toaster.

Feeling thawed out and much perkier after the wash and change, I took a seat at the kitchen table. I was still anxious, of course, pondering in my mind what the next move might be, if indeed there was one. Déjà jumped up and started brushing her wee head against me as I sat contemplatively like Rodin's, 'The Thinker'. Smiling and looking at the wee rascal's furry face, her greeny-yellow, almond shaped marble eyes peered inquisitively at me, as if she were concerned about me in some way. Cats had a tremendous ability to sense when something was wrong and when you were upset or unwell. A kind of psychic link with their guardians. Similar with dogs, of course, and probably many other animals. She was now sensing my anxiety, I guessed. Of course, perhaps she was just wanting me to feed her? Although, as Déjà started to lick her paws, it was evident that my super-efficient lawyer house guest had beaten me to it.

Coming over to the table, Aoife put the pot of freshly brewed coffee on a mat in the center. My wee machine was a modern take on the 1970s filter type, rather than the ubiquitous pod version of today (I did like my retro classics, of course). Much better coffee I thought, especially when made by Ms Gilfeather, and even more so when all I'd had in more than a day was awful 1980s instant. A plate full of buttered toast then arrived - very welcome, indeed - placed in my hands and away from the ever-greedy paws of the furry one. Aoife then took up the seat opposite me and poured out the steaming contents of the pot into mugs for the both of us. In between taking bites of toast and gulps of the delicious brew, I laid bare the gory details of my time-traverse fiasco. This no holds barred account included the fact that I had been careless enough to have had the Hearts v Bayern match program within my leather case, thereby - presumably - confusing the time continuum and delivering me to the 1980s instead of the 1880s, exactly one hundred years out. With considerable shame and embarrassment, I also owned up to losing the all-important 1889 Bannerman & Goudelock auction program, as well as the less critical coat and topper.

As I relayed this sorry tale, Aoife simply nodded, it appeared without casting judgement upon me (although, I would not have blamed her had she done so). After I finished, she started fumbling around in her black satchel bag which hung by its strap over the back of her chair, clearly looking for something. To my considerable surprise, she then produced yet another aged-looking document! Again, it was adorned with a red ribbon and wax seal.

Passing it across the table-top to me like a croupier carefully dealing a playing card face down, she said matter-of-factly, *"Cameron, my firm were additionally instructed by our client, Miss Sgàthach, to pass this letter to you in the event that you were unable to successfully complete the task requested of you outlined in her initial missive. We were to destroy it had you succeeded."*

I chose not to immediately reply, rather nodded in recognition. After giving her somewhat of a grim glance and with more than a little trepidation, I took the ends of the ribbon, pulled and broke the seal to reveal once again a sheaf of weathered and stained parchment papers, albeit with less in number than before, upon which was the now familiar quill-pen handwriting. This time, I read the contents aloud …

15th March 1892 (and 18th September 2082)

Mr Cameron Guthrie,
40 Straiton Place,
Portobello EH15 5BQ

Dear Cameron,

If you are reading this letter, then it means that, sadly, you have been unable to successfully complete the task requested of you - to attain the *Facal an Fìosaiche* manuscript at the 1889 Bannerman & Goudelock auction and, thereafter, destroy it.

Firstly, please be aware that regardless of the particular reasons for your failure, I applaud your efforts (which I am confident you will have made). Traversing in time has huge challenges in itself and, on top of that, the assignment set for you was of considerable difficulty.

Nevertheless, you may recall from my earlier missive that I indicated that a critical crossroads and juncture in time within your 'home epoch' was close to arrival. Further, that were you unable to successfully complete your assignment in advance of this, then after Monday 31st October 2022, certain events would be fully set in motion. Events that would likely be beyond prevention or alteration by a Fìosaiche residing thereafter. I was deliberately a little reticent in that communication on what I meant by this, it being unnecessary to share the details at that stage. Had you managed to attain and destroy the ancient book at the 1889 auction, then such juncture would no longer relevant or a threat. In the current circumstances, however, I may - indeed, I must - elaborate.

I am hoping that upon receipt of this letter by you, it is not yet past Monday 31st October 2022. If that is so, then the good news Cameron is that you still have an opportunity to attain and destroy the malign text. Hence, the purpose of this dispatch is to provide you with guidance as to how to hopefully achieve this – and part and parcel, to outline what your task now is.

However, if you are reading this now and it is already past that critical juncture, then buckle down for a tough ride sir - in basic, practical terms my advice to you would be to: move from your Portobello sea-front home (in the next 3 years, at the latest) to a stone-built house on higher ground (Buckstone, Fairmile-head, Colinton or Balerno all a good call - that is if you choose to stay in the city rather than clearing to the Highlands, as many shall do), ideally containing a large basement; thereafter, install within your new property, a high-quality air filtration system (whilst they are still available and affordable), along with solar panels for energy provision; and, at the same time, begin to stockpile supplies of all nature, including, canned, pickled and dried food, medicines, and items for purposes of water sanitization and self-defence.

Assuming - wishing and praying - that such course of action shall not be required, as it is not yet past the aforementioned critical date and crossroads in time as you read this, then please let me continue.

Regrettably, unlike in my previous communique, I can only offer you limited guidance on how you may now gain possession of the heinous tome in order to enable its destruction. Quite simply, despite my best efforts, I have been unable to establish anything like as much detail to pass on to you as I had wished. That said, what I do know and may share with you is, as follows:

On Monday 31st October, the Noble Order of Eidyn is planning to commence the ceremonial performance a spell, one that is particularly special and unlike any others that they have hitherto incanted – one to grant the gift of 'beatha shiorraidh'. Let me elaborate...

They believe that the reverend John Kellie, whom you will recall I referred to in my previous letter, had pretty much deciphered its wording and instructions back in the 16th century from the obscure Ogham markings within the book's text. Further, that at the time, despite illness from syphilis (due to his frequent visits to Edinburgh's houses of ill repute) he had been preparing to perform the odious magic, however, was ultimately thwarted from doing so due to his detainment and later execution (and with the burning of his remains) for the murder of his wife.

It would seem that when the gentlemen's group purchased the manuscript at the 1889 auction, it contained stuck within its vellum pages, a piece of léine cloth with a rudimentary decryption of this particularly powerful enchantment scribed upon it by Kellie himself. Although, crucially, certain parts of the wording were so faded as illegible.

As alluded within my previous missive, the Noble Order had always believed that the preacher man had developed a deciphering key to the particularly cryptic version of Ogham script within the antique volume. Further, that he'd had some sort of dark spiritual guidance which had assisted him in so creating. Unfortunately for them, however, this interpretive device was never located. Nonetheless, it was clear to them that the decryption scribbled on the fragment of léine cloth had been resultant to Kellie's use of such key.

Engaging appropriate academic sworn to the utmost secrecy, they had the segment of fabric examined. Further to a type of reverse-translation, the scholars were able to match particular components of the cryptic Ogham text to certain letters of the Roman alphabet. This, in turn, permitted the piecing together and assembly of a partial code. The code was sufficient to enable the Order to uncover some of the wider secrets of the aged book and, as part, to decode and perform certain spells hitherto beyond their knowledge and ability to undertake. The exercise of this sinister sorcery bestowing upon them incredible riches, advantages and privileges, such as I alluded to you in my earlier missive.

The problem for the 'gentlemen', however, was that despite this partial code, much of the text within the manuscript remained impenetrable. This, of course, included vital components of the aforementioned special and powerful spell that Kellie had been seeking to perform.

That was until early 2022, when, finally, with their academic assistance and use of the latest optical and scanning electron microscopy, as well as energy dispersive spectroscopy microanalysis techniques, they managed to work out the previously illegible parts of the reverend's léine cloth translation of the extraordinary invocation. The specialist scholars had not created a key to the book as Kellie had reputedly achieved, you understand, but it was sufficient so as to near-fully decipher this particularly important and exceptional spell.

This is the evil enchantment that they are planning to perform on Halloween, 2022. The magic is truly exceptional in nature because it has the power to grant eternal life - including to an individual that has already passed. In this particular case, it will be used to summon the reverend John Kellie - to raise and resurrect him from the dead, and thereupon grant the murderous clergyman immortality (*beatha shìor-raidh*)!

By bringing him, their spiritual leader and inspiration, back to life in such manner, they would have amongst them in perpetuity the holder of the key to the cryptic Ogham text - the individual most capable of fully understanding and deciphering the remaining impenetrable sections of the *Facal an Fìosaiche*. This would effectively unleash the full sinister power and alchemy of the aged text, leading to the catastrophic events for personkind and the planet that I outlined to you in my previous letter. As indicated, had you succeeded in destroying the vile tome in 1889, then, of course, it would never have got into the hands of members of the Gillane group and there would no question of Kellie ever being brought back from the dead, and the monstrous events outlined ensuing. Alas, its destruction in 1889 was not to be.

So, at sunset on Monday 31st October, the Noble Order of Eidyn is to commence the execution of this sinister enchantment to resurrect the reverend. Historical evidence from my home epoch exists which demonstrates that by early November 2022, the reverend was already commencing and undertaking nefarious activities along with his Order disciples – a number of abductions and unexplained murders taking place in Edinburgh and surrounds, in preparation for a flurry of hexes and other sorcery. Being released from a death paralysis of over 450 years, had clearly whetted his appetite for performing such dark alchemy!

As I have indicated, once the clergyman is fully restored to life (and hence, such events are set in motion), it is most likely to be beyond prevention or alteration, at least by a Fiosaiche residing thereafter. Such a Fiosaiche would be unable to traverse back to the resurrection ceremony to prevent it occurring - the appearance of Kellie at such juncture having heralded overwhelmingly dark magic. At the same time, they would be unable to travel back in time to destroy the manuscript.

You may recall from my earlier letter, the conclusion I had reached that a fifth limitation on the powers of time-traverse applied to me. One that had prevented me from travelling back in time and directly ridding the world of the *Facal an Fiosaiche*. The view I had come to was, that due to my being a Fiosaiche residing in a future and home epoch which had been so radically shaped by the evil forces of the script and the reverend's revival and return, it was, in consequence, not possible for me to directly destroy the odious book in an earlier epoch. Whether it were the time continuum railing against alteration in such manner or the malign magic unleashed further to bringing the wicked minister back from the dead, I believed that I had been rendered incapable of traversing back in time to take such direct action.

However, as I also indicated in my letter, I do not believe that such limitation applies to you, at least <u>until</u> the point of his resurrection in your home epoch.

Hence, again assuming that for you it is not already passed the critical juncture of Monday 31st October 2022, you have the power Cameron to prevent the rebirth of the wicked preacher and the bestowing of immortality <u>before</u> it is enabled by the Order's ceremonial performance of the extraordinary enchantment. At least, this is my belief. Any action taken, including destroying the manuscript, will be within your present-day home epoch and thoroughfare of time, and hence not reliant upon the powers of time-traverse to do so.

As to the specific location of the ceremonial event, I cannot, unfortunately, provide you with precise guidance. Wherever it is to be held, it will presumably need to be a private location due to the almost certain use of human remains and potions concocted with gruesome ingredients as part of execution of the unholy spell. This might suggest the Order's mansion in Gillane? Somewhere in Spenton village is perhaps also possible? - the minister's old Kirk or Spenton Manse perhaps?

The village is perhaps the most obvious general location, however, might perhaps lack the necessary privacy to hold the required ceremony, being within a small, tight-knit community of residents. The location, of course, could be somewhere entirely different, perhaps with an occult connection. A place with some sort of direct link to the corrupt church man is most likely.

At the same time, please be aware that wherever the ceremony is to take place, the Order requires Kellie's remains - his ashes - to be present to properly conduct the malevolent magic. If these are buried, this may give a clue to the whereabouts of the ritual. As I highlighted in my previous letter, his remains were burnt further to his execution. However, it is unknown as to where the ashes lie or are stored. Reputedly, they mysteriously disappeared after such cremation. Although, it is safe to assume that the Noble Order will be aware.

Hence, your task now Cameron - with the continued support of the assigned representative from Gilfeather & McLean - is essentially, two-fold: i) stop the resurrection of the reverend John Kellie and, of course, ii) attain and destroy the ancient book. Like before, it is your duty of fate – of Mother Earth - to make every possible effort to carry out successfully. To ensure a positive version of the future and plane of time.

I must warn you that this is a far more perilous task than that previously set. I had sincerely hoped that you would have been successful in your 1889 mission; had that been the case then, of course, I could have avoided making this further request of you.

An important point to note is that the rebirth of the preacher man is only finally concluded when the incantation from the *Facal an Fiosaiche* is fully read (which will almost certainly be in its original Ogham form) and the ceremonial performance of the spell, including provision of offerings or artefacts and use of potions, as applicable, is complete. This might feasibly take an hour or even longer in terms of necessary proceedings as I understand it. You must, of course, halt matters before this stage is reached. Even if Kellie appears during the ceremony, be assured that he is not fully restored and resurrected until the Order accomplish in such manner.

At least this time Cameron, I am not asking you to traverse time in order to attempt the task that I have outlined. I wish you luck. You know how high the stakes are - the future of Mother Earth and personkind being dependent upon your success.

Yours aye,

Sgàthach

Putting the parchment pages down, I looked towards Aoife not knowing whether to feel a sense of relief or greater anxiety. From her expression, it was clear that she had now succumbed to the latter. Trying to lighten the atmosphere, I said rather nonchalantly, *"Well, at least we still have more than a full day."*

But it was like the colour had drained from my legal companion's face, *"You do realise that today is Monday Cameron? Monday the 31st of October, don't you?"*

I shook my head in disbelief, having thought it were still the Sunday, replying, *"Did Sgàthach not say in her first letter that I would return back to my home epoch just a short time, such as a few minutes, after I had first traversed, no matter how long I had spent in the 'destination epoch'?"*

"Not quite Cameron... She outlined that up to a full day could pass in your home epoch - and, in fact, you returned just an hour shy of that, around 23 hours after you had first traversed. I know full well, as I had a cold and uncomfortable night sat in your car at the St Margaret's loch car park waiting for you, hoping that you would be back sooner than what transpired to be the case. In the process, getting propositioned twice by sleazy guys saying that they were 'doggers' and waving their bits at me through the car window! I had to hoot the horn numerous times to frighten them off."

"Jeez, I'm really sorry to hear that Aoife, how appalling! Well, it was a great relief to see you when I eventually did return - a friendly face after such a weird experience - so thank you... thank you so much, for waiting," I responded, at the same time reaching out to take her hand in a comforting gesture, to which she obliged, blushing slightly as she did.

Reflecting that there had been nothing wrong with Syd's clock after all, I continued, *"Time is obviously short, but surely adequate in* order do what Sgàthach asks?" I continued, sounding more optimistic than I was actually feeling. Glancing up at the clock on kitchen wall I could see that it would soon be 2.30 pm, and, at that time of year, only two or so hours from sunset. Of course, this was when the latest communique indicated that the ceremony to resurrect the reverend Kellie would commence.

Obviously concerned about the pressing nature of our predicament, I went on, *"May I suggest that we get our heads together and work out what our realistic options are? Perhaps they are broader than Sgàthach indicates?"* Moving my hand from Aoife's and holding the letter up, I then provided my thoughts on possible ways forward.

"She appears to assume here that I have been to 1889 and for whatever reason have failed to get hold of and destroy the ancient book. If you remember, in her first correspondence she made it clear that a Fiosaiche can only travel back to any particular time juncture or event once and not multiple times, such as to try and any rectify mistakes made. However, as you now know, I have never yet travelled to 1889 and the auction – this being the case, then I must surely still be able to do so, and hence, execute the original plan? This is perhaps a better option than, with the clock ticking, seeking to track down a ceremony taking place goodness knows where, and with no opportunity to prepare for whatever danger that we might face if we actually got there in time? ... What do you think?"

Aoife, however, did not appear convinced, *"Well, my thinking is that travel to the Bannerman & Goudelock event is out of the question now Cameron, not least that you are no longer in possession of the auction program - you would, of course, require that, or something very similar, in order to traverse to the exact destination epoch of Edinburgh, 28th February 1889. How would we get hold of another appropriate 'object' in the next hour or so, as that is the timeframe we have to work to?"*

She continued, *"My firm's client has, of course, firmly indicated in her writing that after the resurrection ceremony has concluded it would be too late, even for a Fiosaiche such as yourself, to stop the malevolence that would be unleashed. So, any travel back to 1889 and destruction of the ancient book would have to be before the reverend Kellie were brought back from the dead - after that event, the dark magic or the time continuum would somehow prevent you from success in any such mission."*

"Well, that is true, Aoife, she did say that, and, yes, the ceremony is due to commence very soon, in just a couple of hours or so. However, could we not avoid such problems if I were to traverse back to earlier last week, perhaps to the Tuesday at noon when you first knocked at my door? When the door is unanswered by the earlier version of me, I would accidentally-on purpose bump into you a few houses down Straiton Place as you walked away – simply saying to you that I had been on my way home. Then, after a discussion between us along the lines of that at the Espy, I would take possession of the letter and auction program as per your client instruction. I'm pretty sure that a free newspaper had been delivered to my house that morning which I'd put in the recycling bin shortly after picking up your business card which you'd posted through my letterbox - it will still be there as, of course, I haven't yet had a chance to put the recycling out for collection - so possibly I could use that as the necessary 'object' to reach the destination epoch of last Tuesday? Once I was in possession of the Bannerman & Goudelock program, I would then be able resume my original intended assignment and journey through time to the event in 1889, would I not?"

Reflecting upon the layered and crazy complexity of that plan, including the risk of my coming into contact with my former self - something that Sgàthach had advised against in reference to the 'second limitation' - I added, *"Or, alternatively, we simply call the police now and advise them of the upcoming ceremony and the danger it presents? That it must be stopped."*

Putting my palms to my temples despairingly, I then stuttered, *"... Jeez, it is all so mind bending,"* contemplating how my life had become such a tangled web in the space of a few days. The fact that I was not now even questioning the bizarre content of Sgàthach's claims - including the bringing back from the dead of an executed murderer and former Kirk minister from the 16th century - was ample testament to that!

Looking a little exasperated, Aoife responded, *"The police Cameron... oh, come on ... they would think you were completely crazy, and you would likely get admitted to a psychiatric institution! And, as for your idea of going back to Tuesday just gone to take possession of the auction program from me, and then use it to travel back to the 19th century event, would that really work? It seems awfully complicated and a long shot. What if we spent the next hour or so making our way back to St Anthony's Chapel, only to find out that you were unable to time-traverse - just as you have experienced before? We really can't afford to waste the short period between now and the ceremony commencing, can we? I honestly think that any effort to travel back in time now is just too risky.*

Looking anxiously at her watch, the lady lawyer added, *"The only credible option for us now is surely to follow the instructions Sgàthach lays out in her letter? And that we find the location of the ceremony and get there fast!"*

"Ok... ok," I readily conceded, concluding that she was talking far better sense than I was (something that any woman in my life was prone to do). After once again checking the clock on the wall and seeing that it was now dead on 2.30 pm, I proceeded to offer some further thoughts:

"By my reckoning sunset is currently around 4.30 pm, maybe shortly after. That gives us just a couple of hours Aoife. The big question, of course, is where the ceremony is to be held? Realistically, with the extremely short

period that we have, we must guess right first time. If we were to travel to the wrong location, it would simply be too late to go elsewhere. So, rather than immediately dashing off, may I suggest that we take a few moments to carefully consider and agree on what the most likely place is?"

My guest nodded in response.

Trying to keep my composure, I continued, *"Ok, and as soon as we decide upon the location, we will go straight there - tactics, in relation to how stop the reappearance of Kellie and destroy the manuscript, we will just have to discuss en route."*

After pausing for a moment, with real concern, I added, *"But I am anxious that we will face danger. The Order are surely not going to give up their revered text willingly. Perhaps best that you allow me to attempt this task alone? You are a solicitor, supporting me as part of a client assignment. Your commitment so far has already been well above and beyond the call of duty. You really must not compromise your safety by going to the ceremony. I certainly wouldn't want that. This is my problem to sort out, not yours."*

She was having none of it though, *"No, no Cameron. I will be with you every step of the way on this. This is my problem as much as yours. This situation is beyond my legal job and representation of a client - it is, of course, far greater and graver than that, we both know it. Like you, I truly believe the contents of these letters from my firm's safe. There is a vital job to do, and I will be there to support you in carrying it out. There is no stopping me!"*

Both of us clearly trying not to panic and to maintain a modicum of level-headedness, we then proceeded to consider the respective likelihoods of resurrection ceremony locations. Needless to say, as part, taking into account Sgàthach's speculative suggestions and points to consider.

Spenton village, either the Kirk or its Manse, we were aware had a proven association with Kellie. A quick internet search on Aoife's phone, however, indicated that in the 19th century Spenton Manse had been burnt down in an unexplained fire. It was now the site of some local authority housing; the present minister of the local parish apparently being housed in a Kirk owned property in the town of Dunpender close-by. Although, on a more positive note, the Kirk building itself, reputedly of at least of the 14th century in origin, appeared to be still standing, and in fact, in continued congregational use.

I mooted to my legal confidant that the gentlemen's group may have the erstwhile churchman's ashes in a casket stored at a secret location, or even in their Gillane mansion, and may bring them to the Kirk building or Kirkyard for performance of the ceremony as dusk was reached? Aoife, however, surmised that perhaps the remains were already at the Kirk, having been covertly stored there since the 16th century, or even secretly buried within the Kirkyard? In response, I expressed my doubts that the ashes would be buried in such place as presumably that would be hallowed ground and any admirer of Kellie would have seen it as an inappropriate location for interment of the remains of the avowed occultist who had turned his back on God. At the same time, we both also questioned the lack of privacy of these places within the heart of the small community of Spenton village, in terms of the hosting of the required ceremony.

Privacy, however, was not something that Gillane Manse would lack, we supposed. But, to our knowledge the property did not have any particular and direct link with Kellie, other than a gaudy statue outside its entrance. A link was something that Sgàthach had alluded may be material, albeit not necessarily essential. Further, there was the extensive security at the property to consider - CCTV cameras, gates and high fences etc. that I had encountered when visiting the mansion to give my talk; I briefly outlined this context to my guest. We agreed that we had no time for such obstacles.

Then, in addition to considering the most likely locations, we each came up with a wild card suggestion. For me, it was vaults at the ruin of Yester Castle. I quickly explained that this had been the 13th century home of the reputed necromancer Hugo de Giffard. That, as the story went, further to a pact with the devil he had raised a magical army of goblins who built him the original keep with special underground vaults, known as the 'Goblin Ha' and where he reputedly practiced his dark arts. Although the castle was in a ruinous state, the gothic-style vaults supposedly remained to this day pretty much intact. Surely, Kellie would have been aware of this place of the occult, perhaps less than 12 miles from his Kirk? The reverend and de Giffard had certainly been kindred spirits, that was for sure. de Giffard may well have been one of the Fiosaichean - I knew that from research for my book and had even mentioned it at my talk at Gillane. Perhaps he had provided Kellie the 'dark spiritual guidance' to which Sgàthach had referred, allowing him to create his reputed key to the ancient book's cryptic Ogham text? I ventured.

Aoife's wildcard suggestion - of which I was not entirely sure that she was being serious, although clearly there was no time for joking - was the "*Brothels of the Edinburgh's old town*". I asked her if she was aware from her work colleagues whether such places were still in existence in that part of town? … before adding in all seriousness, "*If anyone would know, it would surely be Edinburgh's legal fraternity*." Although, it was common knowledge in the city that the nearby 'pubic triangle' of the West Port continued to house a few. Kellie had indeed been a keen and frequent visitor to such establishments it would seem, at least according to the writing of Gilfeather & McLean's unusual client - so fair enough, there was a link there.

Both of us keenly aware that the precious minutes were fast passing, we knew that we could not afford to spend further time pondering. Quickly balancing the pros and cons of our thoughts and suggestions we reached a decision - it would be Spenton Kirk or bust!

Without further ado, we headed off once more from the front door of my wee bungalow on Straiton Place. Firing up Syd, we were determined to get to the old Kirk before the sunset. What we would do once we got there, was an altogether different matter.

CHAPTER 21

Guising

Needless to damn well say, on leaving Porty for Spenton, I noticed that the thirsty beast needed re-fueling, Syd's vintage needle-dial hovering just above the red zone. There was no way we would make it to Spenton without a stop for petrol. I had a bad habit of part-filling the tank up when putting petrol in, perhaps trying to fool myself that the vehicle was not as costly as it actually was to run. Of course, this ignored the fact and necessity of more frequent trips to the filling station. On this particular occasion, with the minutes ticking away on Syd's retro clock, I cursed myself for this daft self-delusion. More precious minutes were eaten up at the garage on Porty High Street just when we could least afford it.

Syd eventually reached the Dunpender roundabout on the A1 around 4.15 pm - Aoife calling out a time-check. At the same time, she had been looking for directions to Spenton as we did not know the exact location of the village, only that it was close to there. Strangely, google maps did not reference the place at all - much to her frustration as she had tried to find the route with that app on her phone. But thankfully, the lady lawyer then located an old, worn road atlas in the glove compartment - alongside the outmoded tape cassettes, another article left by the nonagenarian who had sold me the car - which was marked with a church symbol and 'Spen-ton'. Hence, we took the turn-off in that direction as per the dog-eared map and up a twisty, rural road at the eastern edge of the rather remote Lammermuir hills. I knew that I was pushing Syd too hard and fast for such a thoroughfare, and for an automobilac crooner of its vintage. As such, we could not help crossing the white lines in the middle of the road when taking the corners; at the same time, the engine over-heat indicator light on the dashboard started to flicker orange intermittently. Aoife's heart was clearly in her mouth, as was my own, as a white builder's van came careering towards us in the opposite direction, speeding considerably itself. The vehicles whooshed past each other, with only inches in between! It did not help that the daylight was now fading fast. My resolve to stop the reincarnation of Kellie and seize the manuscript steadying my own nerves to some extent. Not long after my co-pilot, glasses on and road atlas up at her nose, barked at me to take a rather inconspicuous and unsignposted 'B' (or perhaps more aptly, 'C') road on the left. I promptly swung our hulk of a car into it, chewing up half the grass verge on the corner in the process, and we progressed towards a hill.

In order to get the auld fella up what was a steep incline, I had to floor my right foot. Syd juddered as if possessing a sense of reluctance and foreboding at reaching the ultimate destination. Just before the top of the hill, a small road sign came into view - as we closed in on it I could see that it marked 'Spenton'. I felt relief that we had, at least, found the place. After a sharp turn, it was not far before the old Kirk became visible on the right, after a section of quaint Dutch pantile-roofed cottages. Aoife clutched her seat belt with both hands and jerked forward as I brought us to an abrupt halt at the pavement adjacent to the Kirkyard entrance gate.

Spenton's elevated position on the periphery of the Lammermuirs meant that it took the full force of the squalls coming in from the east over the Forth and North Sea. That certainly was the case that afternoon, with the car door being snapped back shut by one such burst just after I had managed to force myself out against the wind resistance. On the pavement, Aoife's fine mane of brunette hair was being tossed around as if she had a 3000-watt turbo hairdryer directed at it. Despite the conditions, I could see further up the pavement and past the Kirk, a mother with her two children, dressed in Halloween costumes, knocking at a door, presumably, out guising, or rather, 'trick or treating' as they seemed to call it these days.

The Kirkyard had heavy gates which took some force to push apart, making a metal upon metal squeal as I did so. Directly inside and on the left, I could see a low roofed, little cottage building. I was aware that such structures had generally been built for the watchmen of old to prevent bodysnatching and the desecration of graves. At the side of my vision, I thought that I caught a glimpse of a dark figure furtively looking out at us from a rectangular sash-barred window at the side of the wee structure. Not wanting to alarm my companion, I chose to ignore this, and we promptly progressed down a lightly graveled path to the old Kirk building itself. A glimmer of dim light emanated from inside via two rectangular, arched windows at the side of the church just before the entrance porch, the shape and positioning of which made me think of a couple of coffins, sat side by side.

As we neared the Kirk entrance - a small side porch additional to the main building - Aoife suddenly stopped, putting out her hand out in a bid for me do the same, and asked, "*Can you hear that?*"

Heeding her, I halted and listened intently. Between the gusts of wind, I could make out the thrash of heavily distorted, low-pitched electric guitars, along with a thudding, fast tempo rapple of drumbeats. This was accompanied by an intermittent tinny bash of cymbals and growling vocals, the words of which themselves were inaudible.

"*Some sort of punky band playing... Pretty shite, eh,*" I replied, adding, "*Local school band practice perhaps?*"

"*Hmm, I don't think so. If I'm not mistaken, it's 'Celtic Frost', a Swiss Death Metal band,*" she corrected.

"*I didn't take you for a fan of such musical genre,*" I put forward, giving her a quizzical look.

"*There is lots you don't know about me Mr Guthrie,*" responded my companion with a correspondingly enigmatic smile. It was admirable that she could muster some humour in the tense circumstances, I reflected.

At the entrance porch itself, I noticed that to the side of the black, weathered wooden door, hung a metal hoop on a chain embedded into the rust-stained stone of the wall. I recognised this from my book research as being a set of 'jougs' - the hoop was in fact a collar fastened around the neck as a bygone means of punishment and humiliation for alleged breach by an offender of the Kirk's strict rules. Sometimes also used to detain the poor souls accused of witchcraft by the Kirk's payment-by-results 'witchfinder', pending their 'trial', conviction and, in most cases, the fate of being burned alive. I shuddered at the sight of it.

As I turned the handle to the door, the music coming from inside suddenly stopped. It was then silent, other than the howl from the wind. The door creaked ajar, but even as I exerted quite a bit of pressure, it would not fully open. However, there was just sufficient room for Aoife and I to edge through and make our way inside.

Setting foot on the ancient flagstones of the porch, I jerked with a start as the music abruptly recommenced, calling out from the main Kirk Hall. The tone however, had changed from the fast, thrashing beat of moments previously. Rather, it was the tinging of a high-pitched bell alongside a slow, pained chanting. This increased in intensity, leading to what sounded like heavy breathing. It did nothing to lighten the atmosphere. My lawyer and muso friend whispered in my ear, "*It's 'Danse Macabre.'*"

As we trod slowly and warily towards a glass and wood partition door to the main hall, further chanting came towards us in waves along with wolf-like howls and distorted wails and moans. It was a rather disturbing cocktail of sound, rather than music.

With my heartbeat quickening along with my rate of breathing, I slowly eased the partition doors apart to allow a gap to peer through, although I was fearful at the scene that we might meet.

However, the hall appeared to be empty.

Creeping in cautiously to investigate further, we passed a number of wooden box-pews. The place did indeed appear to be deserted, that is apart from a circle of white church candles on the floor up near a raised area pulpit area. Lit and burning, the tops of them glowed with little tulip bulbs of yellow-orange flickering light. At the same time, their paraffin wax and smoky odour hung in the air.

As we got closer, I could see that a section of carpet immediately in front of that area had been pulled back. Etched in the stone slab floor underneath was a five-pointed star, surrounded by a circle - I immediately recognised this from my research as an inverted pentagram beloved of occultists and often thought to represent the descent of spirit into matter. The candles were positioned on the stone at each of the five points. Within the triangles beneath each were engraved figures. From what I could make out, they included in one, a ram-headed being, and in another, a winged creature of some sort. The dark and bizarre musical accompaniment of other-worldly keening provided a fitting backdrop to this unnerving sight.

My focus, however, had moved to the centre of the pentagram. A shingle of fear ran down my spine as I observed, lying there in a wee pool of blood, what appeared to be a small, very small, severed human hand, albeit of a strange shape. A child's or small adult's hand, I thought, then, no ... I recognised that it was the hand of a baby! Furthermore, the fingers and bones must have been broken as it had been arranged to mirror, geometrically, the five points of the satanic symbol.

My attention was promptly taken away from this dreadful sight, however, as despite the eerie background music, to the right and from the pulpit, I could hear a light, "*bump, bump, bump.*"

Aoife then shrieked from behind me, "*JESUS... OH JESUS,*" gripping the material at the back of my jacket as she did, as I realised something was rolling down the curved wooden steps which led from the elevated section of the pulpit. The object responsible for the sound arrived, as if deliberately, directly at my feet. Instinctively, I took a couple of steps backward.

At first, I thought it were some sort of ball, then ... the plastic head of a child's doll? In an instant, however, I had the horrific realisation that what we were witnessing was the severed head of an infant. Yes, that of a wee baby! Gentle tufts of light ginger-blonde hair atop and with sad, sad eyes, clear blue, but lifeless and fixed towards us.

"FOR FUCK'S SAKE, EVIL BASTARDS... DOING THAT TO A LOVELY WEE BAIRN," I barked out in sickened anguish, my pounding heart nearly rupturing my chest.

Getting myself together as best I could, I bounded up the wooden steps of the pulpit to see whom or what had set the severed head in rolling motion. The enclosed platform, however, was empty.

In the terrifying circumstances Aoife seemed to be doing a better job at keeping it together than I was. With a shaky but controlled voice she suggested that we check each of the box-pews. We did so, looking within and under each, as well as inside a small anteroom to the main hall. There was not a living soul to be seen.

Just as we completed this search, another high-tempo death-metal track sprang into action. Above the din my lawyer friend shouted over to me, *"IT'S COMING FROM THERE"* nodding and indicating to an old, bulky amplifier on a stand to the left-hand side of the pulpit. A moment later, to my surprise, she launched a rather ferocious kung fu style kick at it - sending it crashing over and smashing to the floor. It was a kick that Eric Cantona would have been proud of.

Not standard solicitor etiquette and conduct I considered, especially from the hitherto fairly demure attorney-at-law. Although, I was grateful that she had managed to mercifully cease that hellish and unholy racket. Aoife was not all that she seemed, I was realising - and certainly a lot more than she generally chose to portray.

With the sudden quiet I ventured to her, "*It would seem that steps are presently well in motion. That the ceremony has already started and has moved on to another location to resume and complete… Exactly where though… any thoughts?*"

She nodded and replied, "*Yes, absolutely. How about the Manse at Gillane? There is certainly no point in us hanging around here any further.*"

"*I would also guess Gillane, just as Sgàthach had speculated … but if that is the case, then I fear we are already too late Aoife, the ceremony being underway, never mind the challenge of our gaining access with its high security, which will have no doubt been ramped up considerably for this evening's proceedings,*" I responded gloomily.

"*Well, unless either of us have a better idea, it's got to be worth a try?*" she responded bluntly, putting things in perspective.

"*For sure, yes. Let's get Syd moving then!*" I swiftly concurred.

As we made to leave the Kirk, despite our haste, I could not help but notice a small poster, or rather flyer, pinned to the 'Church Events' board in the entrance vestibule. It caught my eye as in large, bold letters printed at the top, it stated, '*Samhuinn Festival Bonfire*'.

Whilst researching for my book I had read about Samhuinn. An ancient Celtic religious festival, it marked the battle between the Kings of Summer and Winter, overseen by a fabled 'wizened and veiled old woman' with divine powers, the *'Cailleach'* - the Queen of Winter. It celebrated, with the lighting of bonfires, the transition from summer to winter in the Celtic solar-lunar calendar. Integral to this, was a belief was that those who had died were able to return on this day to walk, once again, amongst the living.

Ripping the leaflet off the Board, I held it up for closer inspection.

'SAMHUINN FESTIVAL BONFIRE

TO ALL SPENTON VILLAGERS

JOIN US, YIN AN' AW

ON NOVEMBER 1ST, AT COMMENCEMENT OF THE DAY

BY THE 'WITCHES' STANE', SPENTON VILLAGE

COME TO CELEBRATE WITH YOUR BROTHERS AND SISTERS

& A VERY SPECIAL GUEST WILL BE ARRIVING TO JOIN US'

This text was accompanied underneath with the representation of a veiled, old woman, with the classic fairy tale witch-like features of hook noose and protruding, wart covered chin.

"*Bingo… this is where they are now … it has got to be!*" I exclaimed in some excitement, holding the leaflet up for my companion to read.

However, looking perplexed and a bit frustrated with me, she replied pointing her finger at the date marked on the flyer, *"But, Cameron, it says the Bonfire Festival is being held tomorrow, NOT today, and in the morning. Odd to be having a bonfire festival in the morning if you ask me, but, in any case, this event must be a red herring. Sgàthach, as you know, said that after 31st October it was too late. We can't risk second guessing that. The ceremony we need to get to, is clearly already underway."*

"Ah… but in the Celtic calendar the commencement of the new day is when the sun sets Aoife," I responded trying not to come across as a bumptious 'mansplainer' before continuing, *"This means that it is already November 1st - not in our Gregorian calendar where that new day is not reached until passed midnight, but in the Celtic calendar. I am guessing that it got dark around 30 to 40 minutes ago, so the Samhuinn Festival Bonfire - the 'ceremony' that we need to locate - has presumably not long started, or at least has recommenced since moving on from the Kirk … and it is taking place here, in Spenton! Clearly, Sgàthach had been referring throughout to our calendar, the Gregorian rather than the Celtic one. Remember what she said: that the resurrection of the reverend Kellie is only finally achieved when the ceremonial incantation from the manuscript is fully read and, hence, the spell complete - and that that might take an hour or perhaps longer. We still have time Aoife."*

At this she nodded in recognition and agreement. Wasting no further moments, we hurriedly exited the Kirkyard. Once outside and on the pavement, I could not help but see to my right, in the distance and in direction of the far end of the village, flickering lights as if from a bonfire. At the same time, coming from that direction, carried upon the bursts of wind, were the intermittent sounds of chanting and cheering. Clearly, this was where we needed to be.

Suggesting to Aoife that we best go on foot rather than in the car, so as to better avoid alerting of our arrival, we jogged towards the lights and sound. As we progressed closer, we could see a few late-comers making their way to the billed event - parents with kids in Halloween dress, a couple of whom were carrying lit sparklers and another, a spinning windmill toy with lights flashing round so fast that the different colours merged. We slowed down do a walking pace, not to draw attention to ourselves. It was definitely the ceremonial event that we were heading towards.

A smell of burning wood was apparent in the air, as was a ruddy-orange glow, which grew brighter as we progressed and eventually reached its location. It was situated in a grassy field at the back of road. Just before the open entrance gate, however, there was a small, fenced enclosure at the side of the thoroughfare. This appeared to contain a stone of around half a meter each-way in diameter. I recalled from my book research that Spenton village had contained such an object to mark the vicinity on which supposed 'witches' had been burned to death, and in particular the last such unfortunate soul at the end of the 17th century.

We progressed through the gate and into the field which was on a slight uphill gradient. Towards the upper end was the bonfire, towering at something like ten meters high and shaped like a wigwam. It was burning like an inferno, most likely aided by the breezy conditions. Further down the slope and a fair bit in advance of the glowing pyre, were a group of spectators in attendance at the 'festival' event, perhaps as many as 100 or so. Deliberately trailing behind the late arrivals, we joined the back of the group, doing our best to remain inconspicuous.

Between the on-lookers and the bonfire, standing in a semi-circle, were a troop of about a dozen robed figures, their backs to the fiery mass and facing towards the assembled crowd. I assumed that they were key Noble Order of Eidyn members, the Elders. We were close enough to observe that the two figures in the centre, unlike the others, had a number of golden tassels hanging from their cloaks, swaying in the wind like pendulums. One of these central individuals, short in height, and with a rotund figure detectable despite his billowing dark robe, sported what appeared to be a ram's head over his own. This resembled the taxi-dermied one which I had seen hanging in the hall on my visit to Gillane Manse, complete with circular twisting horns jutting out from each side at the top. The other tasseled figure, taller, had his hood pulled-up in similarity to the remainder of his associates. Hence, I was unable to see the faces of any of those standing in the semi-circle. After my recent visit to the Order's ostentatious premises, however, it was not difficult to conclude that the two tasseled central figures were almost certainly those of Alister Forbes-Fleming and Farquhar Sutherland, respectively.

The former appeared to be holding a large, weighty tome. My heart truly missed a beat on seeing this as I suspected that this may well be - in fact, it was highly likely to be - THE ancient book, THE *Facal an Fiosaiche*! Was I really so close to it?... the fabled and mysterious artefact that was the root of my life being thrown into chaos in recent days, and which would create far more significant disarray and damage should I not be able to get my hands upon and destroy it. Such catastrophic impact to be levelled not just on me, of course, but all of humanity and the planet, if Sgàthach were to be believed (and after what I had experienced in recent days, I was certainly now a true believer).

At the same time, I realised that although I might be positioned close to it (assuming it were the genuine article), I was still a long way from being able to take possession of it, not least that it was accompanied by a troop of cloaked protectors. Looking like he was struggling to hold the substantial tome up, the likely Forbes-Fleming figure was reading out short passages from its pages, presumably peering out from eye holes fashioned in the ram's head in order to do so. However, he did so in a strange tongue which, linguistically and phonetically, sounded a little bit like Scot's or Irish Gaelic, although at the same time, was quite different. This must be an articulation of the ancient Ogham of the manuscript, I concluded, or at least the bits that the Order had hitherto been able to decipher.

An open area of ground, perhaps 10 to 15 metres in area lay between the semi-circle of cloaked and hooded Elders and the throng of spectators. The latter appeared like they were the mums, dads, kids and grandparents of Spenton village, including those stragglers that we had seen on the way. After all, the flyer on the Kirk entrance vestibule noticeboard had advertised the event as a community gathering for, 'Yin an' Aw'.

I wondered for a moment, were the villagers actually part and parcel of the ceremony and the evil spell that was in the process of being invoked? Perhaps a community exclusively of Noble Order of Eidyn members and their kin, the brotherhood's 'great and good' and their families? Or, had these individuals simply been duped into thinking this was all a bit of amateur theatrics and a spooky Halloween spectacle - fun for all the family in front of the warming cheer of a bonfire? I really did not know which, but I was certainly suspicious that the former may be the reality. In any case, Halloween (or the commencement of Samhuinn in the Celtic calendar) had clearly provided the Order the perfect cover for their ceremony.

Indeed, my suspicions were soon proved correct, as after Forbes-Fleming had read a passage in the strange vernacular (his strident tone audible despite the ram's head-dress and blustery conditions), a particular word was thereupon repeated like a chant - done so communally by each and everyone in the mass of on-lookers (including even the children), in addition to the Order Elders. To my ears, it sounded like, "*Atigenus... atigenus...*" Further, at certain points in the reading cheers erupted from the gathered ensemble. Presumably, those assembled had an understanding of certain passages of the ancient book, including incantations being read by Forbes-Fleming, I concluded. And they seemed to be enjoying the spectacle, with beaming faces all round, some looking rather manic in expression. Yes, these were no ordinary villagers, and Spenton was no ordinary village. It was then that I recognised some of those smiling faces from the attendees at my talk at Gillane Manse. I reflected upon how Aoife and I had been on the verge of discounting Spenton as a venue for the ceremony in favour of Gillane as we had believed the village lacked privacy. Yet, it was clear to see that privacy was not an issue for the Order in Spenton, not only was it a community set within the remote reaches of the Lammermuirs and somehow absent from modern mapping technology, but it was one that appeared to be inhabited solely by the 'gentlemen's' group members and their families.

Standing together at the back of the crowd, clearly anxious, Aoife clasped her hand tightly upon mine. Looking round at her in an effort to reassure, I could not quite manage a smile. My own mind was racing, and I could feel a cold sweat upon my back along with a growing sense of fear and dread. What was I to do in the next few precious minutes (as surely that was all there was) in order to get hold of the manuscript and destroy it? I was really at a loss. We had talked over a few possibilities in the rather frantic car journey to the village, however, they were really no more than articulations of wishful thinking that an opportunity should arise where I could grab the unholy book and we could then make off. Now, in the distinct reality of the ceremony and situation, such a chance seemed highly unlikely to arise. I surmised that we would definitely be apprehended if we made a wrong move; we could even end up murdered - in fact, that was more than likely judging by the Order's track record as indicated by Sgàthach. Shuddering at this thought, I reflected that I should never have allowed Aoife to join me here. So far, at least, with the dark and distractions, no one had noticed us as interlopers.

Just then the loudest cheer of all erupted, followed by the wild chanting of "ATIGENUS... ATIGENUS..." Children were jumping up and down in excitement. The adults present were holding arms aloft, clapping and praising whilst they chanted. It was a fervour akin to religious zeal.

A wave of horror then engulfed me as I suddenly understood what had prompted this animated reaction from the gathered mass. The Sutherland figure had stepped forward a couple of paces from the centre of the semi-circle of Elders and was holding out, at arms' length, the lifeless and headless body of a small, naked baby. He had the poor, dead wee soul by the feet and was swinging their remains slowly in circles around a particular patch of the ground between the group of senior Order members and the onlooking collective. I immediately recalled the equally horrific sight of the wee ginger, tuft-haired severed head of a bairn, looking up at Aoife and I from the stone floor of the Kirk with sad lifeless eyes.

As Sutherland oscillated the infant in a ritualistic manner, blood was dripping from the neck stump, as well as one wrist where the hand was missing, and onto the turf below. At the same time, Forbes-Fleming focused upon the text of the manuscript, continuing his rhythmic incantations. All of a sudden, with casual disregard, Sutherland flung the baby's limp, decapitated corpse straight into the centre of the inferno. More fervent cheers were prompted as a queer sizzling noise emanated from the flames, a sound that I immediately wished that I could un-hear. Then, the tassel robed Paterial Secretary to the Order bent his lengthy frame down, reached into a container and pulled out what appeared to be a piece of meat, perhaps about the size of an orange. No ordinary 'meat', rather I guessed that it was a human organ of some sort. With both hands he squeezed blood from it as if he were seeking to dispense water from a sponge; I guessed it were a heart due to the considerable flow that was discharged. Sutherland did so upon the same patch of turf as before. When the flow and dripping of the dark, ruddy sangre began to exhaust, he shook the organ vigorously, before again disposing of it into the fire, which once more hissed as if it were grateful to receive. Further enthusiastic cheers erupted.

Next, Sutherland proceeded to take out what looked like a small glass vial from a pocket deep within his robe. Removing a cap on the top, he jabbed it downwards repeatedly over the specific area of ground. He did so like he was a Catholic Priest at requiem mass dispensing holy water over a coffin for the soul of the dead or, perhaps as if he were performing a baptism. Under the glow of the bonfire, as he did so, I could see drops of liquid spit out from a nozzle on the small receptacle, hitting the turf below. Strangely, as the droplets reached the surface, they appeared to morph into puffs of smoke or vapour.

It was then that the crazy chanting seemed to reach a climax as the grass and earth upon the patch of ground which Sutherland had been tending to, inexplicably began to move! At first it was like calm water that had been disturbed, the surface undulating somewhat. Then, in several places, tiny eruptions occurred where the soil from underneath the grass appeared to be breaking through and twisting out like muddy worms, as if it were being squeezed out from small tubes beneath.

Exchanging glances with a wide-eyed Aoife, it was clear that our fear was equally manifest and intense.

Following the mud emissions, I gasped in horror to witness the appearance of what looked like the tips of pale-coloured fingers poking through the earth!

Then full fingers ... a hand.... and a second hand. They were grasping and pulling at the soil and turf around, as if they were desperately seeking an escape from under broken ice in a frozen pond with the life of their host dependent upon it. The earth was rupturing as a human form and figure slowly began to emerge - a bent arm at one side of a developing hole, then another... a growing hole... a foot, a bowed leg. The creature manifesting was grabbing, hauling, pushing and crawling in an effort to surface, like a spider breaking out from their web-covered lair.

Here was the reverend John Kellie, I could only surmise, arising from where the casket of his ashes must have been buried over 450 years previously subsequent to his execution and cremation. Whoever had interred his remains all these years ago must have thought the site of countless 'witch' burnings had been a most appropriate and comfortable resting place for the occultist and murderer who had pledged his allegiance to Satan. As he continued to emerge, the crowd reached an even greater frenzied crescendo, including the robed Order Elders. That was apart from Forbes-Fleming who was studiously and diligently continuing to read, in the strange tongue, from the ancient manuscript. The incantation was indeed bringing the malevolent preacher man back from the dead and presumably for eternity!

It was then that my impulses took over, realising that the window of opportunity to do something was fast closing, and I made a dash towards the Grand Pater. With the crowd along with the cloaked senior Order members obviously distracted, I thought that with surprise there was then a chance - albeit a slim one - to topple him, with his over-indulged portly frame, into the flames, along with the manuscript to which he gripped tightly as if it were part of him. Thereby, with success, ceasing the resurrection of the hideous clergyman and destroying the ancient book of dark magic at the same time.

But just as I rounded the preoccupied spectators towards the centre of semi-circle of Order high-heid yins, I realised that I had been rumbled. One of the Elders must have spotted me as he promptly broke from the periphery of group and came charging towards me fast, launching into a robust and effective rugby tackle - no doubt the ability having been developed on the playing fields of an expensive Edinburgh private school. It forcefully chopped me to the ground. Thereupon, with the momentum, I slid along the damp grass, the arms of the tackler still hugging tightly to my legs. Coming to a halt at the border of the hole in the turf which had been opening up, I focused my eyes forward at ground level, trying to regain an element of composure. To my horror they were met with the piercing dark apertures of the reverend John Kellie just as his dirt encrusted head emerged from the muddied depths! This prompted a chill to the very marrow of my bones. In such close proximity, I was confronted by a vile odour emanating from his person, like steam from a recently deposited stool, that of rotting meat and death.

All of sudden, he seemed to effortlessly elevate from the opening in the turf; it was as if he were being pushed up to the surface by forces of the netherworld. As this happened, the hole from whence he had came miraculously closed over, the soil and mud which had discharged in its opening just melting away. Kellie's feet were then on terra firma.

Standing there, right in front of me, he looked every bit like the statue representation in front of the Gillane Manse, albeit not an inanimate golden object, rather, a living, breathing human being - or being of some sort - dressed in the full clergyman's attire of the 16th century. Clearly, he was a powerfully built man, with broad shoulders and over six foot tall. His dark, soulless eyes burning out of the angular features of his face - he was a truly menacing presence. A hush descended as the Order Elders and wider on-lookers gaped motionless in awe at the physical manifestation conjured up by the ungodly sorcery of the *Facal an Fiosaiche* - the reverend John Kellie re-born!

The resurrected clergyman proceeded to glare down upon me with a hateful disdain. Then turning to face Forbes-Fleming or perhaps even the manuscript itself, in the authoritative tones of a minister of the Kirk, he broke the stunned silence with, "*Thy swine requireth slaughter,"* whilst pointing a boney, grey finger towards me.

At this instruction, obedient Elders swiftly broke their inertia and moved into action. Shortly, I felt myself being dragged backwards and then lifted up by the arms and onto my unsteady feet.

"CAST HIM UNTO THE HELL FIRES," Kellie barked commandingly, gesturing to the bonfire.

The several robed Order members which were holding me, then obediently started to drag me towards the still raging inferno. I struggled against them, trying to dig my heels in to the ground in front of me, but it was of little use. The growing heat of the flames met me as I was pulled closer and closer; that was in stark contrast to my blood which had frozen over in terror.

Just then, over the grunts and groans of the men hauling me towards the flames, I could hear Aoife's voice, frantic and urging, *"Cameron, remember… remember that you are of the Fiosaichean… FIGHT THIS."*

As I was being manhandled, I managed to catch a glimpse of her and saw that she had also ran forward, breaking her erstwhile cover. Likewise, she was being detained, with the hands of several persons from the crowd upon her. It seemed certain that poor Aoife would soon suffer the same fate as allotted to me by the demon preacher.

Yet, her words prompted something to emerge from deep within me. And, as if reinforced by telepathy, I could then also hear Sgàthach urging me similarly and speaking as if she were standing right next to me, *"Have belief in your abilities Cameron…*

BELIEVE." I shut my eyes fully expecting any moment to feel the harsh burn of the fire and with unimaginable pain and agony, the melting away of my skin. However, from such prompting, I found the strength in that moment to collect my thoughts and focus. In my mind's eye I concentrated and reflected upon on those poor souls that had been victims of the Order over the many years since they had taken possession of the evil manuscript. Those lost souls … the lost souls… I searched for them…. I called out to them.

It was merely an instant before this searching and calling was answered. I started to sense their presence nearby, the ghosts of victims of past atrocities of the Order. There were quite a few already I felt sure, and more and more of them were manifesting. Amongst them, I also perceived as present at least one and perhaps more direct victims of the wicked preacher man himself.

Just at the moment I was about to be finally hurled into the flames of the pyre, suddenly it was like my feet were lodged in cement and that I was made of rigid steel. I opened my eyes and observed that despite the strength of the four or five men around and upon me, they were unable to shift me anymore, not even by an inch.

On witnessing this, the reverend, his gaunt face etched with impatience and frustration, roared angrily, "CAST HIM, I DEMAND OF YEEH, CAST HIM UNTO THE BLAZE."

The remaining robed Elders except for Sutherland and Forbes-Fleming, as well a number of those from the throng of villagers, joined in the effort to comply with his instruction and hurl me into the inferno. I felt hands and arms upon me everywhere - on my legs, arms, waist, neck, and head - but strangely I could not feel any real force from them whatsoever, rather that it were merely light touches. Yet, I could see that they were trying everything to lift me, to prize me from the spot on which I now appeared to be rooted, tugging, pulling and pushing, but they were simply unable to budge me.

As the same time, I could see Sutherland and Forbes-Fleming close by frantically scanning through the pages of the manuscript together, presumably to incant the final parts of the resurrection spell.

My sense of the presence of the departed, the desecrated, the murdered, became stronger and more powerful. Then their voices came to me, along with wider materialisation.

Firstly, that of 'Chloe', as she told me. Through the various hands and arms grappling upon me, I could make her out, perhaps ten meters away. She was walking into sight from the darkness and into the glow of the bonfire, a bonnie lassie of perhaps 12 or 13 years old. And, in her arms she lovingly cradled a baby, an angelic cherub of an infant, with wispy, light ginger hair and deep, sparkling blue eyes.

"*This is baby Mia. And I'm looking after her,*" Chloe informed me, smiling with pride.

At first, a haze of soft light surrounded them, as if gently caressing them. However, it then dissipated, as if it had opened its arms in order to set them down upon the mortal earth. At the same time, other ghostly forms were moving into sight from the shadows. There were men and women, old and young, as well as other children and infants. Yet, it was only me, so far, that appeared to register and acknowledge their presence.

The diabolical clergyman, presumably frustrated that the group of men had so far failed to throw me into the bonfire, bellowed at an even higher volume than before, *"YEE USELESS WRETCHES."* The group nervously glanced up at him with a mix of deference and fear, like hounds fearful of a cruel master's strike.

"I shall cast thee myself, progeny of a syphilitic Port o' Leith hoor!" Kellie uttered more quietly this time but with real menace, fixing the gaze of his dark eyes directly upon mine. He then started to attempt to move, for the first time, his formidable frame from the spot from which he had emerged from the muddy depths of below.

At that moment, however, a murmuring commenced within the throng of village spectators, panning out like a wave amongst the assembled group. This was promptly followed by a number of shrieks and screams. Children were crying and whimpering, clutching on to their parents. Throughout the crowd, eyes stared in terrified disbelief at the ghostly figures and shapes which were emerging from the darkness - clearly, the apparitions were now visible to all and not just myself.

The men who had been trying to cast me into the fire, promptly released their grips, as they too gaped in shock and horror at what was appearing from the black of the night, illuminated by the flickering amber light of the bonfire.

The ethereal figures, now numbering thirty, forty or more and growing by the second, were clothed in a variety of attire and dress reflecting, I presumed, the different ages and eras when their lives had been taken and cut short. The glow from the blaze revealed the marks of murder upon many of them, slit throats with blood still oozing, severed extremities and stumps, open wounds from scars and slashes upon faces, torsos, limbs and the like. A desire to exact revenge universally apparent within their eyes and written upon their faces. They had been wronged, they had been defiled, they had been cut open, they had been murdered, and more… - they were indeed, angry and vengeful spirits.

Despite his efforts, it was clear that the reverend was unable to progress more than a step from the spot from which he had surfaced. A panicked expression came over his grey face as he looked down at his feet to see that a muddy hand - part bone, part rotting skin - had risen up through the turf and was shackling itself upon one of his ankles with a vice-like grip.

I could hardly believe what I was witnessing. At the same time, from his increasing agitation, I could see that he was also cognisant that figures from the darkness were now approaching him.

This prompted Kellie to boom a commandment at Sutherland and Forbes-Fleming,

"INCANT FROM MY DIVINE BOOK, I BESEECH THEES. INVOKE ALL THAT IS REMAINETH EXTANT FOR MY RESURRECTION. DO IT YEES, DO IT NOW."

The pair, looking flustered and anxious, appeared to finally settle upon a particular page of the weighty tome which they were now holding between them. In unison, they hurriedly began to chant words in the peculiar and uncanny Ogham tongue.

But as they did so, eyeing the preacher man with incredulity, I could see that another hand, cut and bloodied, was emerging up from the ground and taking grasp of his other ankle.

Moments later, a further paw pushed out from under the turf and fastened its muddied, decaying fingers upon him; then another, following suit. Even in such sorry state of decomposition, I thought that they had the size and shape of women's hands. It was clear that they were not simply trying to stop the malign minister from moving, rather that they sought to pull him back into the abyss from which he had arisen. The reverend struggled, screaming out some words in the same strange tongue as his Order protectors who were continuing to desperately dictate from the unholy volume. Flailing his arms around and over his legs, Kellie was evidently trying to free himself from the grasping mitts upon him. However, I could see that it was to no avail - he was ever so slowly succumbing and being dragged downwards into a new hollow that was forming in the ground.

On witnessing the predicament of the being whom they held as inspiration for their brotherhood, Sutherland and Forbes-Fleming redoubled their efforts, chanting script from the ancient tome ever more frantically and loudly, whilst swaying back and forth like they were in a religious trance. It was clear that they believed the resurrection was very near to completion and that, when reached, their spiritual master would be safe from the deathly hands upon him along with any vengeful spirits that dared approach.

At this point, I could see once again the apparition, the soul which had announced herself to me as Chloe. She was closer to me still and a bloodied opening on her temple was visible with a fragment of skull bone jutting out. Very gently, she was releasing the infant Mia from her embrace and onto the grass at the side of her. From smiling lovingly at the bonny baby,

Chloe's expression changed mercurially to that of pure hatred as she fixed her eyes towards the Order Elders.

Suddenly, and at some speed, she ran charging towards the group of individuals still surrounding me. With all the athleticism of a skilled and talented dancer, launching herself at one of the robed figures and toppling him backwards like a skittle towards the bonfire. Although he somehow managed to avoid falling in, at the very edge of the inferno his lengthy cloak caught alight. The flammable velvet fabric was such that he was enveloped in a lick of flames in a matter of seconds. Screaming and wailing, he ran, arms flapping and moving like a Dervish, into the panicked crowd, which was now swiftly dispersing, terrified, in all directions.

Baby Mia would clearly not have been old enough to walk in her mortal body, however, in her ghostly spirit form she abruptly took to her chubby wee legs from the grass. As she did so, I noticed a bloodied scarring travelling the circumference of her delicate neck. She toddled towards Chloe, who reached down to take her tiny hand, the wrist of which had a similar marking. In silence, but with a look of grim determination upon their pale, spectral faces, they charged together towards Farquhar Sutherland like a phantom tag-team, at the same time shrieking in a high-pitched and unearthly manner.

On hearing this strange sound, the Paterial Secretary of the Order promptly ceased his chanting, looking up in clear terror as he witnessed the otherworldly duo racing in his direction. The lanky gent thereupon dropped his grasp upon the manuscript and reached within his robe, producing in an instant what I thought looked like a German WW2 pistol, a Luger perhaps, with a swastika insignia visible upon the base of the grip. Just as the two spirits were nearly upon him, he fired randomly at them, jabbing his gun as he did as if he were in a gunfight scene in an old Western movie. Of course, this was of no use whatsoever, the bullets simply whistling through Chloe and Mia's ethereal forms - he could do them no further harm. In a moment, the pair collided with the lanky gent with a superhuman force, sending him flying backwards with such momentum that he disappeared wailing right into the burning cone of the towering inferno. For a few moments, I could see his outline blindly thrashing and writhing as the searing heat incinerated his mortal frame, the bonfire crackling and spitting in the process.

At this point the other spirit figures which had emerged from the shadows, were likewise making for the robed Elders, some of whom were now desperately trying to flee, whilst others sought to stand their ground, like Sutherland had attempted pointlessly drawing side arms upon the specters. One such senior Order member was shooting repeatedly at the spirit figure of balding, middle-aged man in a sober grey suit. Visible on the lapel of the specter's suit jacket was a bronze badge which I recognised as displaying the logo of the Kirk of Scotland, a church building within cupped hands. The spirit's mouth hung open, gaping and bloodied, revealing the absence of an entire front row of teeth. Further, as his jacket flapped open in the wind, I could see a gory and gaping hole his chest, just left of the centre. Closing in upon the now frantic Elder, the suited apparition reached out towards him with hands that bore bloodied holes, like stigmata, within each.

Within a moment the aggrieved spirts descended like hungry wolves, grabbing the remaining cloaked 'gentlemen' and tossing each into the still raging fire, like logs being casually chucked upon a hearth - the flames lapping ever more vigorously upon welcome receipt. Just deserts were being served with relish - the Noble Order miscreants pitiful wails disappearing along with their flesh, evaporating in the flames.

Noticeably, the smoke emitting from the bonfire was now taking on a pungent, meaty quality and aroma akin to that of a barbeque or hog roast. My stomach churned.

There was still one robed figure left standing, however - Alister Forbes-Fleming. He had taken off the ram's head and seemed unable to chant anymore, his ruddy, puffed and sweating face quivering in fear. The *Facal an Fiosaiche* manuscript was now closed and drawn close to his chest, his arms wrapped tightly around it as if dear life depended on it. Perhaps it had somehow already saved him from the vengeful spirts, I considered. The Grand Pater of the Order was looking in horror and despair towards Kellie.

Now more than a third of the reverend's long frame had been pulled under the ground by the now forest of grasping hands of the dead upon him. I wondered whether these bloodied, rotting hands, many with flaps of part-burnt skin hanging off exposed finger bones, were of the souls of the burned 'witches' of Spenton, seeking retribution against a clergyman who, no doubt, had had a hand in the fate of many as he, along with Kirk 'witchfinder', sought to control the 16th century villagers with fear and terror.

The figure of a woman then appeared, floating in from the darkness. It settled directly in front of the diabolical preacher, head askew upon a broken neck. She held in her hands a rope with a noose at one end and then promptly began to manoeuvre it over Kellie's head.

"*Margaret, aye beg o' yeh… Wi can be the gither again,*" he pleaded at the specter of his murdered spouse, whilst desperately trying to prevent the loop of the rope from progressing further.

The pitiful begging, however, curried no favour with the apparition. She was now assisted by a second spirit which had materialised, that of a slight young man whose face seemed inverted with facial bones and features coming in on themselves. His brightly coloured trousers had what appeared to be a dark soaking of blood at the crotch. He sought to thwart the efforts of the clergyman to resist.

Without further ado, and despite his continued struggling, Margaret, with a strength not afforded to her in mortal life, then managed to force the noose right over her husband's head, roughly tightening it around the neck. The preacher's dark eyes burned in anger and perceived injustice. The spirit of his spouse then draped the other end of the rope down towards the hands of the dead that were upon him. Decaying fingers and palms eagerly reached out and tightened their grip upon it. Then, with a series of forceful tugs, I could see Kellie being bent double. Choking, he clawed with his bony fingers at the tight circle of jute around his neck, before his head, followed by the rest of his sorry being, disappeared in an instant down into the dark, muddy abyss. The sides of this void and channel to the netherworld thereupon slapping shut, like the surface waters of a still pond closing over directly after having been broken by the throw of a stone, the ground in a moment appearing undisturbed.

The stench of cremated Order Elders hung in the air as the last of the throng of villagers scurried away from the field in terror and fear for their lives. I could hear cottage doors being hurriedly opened, then slammed shut, with locks turning and bolts clunking.

It was time for me to complete my task, that which fate - Mother Earth - demanded of me. Moving towards Forbes-Fleming, he cowered like a cornered animal, the alcoholic rosacea of his cheeks appearing brighter than ever with the heat of the bonfire. Stepping backwards from me, he continued to tightly embrace the manuscript, seemingly both protective of it as well as wishing it to be his saviour.

"*Hand it over, NOW,*" I directed him firmly. However, perhaps unsurprisingly, it was evident that he was not going to do so voluntarily. Hence, without wasting a further moment, I grappled with the Grand Pater and roughly, but quite easily in the end, extricated the fabled tome from his defeated grasp and crumbled resolve. At this, he whimpered and cried like a child who had been dispossessed of a much-coveted toy.

On taking hold of the ancient tome in my hands, I experienced an immediate and quite extraordinary feeling. It was like it was fully aware that it was in a perilous situation, possibly close to destruction - that it had a consciousness in its own right as a sentient being - and was urging me to be its protector. The text was communicating with me, seemingly trying to bargain and negotiate for its safety. Its cover of rough hide, imprinted with various strange symbols, seemed to be reaching out to me, tempting me with all sorts of gifts and promised powers. At the same time, it was trying to convince me that it could be a positive force for the world if that were what I wanted of it. It was probing and calculating, seeking to sense my weak spot.

For a few moments I felt myself succumbing to its charms, thinking that if I kept it safe, saving it from the fate of the flames, I could indeed use it for the good of humanity. That, perhaps it could be employed as a tool to find cures for terminal illnesses, and to halt us frail and hapless human beings from destroying each other and the planet? That its positive uses could truly be infinite and for the benefit of personkind?

But the good intentions it plied me with, thinly veiled a deep malevolence within its very essence. Coming to my senses as if waking from a daydream, I recalled and recognized its true nature. It may be able to deceive others with promises and fools' gold, but not me - I was one of the Fiosaichean, just as Aoife's mysterious client had said in her correspondence. I saw it for what it was - a two-faced demon! Sgàthach's instructions had to be followed and without further ado lest it may find other means to attempt to halt and prohibit me, as it had strong powers of self-preservation, that was for sure. Thereupon, with some force, I cast the aged book directly into the core of the burning pile, now rejuvenated further to incineration of the robed 'gentlemen'. Its hide cover curled with the heat in an instant before fully igniting.

"NO, NO… YOU FOOL.… YOU FOOL," a horrified Forbes-Fleming bellowed in strangulated Edinburgh private school tones. He stumbled forward and reached into the inferno in a frantic effort to rescue the burning text from everlasting destruction. However, like the Order members before him, he quickly found that the luxuriant fabric of his tasseled robe was considerably combustible. The bumptious Grand Pater of the Noble Order of Eidyn was within seconds engulfed in flames himself. Tottering on his feet, his considerable girth then setting him rolling forward like a fireball and into the body of the furnace.

Despite this, and for a few seconds, he continued to reach out blindly and in desperation for the heinous book, until he writhed and convulsed for the final time. From what I could make out peering into the blaze as close as I could comfortably get, the *Facal an Fiosaiche* manuscript had disintegrated into burning embers, just inches from Forbes-Fleming's vanishing grasp.

Taking a couple of steps back from the fierce heat, I felt an overwhelming sense of relief.

Just then an arm gently reached around my waist. It was Aoife, smiling up at me with clear relief and admiration. Kissing me on the cheek, she simply said, "*You did it, Cameron... you did it.*"

Smiling back at her, my eyes welling up, I replied, "*We did it, Aoife, the both of us.*" Tears of relief then came, and we hugged and greeted for some moments.

As we released each other, I looked around. The spirit figures - the apparitions - which had avenged themselves against the atrocities of Order Elders and the wicked preacher, had faded away. That is all apart from Chloe, who stood towards the darkness. In the remaining glow of the bonfire, I could see that she once again held baby Mia lovingly in her arms. In turn, the infant, with her beautiful blue eyes, gazed upwards and adoringly at the young teenager. Before departing, Chloe looked towards me with a warm smile, then turned and disappeared with the bonny wee baby into the night. My sense was that both of them were now at peace.

CHAPTER 22

Work as if You Live in the Early Days of a Better Nation

S atisfied that the malevolent manuscript had been fully destroyed in the flames, Aoife and Cameron hurried back to
Syd. They thought it best not to hang about in Spenton
village any longer than necessary for fear of reprisal, not least
from the folks living there who appeared to have been allied to
the Noble Order.

On the drive home they did not say much to each other, rather
were equally dumbstruck by events. Of course, they had the
quiet satisfaction and tangible relief that the despicable book
had finally been destroyed and the resurrection of the reverend
John Kellie thwarted. At the same time, however, they were
acutely aware of how close they had come to failure and paying
the ultimate price with their lives.

Aoife tenderly placed her hand upon Cameron's as he slipped
Syd in and out of the necessary gears to traverse the winding
roads leading from the village back down to the A1. Before long
they were arriving back in Porty, without any discussion of
dropping the lady lawyer at her flat in advance. The retro clock
on the dashboard showing that it was approaching only 9 pm.
That, of course, was a very long time from when Cameron had

awoken at the Artisan hotel that morning, or rather the morning of Wednesday, 1st March 1989, contemplating the day ahead.

As he opened the front door to his bungalow, he was promptly greeted by Déjà, rubbing against his legs and then nearly tripping him up as he made his way to the kitchen. Of course, she was looking for food as per usual. Lifting her up to give her a wee clap, Cameron then placed the cat down by her bowl. Contented purring ensued soon after as he filled it with half the contents of a can of tuna.

It was a special occasion, that was for sure, so he fished out from the cupboard a bottle of very fine Chianti Classico, the 'gallo nero' logo proudly displayed upon its neck. This had been on special offer at the local offie a couple of weeks previously and Cameron had convinced himself that it would do with Christmas dinner that year. He knew, of course, that it would never last until 25th December and, indeed, was surprised that it had lasted as long as it had done, to that evening. There was no better time than this to uncork it, he considered. Pouring two large glasses, he handed one to a grateful Aoife who had joined him in the kitchen. Taking a sizeable slug, it tasted divine, but he resolved to better savor the rest of the contents of the glass.

"Hang on you… We need to clink glasses," his guest interjected with a smile.

"Oh yes, my apologies miss," Cameron replied with a grin, obliging to the ping of crystal upon crystal.

Grabbing the bottle, he then led Aoife through to the front room. About to light the wee woodburning stove, he thought better of it and instead flicked the central heating on, along with his wee Himalayan salt lamp which filled the room with a gentle warming light. Thereupon, they both collapsed onto the couch, not even bothering to pull the curtains shut. The buzzing energy and excitement, together with real fear provoked by the days' events had gradually started to dissipate and nervous exhaustion was beginning to envelope them. Aoife rested upon Cameron's chest, and he put his arm affectionately around her, gently kissing the back of her head which nestled just under his chin. Perhaps it was the tiredness, but he felt no urge to progress matters on to a sexual footing and was happy as things were between them that evening. She was just enjoying the warm and tender moments they were sharing. Déjà jumped up to be next to the pair, purring and clearly pleased that the nice lady was back. Resting there, nestled together, the couple quietly contemplated the day's crazy events. On finishing the wine, they hugged a little before drifting off to sleep in unison.

For the second time in a week, Cameron then experienced vivid dreams of the future. This time, however, they did not prompt a restless night and troubled sleep...

Again, it was 2082, 1st November, and not long after 3 pm. The scene, however, had very much changed from the previous dream and vision of the future. He and Aoife were on solid ground, walking along Great Junction Street, Leith, and turning into the Walk. The air smelt fresh and pure, and it was a pleasant day for the time of year, just cold enough so that they were wearing coats, and with some light sunshine. On the Walk, there was the hustle and bustle of Leithers going about their daily business, absolutely none of whom sported the plastic head bubble gear which he had previously witnessed - clearly, there was no necessity for that.

The pair of them walked past the Spey Rest, no longer a water-side tavern, although remaining a bit dingy and down at heal, sticking out like a sore thumb against the sophisticated neigh-bouring establishments. As Cameron glanced in the window, he could see a small group of auld Port worthies gathered at a small, circular table, laughing and joking with each other whilst playing dominoes. Each with a half-pint and a nip glass in front of them. As hands deftly shifted to move dominoes and con-sume drinks, he could see no sign of blistering sunburn upon any of them. The ruddy complexions on the coupons of the punters, however, remained, albeit this time definitely not the result of fierce sun damage.

The Walk had been transformed into a rather majestic tree-lined and pedestrian friendly avenue. Birds chirped in the branches of the trees, and it had a very cosmopolitan and wel-coming air with a diverse mix of interesting and stylish looking folks taking a stroll or relaxing at one of the numerous pave-ment cafés and brasseries. The wide boulevard linking Edinburgh city with Leith had become a kind of a Barcelona-style Ramblas of the north. ... And finally, to Cameron's great surprise, there appeared to be fully functioning tram system traversing its entire length! The roadway and waterway had gone, hence there was a total absence of cars, amphibious craft and indeed 'waxis', and hence the choking exhaust fumes and noxious pollution of the past. In its place, were small communal vegetable growing plots for the local tenement flat dwellers, garden zones, children's play areas, tasteful street furniture, out-door gym equipment, and what seemed like public remote workspace or office pods, all dotted around at suitable intervals.

A lane was cordoned off, out of the way of pedestrians and adjacent to the tram lines, upon which an assortment of very sleek pedal bikes, scooters and more unusual personal transit vehicles, no doubt all sustainably powered, made their way to and fro.

Enjoying the pleasant surroundings and the freshness in the air, the couple progressed to an equally impressive Queen Street. At the grand neo-gothic palace of the Scottish National Portrait Gallery (which Cameron noted with a smile, had first opened its doors to the public in 1889 according to a plaque on its side wall) they turned in to St Andrew's Square. He looked with some delight to see that the ostentatious pillar and statue to slave trade protector and corrupt politician, Henry Dundas, Viscount Melville, had been removed. It was now stored within a museum accompanied by appropriate interpretation, he hoped. A far more modest and understated replacement stood in its place. It was the portrayal of a rather elegant, diminutive elderly lady. As they passed through the verdant space in which it was situated, they noticed writing engraved upon the statue's plinth and paused for a moment to read the inscription:

"Karen Ferguson CBE
(Citizen Bringing Excellence)
Former First Minister and President,
known as 'Mama Alba'
19th July 1970 – 18th August 2070
In honor of her role in re-establishing
Scotland as a proud, independent,
sovereign European nation"

The fine, autumnal gardens of the Square looked resplendent with families and folks of all ages enjoying the welcoming outdoor space. Cameron and Aoife smiled at one another. They were enjoying the simple pleasure of being in each other's company, along with the nurturing and inspiring environment of Edinburgh, November 2082.

With a shaft of sun light coming in through bay window and placing itself upon his face, Cameron awoke from his dreams at around 7am, feeling refreshed and positive. He was now alone on the sofa and figured that in the middle of the night Aoife, getting cold, must have made her way to bed; that she would presently be there, snug under the duvet. He was tempted to join her.

Proceeding to check the local news headlines on his phone, he noted that that there was no mention of Spenton village and the strange events of the previous evening. Of course, he was quite happy, even relieved, about that as, after all, the two of them had been witness to a bizarre series of deaths, of which Cameron had been directly and intricately involved. He suspected, however, that the residents of Spenton would be in no rush to involve the police. Further, that without the power of the ancient manuscript and their central figures, that the Noble Order of Eidyn would quietly disband and melt away. Although, he considered that he may still anonymously alert the authorities and media to the nefarious activities masterminded from their Gillane HQ (the power of the 'gentleman's' group to nobble senior officials and reporters now, surely, much diminished). Cameron sighed with relief and got up to put a pot of coffee on.

After doing so, he checked both the fridge and bread bin for breakfast supplies, then went through to see if his lady visitor was awake and, if so, ask what she might like to eat - it was his turn to do the honours, of course. Peeking in the door of his room, then that of the spare room, however, she was nowhere to be seen. Neither was she was she in the bathroom, the door to which gaped open. He could not help but feel a pang of disappointment, as he realised that Aoife was not in the house at all.

Of course, unlike him, she did have a proper day job after all, he reflected, and had already taken a considerable amount of time away from her normal duties to assist him with the very unusual client instruction. She must have gone home, he concluded, probably early in the morning before he had awoken, to get a shower and change clothes so as to head to her work at Gilfeather & McLean. The considerate lassie that she was, he imagined, must have quietly crept out the house so as to avoid rousing him from much needed recuperative sleep. He would message her later, he resolved, and see if she might like to meet for lunch or dinner. He could not wait to see her again, that was for sure.

It was then that he spied a handwritten note marked with his name propped up by the toaster on the kitchen worktop. Grabbing it, he moved through to bay window of the living room so as to read in the better light…

Cameron,

I can't tell you how happy I am that you have achieved what you set out to do last night. If the task put to you by Sgàthach was indeed your duty of fate to undertake, then destiny is surely smiling upon you.

It has been a joy to support you in your success, albeit in a small and indirect way. This is despite the truly frightening and dangerous circumstances and events that we faced. By your actions you have, of course, done good, immeasurable good, for the world. Trust me, I know that for certain.

Equally, it has been really special for me to have been able to spend some time with you, even just for few days, and to get to know you a little.

But Cameron, I have a confession that I must make.

It is difficult for me to admit this, but I have not been straight with you about myself, as well as more broadly. Neither has Sgàthach. We had never wanted to deceive you in any way, but it was the best thing to do in the circumstances, I am sure of that. At the same time, do please know that most of what we said to you was genuine.

For example, it is true that I was acting on the instructions of Sgàthach. Further, the vast majority of what she wrote to you in her letters was accurate, including the fate of the world had you not been successful in achieving what you did. But as her primarily goal was to ensure such success and to avoid that fate, certain parts of what she said were fabricated out of necessity. This was, in part, to provide a cover story for myself.

And why would that be needed? ... Well, Cameron, it is because you are my father, and I am your daughter!

I know that this revelation will be somewhat of a shock for you. That it shall seem strange, unbelievable even, not least with the apparent, relatively short age gap between us, along with the fact that we have become so close, particularly last night. It was all platonic, of course – I think you sensed that that was the way it should be between us, despite our obvious mutual bond.

The fact is Cameron (… or should I now say father?), I am from the future, just like Sgàthach.

I shall not be born until June 2057, some 35 years from now. It is true that I am a solicitor working for Gilfeather & McLean (which is, indeed, a long-established firm dating back to the 19th century), however, not in 2022, but rather in 2082 (my qualification from law school is not until 2079).

I can imagine that you will currently be thinking that, if you really are my father, then who is my mother and how it is so that she bore a child to you? Well, my mother is none other than your letter writer, Sgàthach. Being a child of you both, I am also one of the Fiosaichean. As to how I was conceived, I shall explain, shortly.

Firstly, however, may I confess that the communications written by my mother were not actually lodged in Gilfeather & McLean's safe in 1892 for provision to you some 130 years later — that was a necessary fiction. Rather, she provided them to me in 2082, in order to hand deliver to you, as applicable, in 2022. Exactly when she first wrote them, I do not know, although, clearly, they were made to look antique. She felt it best that the truth about me was not divulged to you when we met as it would surely be too much for you to take in, along with all the other revelations in the letters. Further, that telling you might possibly compromise the carrying out of your vital assignment to safeguard the future; perhaps, even giving you a false sense of security that it had already been achieved. This pretence, however, allowed me to indirectly support to you in the successful completion of your task (a duty which I believe Mother Earth had, indeed, provided you).

The fact is that the future you have ensured Cameron, is the one that I was born into. I was sent back in time to seek to make sure that you achieved what you needed to do in order to protect that precious thoroughfare of time. My mother's correspondence was written from the perspective – and fear – of a possible dark future where that positive plane of time had been denied and with a negative and destructive throughfare in its place.

As stated in her first missive, it is correct that in 2056, after she failed in her efforts to destroy the malign manuscript, she began to sense your presence as a fellow Fiosaiche. And, yes, at that time, she noticed that her powers of time-traverse were waning. However, before theses abilities abandoned her completely, in that year she was able to make one further return traverse ... to 2022.

To be precise, it was to the night of Tuesday 25th October 2022; so, for you, Cameron, just one week ago! As I understand it, this trip was in order to – I must say bluntly – congress with you physically. You may know of this meeting, having recently experienced it... perhaps having thought it were a dream? She got you to deliver the goods, or should I say, the sperm (I am blushing writing this you know.... and may I apologise for the rather mechanical description). I am sure that you will have confused feelings and emotions about this happening to you, however, do know that my mother said that it was essential. She explained to me that, at the time, she had sensed that it served a higher purpose; that her psychic mind had impelled and drove her to seek congress with you for the purpose of receiving your manly emissions and conceiving your child; however, without revealing to her why it had been so vital – that would only later become apparent.

Not since that trip, has she been able to travel time. The fact is that there had never been any traverse by her to 1892 (from 2082 or otherwise) as she had indicated to you in her writing. As for the Bannerman and Goudelock auction program that she had claimed to have procured on such visit, she had, in fact, already attained it on a previous time–traverse (which had turned out to be a further failed attempt to destroy the ancient book); that was, of course, prior to her powers of travel between the dimensions leaving her.

Please also be aware Cameron, that it was only one month ago, in my 'home epoch' of 2082, that my mother divulged to me for the first time the details which I am relaying to you now. As part, she explained that the time continuum was fragile and may continue to rail against its earlier alteration; that we must ensure that the positive future enabled by your actions remained. That we could not risk it collapsing back in upon itself, prompting calamity with the evil text, the Order and the resurrection of the wicked reverend Kellie. So, as indicated, I was tasked with traversing back to 2022 to give you at least her first letter and to assist and support you in undertaking your vital duty. She explained that this was my own pre-ordained destiny, just as it had been hers to visit you on the night of Tuesday 25th October 2022 in order to conceive me.

When she came to you that night from 2056, as I indicated, it was with that sole purpose. At such juncture, she could not, herself, have been able to give the support and assistance that I have, in recent days, provided to you. She lacked sufficient knowledge and understanding of what needed to be done. It was only in the years hence that she became clear as to what our respective roles were — our 'higher purpose' if you like. As part, that it was you who must destroy the Facal an Fiosaiche manuscript and stop the resurrection of the corrupt preacher man – that it was you, and only you, who possessed the necessary ability to do so directly. Further to accumulating such knowledge, the letters she wrote were her means of outlining and communicating to you what needed to be done in order to preserve the future.

My mother believed that my capabilities as a Fiosaiche were restricted, in the same manner as hers, by the 'fifth limitation' (of which you will recall she had referred to in her correspondence), as I was of the same home epoch. Hence, my role had to be one of provision of indirect support to you, including prompting you to take direct action yourself and more broadly to successfully carry out your critical mission. She did not, of course, believe that this fifth limitation applied to you for the reasons she outlined within her text.

At the same time, my mother explained to me that, from the future, she only had partial vision and insight as to what actions you may or may not take in response to her letters. Nevertheless, that the 1889 auction would most likely, in her view, allow you to attain and destroy the manuscript and protect the positive version of the future and plane of time. Hence, the instruction to you within her first letter. Her second letter was, indeed, meant as a back-up plan, only to be provided to you in the event that you failed in the 1889 mission.

May I say again that being able to support you in your task has made me very happy. Had you not accomplished what you did, the time continuum would have surely fallen back in upon itself as my mother had feared, so that our future, along with yours and that of the wider world itself, would have been very bleak indeed.

Alas, I must say that it is now the moment for me to return to my mother and the positive time ahead that you have allowed and preserved for us, and many millions more. May I apologise for providing you simply this note to explain matters, rather than speaking to you face to face. I feared that if I took the latter course of action, I would have been unable to part from you for my mother. She needs me, please understand that.

Through these last few days, I have got to know you, I have got to like you and to care for you... so I shall miss you. You... my father. Remember me and miss me too please. We will meet again, be assured of that.

In the meantime, may I ask you please to reflect upon the famous words associated with the writer of your era, sadly passed, Alasdair Gray –

> *"Work as if you live in the early days*
> *of a better nation"*

Indeed, you are living in such days Cameron, but also those of a better world and civilisation. And those times ahead that shall only be forthcoming thanks to your brave actions.

To these days hence, and until we meet again.

Aoife x

Cameron's hand shook a little, the piece of paper wavering in its grip. A tear then dropped down from the corner of one of his eyes, landing upon the note and blotting some of the writing. At this, he dabbed his eye with the back of his other hand.

The emotion was partly due to his joy at the realisation that he had a daughter but also sadness at the fact that she was gone. In addition, of course, it was prompted by the wider events of the past week, taking bizarre new twists and turns under the contents of this new communique, and his bewilderment at the strangeness of it all. It seemed that he was living through the craziest reality. Could it all really be true? Was she being straight with him?

Having experienced everything that he had done in recent days he knew that it must be genuine. He also trusted Aoife implicitly, despite her earlier and now self-confessed subterfuge. Her support and encouragement had helped to save him from the fate of the bonfire after all, along with his ultimate success that evening. There definitely was a deep bond between them, something that he had already sensed were present, but one that he now realised was of father and daughter rather than anything else.

What would he do now? Today was the first day in the rest of his life and, yes, true, as she had quoted, the early days of an almost certainly better one - for him, Scotland, Mother Earth and all - than would otherwise have been the case. Of course, it would be a very different life to that he had hitherto anticipated - now that he was aware of his special powers and abilities as one of the Fiosaichean.

Looking up from the note, he gazed out of the bay window in further contemplation. Suddenly, his heart lifted as he noticed the figure of Aoife standing in Straiton Park, right by the exit to the Promenade. She was looking towards him affectionately... her father. Without the unpleasant mugginess of late, it was a typical day for the time of year, with clouds interspersed with rays of sunshine. As shadows of the former lifted and a beam of bright golden light rested upon her, Cameron reflected on how beautiful she was... his daughter. With tears further welling up in his eyes, he smiled over at her warmly. Just then, Déjà jumped up onto the windowsill giving him a start so that he momentarily glanced downwards at the feline. When he looked back up, Aoife was gone.

Acknowledgements

A word of thanks to my good friend, the author and historian Roy Pugh. Not least for demonstrating to me that you do not need to be under 30 years of age to write your first novel. His passion for writing and history helping to inspire me to write this book.

My gratitude also to Ian Yule for undertaking the task of proof-reading.

Further, I must give credit to 'The Edinburgh Reporter' and journalist, Mike Smith. Mike's 30th anniversary article in the publication, entitled 'When Hearts humbled Bayern Munich', painted a vivid picture of the match, helping to ferment my ideas on my lead character's account.

Last but certainly not least, may I provide recognition to those who have provided support to me during the difficult pandemic period in which this novel was written, including my family and friends.

About the Author

George Murray Wilson has had a long career in human resources prior to writing his first novel, ultimately choosing that career path after completing an MA in law and solicitors' finals in his early twenties. In advance of setting up his own small consultancy, Online HR, he was employed in numerous job roles over the years, latterly as director of human resources for the National Trust for Scotland. In a consultancy capacity, as well as supporting many different organisations, large and small, George has authored over 80 guides on international employment law, employee benefits and corporate governance, covering more than thirty countries.

Edinburgh born and bred, he is now based in the coastal town of Dunbar, East Lothian and has two grown up children. In his debut novel, 'The Word of the Seer', George has sought to channel certain aspects of his experience of living with obsessive compulsive disorder and Tourette's syndrome under the guise of the lead character's 'unwelcome gift' of psychic abilities.

A social democrat and an internationalist, over many years he has campaigned for environmental issues as well as regaining Scottish independence. Passionate about history and particularly local myth and legend, George's writing seeks to invoke the spirits of the past within the context of the present and the future.